T0690724

AIRSHIP 27 PRODUCTIONS

All-American Sports Stories Volume Two

"Brooklyn Breakdown" © 2020 Derrick Ferguson
"Baseball in December" © 2020 Dexter Fabi
"The Kicker" © 2020 Ron Fortier

Published by Airship 27 Productions
www.airship27.com
www.airship27hangar.com

Interior illustrations© 2020 Rob Davis
Cover illustration© 2020 Adam Shaw

Editor: Ron Fortier
Associate Editor: Jonathan Sweet
Marketing and Promotions Manager: Michael Vance
Production Designer: Rob Davis.

ISBN: 978-1-946183-96-5

Printed in the United States of America

10 9 8 7 6 5 4 3 2 1

Volume Two

BROOKLYN BEATDOWN

Derrick Ferguson

ROUND ONE
Too Sweet's Bar & Grill
Bedford-Stuyvesant, Brooklyn, N.Y.
1955

The profane screaming, cheering and general mayhem of the crowd reached such a wall-vibrating level that it could easily be heard from a block away but Levi Kimbro had long learned how to tune that out. He cared about nothing but putting down the man in front of him. He cared about nothing but seeing this man lying unconscious at his feet on the blood-splattered concrete floor.

Cornbread Broughton approached him with that easy, deceptively unhurried style that he had mastered. Cornbread came at you slow as a pastor's sermon on Sunday morning until he had just a few feet separating you and then all of a sudden, he was inside your defenses and whaling away like a demented lumberjack going to work with an axe on a helpless tree. A testament to how Levi had fallen for that attack a couple of times already was the swelling around and above his left eye where Cornbread gave him a couple of good bangs in the second round.

Levi threw out that blindingly fast jab he'd been working behind all night long and it continued to work. Cornbread kept his distance. That jab stung him enough times during the fight that he developed a healthy respect for it early on the fight. Levi's feet kept moving, keeping him out of range of those sledgehammers Cornbread used for fists. The cat had the heaviest hands Levi had ever felt.

"That's it, baby!" the shrill, drunken woman's voice cut through the chaotic din. "You keep on dancin'! I sho' love to watch you dance!"

A lot of people did. That was how Levi Kimbro had gotten the nickname of 'Dancer' in plenty of backrooms like this one. Because this was where he danced and he did it good.

Time to remind Cornbread of that fact. Levi threw hooking jabs at Cornbread's head, knocking sweat and droplets of blood into the howling mob surrounding them. No ring here, just a ragged square marked out with duct tape surrounded by men and women bawling for blood. Crumpled currency changed hands as men bet their week's pay on the outcome of the fight. Bottles of liquor were passed around and greedily upturned. Hastily rolled joints were exchanged. No time for glasses or nice polite behavior. This was all about the blood.

Levi slipped Cornbread's straight right punch and gave him a right hook into his ribs that made Cornbread back up, wheezing and grunting with the effort of trying to get air back in in his lungs. Levi brazenly dropped his hands, waggling his head back and forth, clowning for the crowd and they rewarded him with whoops of delight.

Cornbread snarled and leapt forward, wrapped his arms around Levi's arms and torso. He cleaned jerked Levi straight up, lifting him up completely up off the floor. They stood there like some bizarre statue. Cornbread snapped at Levi's throat like a hungry dog.

"Let 'im go! Knock it off!" The lead weighted end of a cosh came down on Cornbread's left shoulder. "Let him go! I ain't going to tell you agin'!" And Bendigo Cribb meant what he said. For going on twenty years now he'd been the referee of more of these backroom bareknuckle brawls than could be counted. He was well respected for his fairness and his handling of the crowds that turned out to watch the brawls. He enforced his word with his cosh and if that wasn't enough, the gold-plated .45 automatic stuffed in his waistband did. And if that still wasn't enough the half-dozen men he employed as security for these fights and their weapons were more than enough to finish any argument.

Cornbread let go of Levi who got in a last jab as his feet hit the ground. The bell rang, signaling the end of the round "Corners!" Bendigo hollered. Levi went to his corner, signified by the sudden appearance of a three-legged stool. His corner man, Nappy Johnson shoved the crowd back, yelling, "Give 'im room, dammit! Let the man breathe!"

Levi dropped onto the stool and let Nappy work on his swelling eye. "That is one tough boy, man," he gasped.

"Here, drink some water and save your breath. Didn't I tell you he had some heavy hands? But he don't watch his right side. And he didn't expect you to last this long. He's too used to lettin' them heavy hands of his do all the work. You keep on banging away at that right side an' the second he lose his temper, you ring his bell but good. An' I want to see more doublin' up on them jabs, y'hear me?"

Levi didn't answer, just spit in the battered tin bucket Nappy seemed to pull out of thin air.

Bendigo signaled for one of his men to whack the bell and the two fighters came back out for the fourth round. Levi immediately went to work on Cornbread's right side and saw red murder in the man's eyes. Levi ducked back from the whooshing overhand right and pounded Cornbread's right side some more since he obligingly left it open. Cornbread's entire right side seemed to be glowing red. His light-colored skin on that side looked as if he'd been beaten with a barber's strop.

Cornbread came back with a dangerous short uppercut that scored a glancing blow off the side of Levi's head but even a glancing blow proved enough to knock him back into the clamoring mob. Eager hands caught Levi, prevented him from falling. A woman's slim arm darted out and delicate fingers stroked his brawny mahogany shoulder. The woman looked at the blood and sweat on her fingers, large dark brown eyes sparkling with intensity as she slowly rubbed her thumb on those fingers, one by one.

The helping hands threw Levi back into the fight and he used that momentum to add to his straight right punch that snapped Cornbread's head back so fast and so hard that somebody yelled out; "He done gon' an' broke that sucka's neck!"

Not quite but it was a blow that plainly disoriented Cornbread long enough for Levi to dive on in, looking more like he was doing a samba than fighting but the result was all that counted and that result was a smashing hard right that snapped Cornbread's head to the left. Levi gave him another right, another right and one more just because.

Cornbread tripped over his own feet trying to recover and crashed to the concrete floor, leaving a wide blood-streaked, sweaty smear as he rolled over on his side, already trying to get back up on his feet, to continue the fight. His eyes rolled madly, trying to focus on something, anything.

Bendigo waved Levi back. He didn't have to lift his cosh in warning. Levi was all right with him. They never got into any beef in or out of the ring. Levi backed off while Bendigo bent over Cornbread who got to his knees, struggled to get to his feet. Cornbread's corner man was at Bendigo's side, insisting that his man could continue the fight. Bendigo waited until Cornbread got to his feet by himself. Cornbread nodded at Bendigo.

The yelling of the mob amazingly seemed to increase in volume as Bendigo waved for the fighters to resume. Cornbread tried to switch up his style and popped a series of jabs at Levi, looking to keep him back, give his head more time to clear and his legs to get a little steadier.

Levi was having none of that. He was ready for a hot meal, an even hotter bath and a cool bed. He threw left, right combinations at Cornbread who was simply too slow to counter or block. Cornbread's lower lip split and blood spurted over his chin.

Levi risked turning his head away from Cornbread, looking at Bendigo. His eyes and face plainly asking the ref to call the fight over. Bendigo's answering look was just as plain; you know the rules, son...put your man down.

Levi delivered an uppercut that did indeed put Cornbread Broughton down. There was no doubt in anybody's mind that the fight was now over. Levi winced from the many backslaps he received as the mob surged forward to congratulate him. Several men picked up the unconscious Cornbread. They would take him to the storage room where only his corner man would console him when he came to. There was nothing for the loser of a backroom brawl. Nothing at all. Not even a "good fight, man."

Nappy threw a towel around Levi's neck. He reached down to Levi's bandaged hands. The tape had been white as typing paper when Nappy wrapped them on earlier that evening. Now they were dark with blood and sweat. "Lemme cut them offa you."

"Go get my money, Nappy." Levi said, accepting a fifth of Jonnie Walker Red.

Nappy sighed. But he turned away and disappeared into the crowd that hung around even though the fight was over. These were the winners who had bet on Levi and now were high on their fat pockets. The losers were on their way home, coming up with elaborate excuses for their wives as to why the electric bill would have to wait to be paid or why meat wouldn't be on the shopping list this week.

Women pressed themselves against his still sweat-dripping body. Women plainly turned on by the brutality they just witnessed. Levi took a healthy swig from the bottle, enjoying the burn from the liquor as it went down. It wasn't anything like the burn he felt when he was fighting. It was nowhere even close but it helped him come down from the adren-aline rush. He could have taken any of these women home and he had on many nights past. But he didn't want a woman tonight. He just wanted his money and his bed.

Nappy returned bearing a gift. In one hand he held a sizeable hunk of green, held together with a thick rubber band. "It's all there."

"You take your cut?"

"You know better than that." In all the time they'd been working together Nappy had never taken his cut. He waited until Levi gave it to him. "C'mon over here, I wanna talk to you." Nappy took him by the elbow and pushed out of the circle of well-wishers until they found a relatively quiet corner of the back room. But it was emptying out rapidly as everybody moved back into the bar. Big Maybelle's "Whole Lotta Shakin' Goin' On" started playing as the bar's owner, Too Sweet, plugged the jukebox back in.

Nappy unfolded his pocket knife and started in carefully cutting off the tape off Levi's hands. "What's goin' on with you, man? You haven't been the same last coupla days. Can't be money troubles 'cause I know you don't spend none on anythin' you don't need. You won't even buy a car."

"What do I need a car for, Nappy? I like walkin'. It gets me where I want to go. You buy a car then you got all these flash women…" and here Levi jerked his chin in the direction of a few women who still hung around, obviously hoping to catch his eye. "…hanging offa you wanting to get in your pockets. I don't have time for that."

Nappy threw the bandages on the floor. Too Sweet's nephew Deaf Jimmy would clean up in here after everybody was gone. "When was the last time you had a woman, man? And don't forget who you talking to. I done seen you take more than your share back up to your room. A woman is prob'ly what you need. After a fight you all keyed up, still got juice in your system you got to get rid of. You know what I mean." Nappy winked.

Levi went over to where his neatly folded clothing rested on a stack of Rheingold beer cases. Dressing rooms were a luxury in this sport that participants frequently had to go without. "It ain't that, man. It's just I…I don't know. I'm just getting used to this life. Settling in, know what I mean? I ain't hungry no more for what I got planned. It's not that I'm getting to like this. But it's becoming okay for me. Am I making sense?"

"Yeah, yeah, you are." Nappy picked up Levi's folded shirt, opened it with an expert snap. "If you had told me forty years ago I'd be runnin' a fourth-rate boxing gym on Fulton Street and being the corner man of backroom bareknuckle fighters, I'd have laughed myself into a hernia. Yet here I be." Nappy gestured at himself, at the smoky room, at the outside world. "And you know what? I come to terms with it a long time ago. Nah, it ain't the life I wanted. But I own my place free and clear, my car's paid off, I done outlived two wives, I come and go as I please and men tip their hats to me and call me Mr. Johnson when they meet me in the street."

"Your point?"

Nappy shrugged. "Sometimes there ain't no point. You get up in the morning, go about your business and hope others do the same. You don't like where this is goin', do something about it. I been telling you for the longest that you're just wasting your time in these brawls. You got what it takes to go pro. You got speed, you got stamina, you got heart and most of all, you got the brains. You know how to think in a fight."

Levi tucked his shirt in his pants, zipped them up and belted them. "And give over most of my winnings to some manager who ain't no better than a mobster? Sign some contract that keeps me on some white man's leash like a dog? Be told when to take a dive and when I can win? Bullshit on that noise, man. I know how the fight game goes. Leastways here I get to keep what I earned with my own sweat and blood and not watch it go into another man's pocket."

Nappy sighed. "It ain't all that, man. I know the right people. I'm not gonna stand here and tell you we can stay clean. But we can go places."

"I don't want to be a boxer, Nappy. Not that kind anyway."

"You ain't got long to be this kind, either." Nappy nodded at the dried blood on the concrete floor. "You been lucky this past year, Levi. Cats get crippled in these kinds of fights they stay in too long. Or worse."

Levi shrugged into his hooded black pea coat and slapped his well-worn flat cap on his head. "You want your cut now?"

Nappy shook his head. "You give it to me t'morrow. Give it to me now and I'll be spending it on one'a them flash women you were just talking about!"

Nappy Johnson's roaring laughing followed Levi as he made his way to the delivery entrance and then out into the street.

ROUND TWO

March in Brooklyn meant a lot of things but the one that mattered most to those who depended on their feet to get them where they needed to go was if The Hawk was talking. That's all folks wanted to know if they were fixing to go out for the evening; "The Hawk out there tonight?" "What that ol' Hawk doin' tonight?" "Man, The Hawk is out there waitin' for me." The Hawk being the brutally cold wind that when it really blew as it did tonight sounded like the hunting cry of that bird of prey. It flew up and down the canyons of Brooklyn with icy talons that dug deep and stayed in the bones.

But it was a cold that felt good to Levi Kimbro. He never was one to complain during the winter months. Shucks, it was supposed to be cold. That's why they called it winter. And he still had that fifth of Black in the inside pocket of his pea coat to warm him up a bit if necessary. Not that he planned on going anywhere but home. He walked west on Fulton Street, passing by the other bars that were open on both sides of the street. The other shops and businesses were dark, locked up for the night and had been for hours now. But the places where the party people hung out stayed open late and long. Six blocks further on east was Nappy Johnson's Gym where he worked. But Levi's studio apartment lay to the west, on the corner of Tompkins and Decatur, no more than a brisk fifteen-minute walk.

As he walked his thoughts replayed the conversation he had just had with Napoleon Johnson and he regretted not being more honest with him. God knows the man had treated him like family ever since Levi came to Brooklyn after his honorable discharge from the Army. Levi had written Father Tim just after leaving the Army to tell him he was going to New York, try to make a life there. Father Tim wrote back, telling Levi that any time he wanted to come back to Chicago and St. Vincent's he was more than welcome. Cholly Dougan, the janitor/maintenance man at St. Vincent's for forty-two years had gone home to be with The Lord, praise Jesus and he had taught Levi everything he knew about boilers, carpentry, masonry, electrical and plumbing work. Father Tim would be delighted to have Levi come and take Cholly's job.

Much as he appreciated Father Tim's offer and he knew where it was coming from because Father Tim was a man in every sense of the word, Levi knew he couldn't do it. If he took that job in twenty years he'd be exactly like Cholly Dougan, living in the basement of St. Vincent's with books and bottles of booze as his only family. And as much Levi had loved Cholly, Lord have mercy on his soul, Levi sure as hell didn't love him enough to want to be him.

And so, he'd come to Brooklyn as he'd had enough of the South during his time in the Army and he wanted no more truck with that part of these here United States, thank you, sir.

He made his left turn on Tompkins, lost in thought but not so lost that he didn't snap into a defensive stance as four youths came out of darkened doorways and from behind parked cars where they had been lurking. You always had to keep one eye and one ear open for trouble in Brooklyn no matter how hard you were thinking. It didn't take Levi long to learn that if you didn't look out for yourself in Brooklyn, it would eat you alive and pick its teeth with your bones.

The punks spread out. Teenagers, all of them, barely old enough to wipe their own behinds. The leader snarled, "You know what this is, nigger! We know you won that fight so jus' go on an' give it up!" The leader reached in his pocket and pulled out a linoleum knife.

Levi's lips drew back from his teeth. This wasn't even going to be a fair fight. He went on the offensive, surprising the leader who recovered, tried to cut Levi with the linoleum knife. Levi's right hook landed with explosive force on the side of the youth's head and his partners all heard something in his head break with a meaty POP! And in the frosty harsh light of the streetlamp they saw two teeth go flying, trailing bloody roots.

Levi kicked him away and went after the second one, delivering a blow to that boy's stomach so hard that the boy immediately dropped to his knees and gave up his dinner, lunch and probably breakfast as well. The two others had seen more than enough. They broke out of there, splitting up and hauling ass in two different directions. Standard stick-up kid loyalty.

Levi was in the mood to play. With wanna-be's like these punks, a message had to be sent so that they'd spread the word. Levi picked his victim and gave chase. Shoot, the boy couldn't even run right. His feet slapped against the pavement so loud he might as well have been wearing wooden clogs. And he kept looking over his shoulder to see where Levi was and how fast he was gaining. Anybody with any sense knew that if you going to run, then run dammit. If you got caught, then you just got caught. But you couldn't run and look at the same time. If you were going to look then you might as well stand and fight.

Levi let the boy go half a block for the fun of it before cranking up the speed a couple of notches and seizing him by the neck. He slammed the boy up against a parked Chevy, spun him around so he could get a look at him. "Boy, how old are you?"

"Sixteen! Sixteen! Please, Mr. Levi, I'm sorry!"

Levi dragged the boy further into the light so he could see his face fully. "You know me? And you still tried to jump me? Boy, I coulda killed all'a you if I wasn't in a good mood." Levi yanked the boy's knit cap off his head. "What's your name?"

"Michael Allen! You know my father!"

"Mikey Allen? Sam Allen's your daddy?"

"That's right! We live over on Gates Avenue! You been to our house!"

"What you doing out here on a freezing cold night trying to play stick-up kid?" Levi demanded. But he already knew the answer. Sam Allen had disappeared on a night much like this one last year. Along with three other would-be gangsters who boasted and bragged how they were going to loot this Jew warehouse full of stereos over in Williamsburg. They drove off in a beat to shit box truck and from that night to this, they had never been seen again. The way Levi had heard the story, Sam's wife Rose had called the police and they sent over two detectives. Once she told them about the proposed heist and where her husband and his cronies had gone, the detectives put away their pads and suggested to Rose that she treat the whole incident as if her husband had run off with some woman. Levi believed the story because he had heard it from Rose herself the night he had beaten Tommy Thompson after fourteen bloody rounds. Rose had been at the fight and she had looked oh so fine in that green semi-transparent lace top with matching chiffon skirt.

Rose had told him that story after the fight as they lay in his bed, the sweat on their bodies drying. She was lonely and looking for a man to help her raise three boys. But Levi wasn't that man. He'd cut off relations with Rose soon after. Levi wondered if Michael knew.

"It was my boy Streety! He said that it didn't matter how good you were supposed to be, you'd be all wore out after a fight. He said that the four of us could take you if we hung together."

"Yeah, I saw how you all hung together. I bet that other punk is clear on over to Flushing Avenue by now." Levi let Michael go and stood back. The boy wiped his runny nose with the sleeve of his corduroy coat. "Where's your momma? Home?"

"Naw. She went out. I waited till she turned the corner then I come out."

"How'd you know she wasn't coming back home?"

"I heard her on the phone. She going around with The Duke's crowd these days."

The boy needed to say no more on that score.

"You need money, why don't you get a job?"

Now that it appeared that Levi wasn't going to beat him to death, Michael had gotten back a bit of nerve. "A job's for suckers, man."

Levi gave him a right smart clout upside his head for his answer. "Don't you talk to me like that. You ain't grown."

Michael remembered his place and rubbed the side of his head, standing up straight. "Yessir," he mumbled. "I'm sorry."

"Yeah, that you are. You go to school?"

"Sometimes."

"You go t'morrow. And then after school you come by Napoleon

Johnson's gym. You know where that is? You know Mr. Johnson?"

"Yessir. My brother Sly, he goes there to workout sometimes on Saturdays."

Levi nodded. "You come by the gym. You'll work for me."

"Doin' what?"

"Doin' whatever I tell you to do! Boy, don't test me. You got me standing out here in the cold trying to do your dumb ass a favor an' you ain't co-operating. Way I see it, you owe me plenty. But me beating on you wouldn't teach you nothin'. You need money? Then you work for it. You don't want the job, we can settle up another way..." Levi cracked his knuckles.

Michael got the point. "I'll be there, Mr. Levi."

Levi grunted. "You better. And don't even think about not coming. Like you said, I been to your house. I know where you live. I got to come looking for you and I'll give you the beatin' I shoulda give you already."

"You won't have to come look for me, Mr. Levi, I swear!"

"Go on and get outta here then. Go straight on home and stay there."

The boy took off so quickly that Levi could have sworn he left behind a Michael Allen shaped cloud of dust that lingered in the frigid air for a few seconds after he was gone. Levi sighed and went on to the three-story brownstone where he lived, jogging lightly up the stairs, keys in hand. He opened the door and walked up the three flights to his studio apartment. Levi had specifically looked for a top floor apartment so that he had to walk up all those flights of stairs. His studio apartment suited him just fine. He greatly disliked clutter and so his apartment was a model of bare necessities. He had friends who had apartments packed with junk they didn't need and rarely used. One thing he appreciated about both St. Vincent's and the Army, they'd taught him how to be satisfied with very little.

Not that he didn't want more. Not having grown up with a real family, Levi wanted one of his own, a wife who wanted kids as Levi planned on having three or more. A house out in Jersey or Long Island. And he wanted to be his own man more than anything. He touched the rubber-banded bills in his pocket.

Once inside his apartment he firmly locked the door. He had drawn the blinds and curtains before he left so nobody from across the street could see in. Being nosy was practically a neighborhood responsibility in this part of Brooklyn. Levi took off his coat and hat then went over to his bed. The biceps on his arms swelled and writhed as he carefully lifted up the end of his bed, moved it about five feet to the right and set it down quietly. He knelt down to a section of the floor that had been covered by the bed.

He used his pocket knife and pried up a rectangular section of the hardwood floor. Within was a gap. A gap filled with money. Thick wads of money held together by rubber bands. Levi took the money from his pocket and threw it in to join the rest. He counted it about once a month just to make sure he had an accurate count but by his reckoning he had something like $50,000 in there. Another four, maybe five fights and he would give it up for good. Levi carefully replaced the board and moved the bed back in place. Nobody knew he had his money there, not even Nappy. Levi supposed he should have kept it in a bank but he didn't trust banks. And he knew himself, knew that even though the money would have been perfectly safe he would lie awake nights worrying. But he knew it was right there at all times. Not even his landlady had a key to this apartment. He'd changed the lock himself quietly and never told her. He had his suspicions about her after hearing from a couple of the building's other tenants that they'd come home from work and found doors open inside their apartment they knew they had left closed. Or stuff in their bureau drawers looking as if somebody had been rummaging around in them. The guy on the second floor who was a bachelor like Levi and lived alone said that from time to time he'd come home and found the toilet seat down.

Levi walked over to the fridge and removed a plate with a couple of raw steaks on it. He started a fire on the stove, threw the steaks in a cast iron skillet and put that on the fire. While the steaks cooked he took out ice trays from the freezer, dumped the ice into a bucket and took it over to the square folding table he sat at to eat his meals.

Over on the wall across from his bed stood a waist high wooden bookcase he'd built himself. He selected a battered hardcover copy of Chester Himes' "If He Hollers Let Him Go" which he'd picked up in his favorite used bookstore on Livingston Street. He sat the book on the table along with a plate, knife and a fork. The bottle of Johnnie Walker joined the book. Levi returned to the stove and seasoned his steaks with garlic, green peppers and onions he cut up, threw that on top of the steaks. When they were done he took the skillet over the table and forked the steaks onto the plate.

He sat down and ate his steaks in silence. After the overwhelming noise of a fight, Levi appreciated a few hours of quiet. And he needed the time to think about what he getting into with the Allen boy. After he ate, he took himself a healthy slug of Scotch then opened up his book to read for a bit before bed. He stuck his other hand in the bucket of ice.

Levi carefully replaced the board....

ROUND THREE

"What do you mean you hired an assistant?" Nappy Johnson frowned slightly. He sat back in his ancient leather wingback chair that creaked as if it were being tortured. Levi never liked going into Nappy's office which is why he only went in there when he absolutely had to. Nappy had file cabinets full of yellowed papers that Levi knew he only kept for show as anything Nappy had worth remembering was in his head. The window looking out over Fulton Street appeared to have not been washed in a year. Nappy had over a dozen photos framed on the wall behind him. Most of them were of Nappy and his two dead wives. The others Levi didn't care about. The only one he was interested in and the only one Nappy would never talk about or explain was the one of him and Sam Langford on Miami Beach. According to words scrawled in the lower right-hand corner the picture had been taken in 1916.

"What part you didn't understand? I'm taking on an assistant. Somebody to help me out 'round here. Sam Allen's boy, Mikey. You know him."

Nappy nodded, reached for the stub of an unlit cigar resting on the edge of the desk. "Yeah. That the fool that went messing 'round with them Jews last year. An' ain't nobody seen hide nor hair of him since. You was layin' up with his wife for a while, weren't you?"

"Yeah, for about a minute."

"That got anything to do with you hiring this boy?"

Levi told him about the attempted stick-up last night after the fight. Nappy thought it pretty hilarious and took about ten minutes to laugh himself in a coughing fit. Levi got him a paper cup of water from the sink in the bathroom. After getting himself under control, Nappy said; "Still don't explain why you want to give this boy a job. You feel guilty 'bout layin' up with his moms?"

And even though they were good friends, Levi knew he could never make Nappy understand why he was doing this for the boy. Now Father Tim, he'd have understood. And he would have approved.

"Look, Nappy, I ain't gonna be around here forever. We both know that. It's about time I started training somebody how to handle the boilers, do the repairs around here and why not him? He could use the money and learn some responsibility. It'll keep him off the street and away from them knuckleheads that almost got his tail beat to a crisp last night. Next time he might try to stick up somebody who'll cut or shoot him. And then I would feel responsible, like I had my chance to do something and didn't take it. If you don't want to pay the boy, I will."

"Daggone right you will. He's your assistant so he's your lookout. And mind me good now; I don't want nunna his friends hangin' 'round here and I don't want to hear a single complaint about him from nobody. You hear me?"

"I hear you. Thanks, Nappy."

Nappy grunted and hauled himself out of his chair. "When he comin'?"

"Not until this afternoon, after school."

"What you got planned for today?"

"First of all, I think I'm gonna wash your windows. God knows you're too damn lazy to do it yourself. How do you see out of that thing?"

"I don't," Nappy said briskly. "What I need to see out the window for? I know what Fulton Street look like. C'mon with me for a minnit. I want you to take a look at somebody."

They left Nappy's office and stepped out into the gym proper. Located on the top floor of a four-story building, Johnson's Gym was one of the few places where Levi Kimbro felt completely at home. There was nothing on Earth like the smells and sounds of a gym. Especially when it was filled with boxers busy at training. Even at this early hour there were a dozen men busy working up a sweat, their dark skin shining with the fruit of their exercise. The thump of fists against heavy bags, the odd rhythm of speed bags being properly worked, the harsh slap of medicine balls against bare skin, the profane words of encouragement and instruction being shouted... it all blended into a sensory swirl that Levi had always found comforting.

Nappy's gym had three standard sized boxing rings and they were all being used. Nappy led Levi to the middle one where two lanky youths banged away at each other with more enthusiasm than skill. Nappy pointed with his cigar stub. "The one on the left is Billy Rico. He's one'a Duke Williamson's fighters. New boy he brought up from Florida."

"Duke's going to put him in the backrooms?" Even as he asked the question Levi knew what the answer was. Duke Williamson didn't have a hand in anything legal. All his fighters were straight-up backroom brawlers. But when it came to Duke Williamson, Levi made it a point to play dumb. Even with Nappy. When men like Duke Williamson were involved it was always safer to play dumb.

"You think he shouldn't?"

Levi shrugged. "Don't make me a bit of difference but I'd put a good thirty more pounds on him before throwing him in a fight. His neck's a little too long but if you put somebody good to work with him on that…" a sudden thought struck Levi and he looked at his friend with suspicion. "Nappy…you ain't thinking about training this boy, are you?"

"Duke's made me an offer is all. All I'd have to do is train. I wouldn't be corner man or nothin' like that. And it wouldn't have anything' to do with our deal."

Levi still didn't like it. Duke Williamson had approached Levi a couple of times about Levi coming to fight for him and Levi turned him down. He didn't like this idea at all. But Nappy was a grown man who could look out for himself. Still, Levi couldn't help but feel that this was a situation that had more cooking under the lid of the pot than what had originally been put in.

"Who's the other kid?" Levi asked. This kid actually had some good footwork going for him. He easily slipped punches Rico threw at him as if Rico were moving in slow motion. And every time Rico missed a punch, the kid made him pay for it by jabbing out a nice little beat on his ribs.

"Dunno much about him. Calls himself T-Bird. Says he works for Duke."

Levi turned away. He was hearing entirely too much of Duke's name between last night and today. "I'm gonna get to work. Call me…"

The sharp female voice cut through the sounds of the gym like a gunshot; "TEDDY! GET YOURSELF OUT OF THERE RIGHT THIS INSTANT!"

Levi swiveled his head to look at a woman so striking and so beautiful that he simply could not take his eyes off of her. She crossed the distance between the exit/entrance of the gym and the ring in three-inch heels that sounded like firecrackers going off, so sharp and firm were her precise steps. Even with the heels she still was an itty-bitty thing. Fine boned with brown skin and tight curly ebony hair under a pillbox hat.

"Boy, don't make me tell you again! Get your tail out of there right now!" the woman whirled on Levi. "Are you the manager here?"

Levi couldn't say a word. Just grin rather stupidly. He couldn't help it. This woman was like dynamite given human form. He could swear sparks were flying from her in all directions.

"What is your problem? Can't you talk? Who's in charge around here?"

"That would be me, ma'am." Nappy stepped forward, extending his hand. "I'm Napoleon Johnson. And you are…?"

"That's my sister Dorothea, Mr. Johnson," the youth nicknamed T-Bird said. He had stopped sparring and leaned on the top rope, breathing heavily. "Go on home, Thea. What you doin' here embarrassing me like this?"

"I want you out of there right now and I mean it. You haven't been embarrassed yet but if you don't mind what I say you'll know what being embarrassed really is." The young woman rounded back to Nappy. "My name is Dorothea McBricker and I want to know why you have these young boys beating up on each other when they should be in school!"

"Ma'am, the time for this ring and sparring session done been paid for. You got a problem, you need to take it up with the man who paid for it."

"You don't take any responsibility for encouraging delinquency in minors? You shouldn't be allowing boys their age in here during school hours!"

"Stop callin' me a boy!" T-Bird shouted. "And go on home!"

"Don't you dare speak to me in that tone of voice!"

"She's right, son," Levi said. "You need to take that bass outta your voice."

T-Bird glared poison at Levi. "Mind your bidness, man. This is between me an' my sister. An' don't be callin' me 'son.' I don't know you."

Dorothea McBricker turned to Levi and said wrathfully, "My brother's right. This is a family matter and we'll settle it ourselves and thank you to keep to your own business!"

"Hey, I'm only trying to help, Miss McBricker. And brother or not, he's got no call to be yelling at you like that. You're a lady."

That appeared to mollify Dorothea McBricker some. She ran her eyes up and down Levi's compactly muscular 5'10" worth of a hundred and fifty pounds. "You seem like you might be what passes for a gentleman around here. Why are you letting these boys hang out in here beating on each other when they need to be in school getting an education?"

"First of all ma'am, boxing is hardly a waste of time..."

"You can save your breath, Mr...?"

"Kimbro, ma'am. Levi Kimbro."

"Mr. Kimbro, my father and three of my uncles boxed. They taught me and my brothers how to box so I know all about the virtues of the sport. And I have no problem with Teddy coming here to spar. After school."

"I ain't wasting my time here, Thea. I'm getting paid for sparring with Billy." T-Bird McBricker waved a gloved hand at Billy Rico who had moved to the center of the ring where he shadow boxed, keeping warmed up while the family drama played itself out.

"I don't care. Get out of that ring and put your clothes on. I'm taking you to your school myself to make sure you get there. Afterwards is your own time and you can waste it any way you want. But you're going to go to school if I have to..."

"Hey, hey...it's too early for all that hollering and yelling, y'all."

The pure velvet and honey voice, delivered in a smoky South Carolina accent came from the throat of Duke Williamson. He entered the gym as if it were a grand ballroom. Duke Williamson's sartorial elegance had been legendary in Brooklyn for years. He changed his thousand dollar imported Italian suits three times a day. This particular suit was sapphire blue with a matching homburg sitting atop Duke's head at a rakish angle. He held a brass headed walking stick in his right hand. Duke Williamson moved with the stylish grace of a panther, leading with his lethal charm but he backed it up with plenty of guns and muscle he could call up with the snap of a finger.

Levi watched him approach warily. At his back were his usual entourage; his latest sportin' girl Lillian who had lasted longer than most. Levi heard the stories that Duke was supposed to be married to a white woman beautiful enough to be a movie star he kept in a mansion somewhere way out in Long Island but he didn't believe that. Duke spent too much time in Brooklyn to be married and had too many women. His right-hand man Curtis Sapp stayed at his elbow. Sapp never said or did much. There were stories about him as well. The most popular one was that he had one of those memories where he never forgot a thing he saw, heard or read. Duke used him as sort of a human filing cabinet. It was said that he had all of Duke's business dealings committed to that freaky memory and so Duke had nothing of his illegal activities on paper anywhere. It was all in Sapp's head.

Two of Duke's top leg breakers spread out to take up positions in the gym where they could watch the exit/entrance and cover their boss. They eyed everybody in the gym, communicating quite clearly that it would be wise to just go on with their business.

The final member of Duke's entourage was also the largest. Standing at an even six two and two hundred sixty pounds, Calvin Ballantine scowled at the world with a face that looked like it had probably been frightening folks all his life. Starting with the doctor that delivered him. Calvin Ballantine was just pure flat out mean. Nobody except for Duke had any affection for him at all. He didn't take pleasure in women as much as he used them up and threw them away. Even though he drank liquor like most men drank water nobody could ever remember having seen him drunk. The one thing everybody could agree on was that he was the deadliest and most dangerous fighter in Duke's stable as well as his personal bodyguard. Nicknamed 'Deathblow' he had killed two men in backroom brawls in the last five years. Calvin had lasted a lot longer than most in the backrooms.

Duke shrugged off the ankle length leather trench coat draped across his shoulders like a cape. Lillian easily caught it, casually threw it over her forearm. Duke walked on over to Nappy. "What's the rumpus, Nappy? I come to watch my newest investment spar." Duke's bright eyes went from Nappy to Levi. "Hey, Dancer…heard you whooped Cornbread last night. You think you're finally ready for my main man here?" Duke waggled his head in Calvin's direction.

Levi forced a smile. It was easier than he thought. "I don't think I'd be ready for ol' Deathblow unless I had a couple'a .45's in the ring with me."

Duke laughed, lightly punched Levi in the shoulder." Anytime you want to stop wasting your time with punks and fight a real man, let me know. I'll make it more than worth your while. So, what's the holdup?" he said, returning his attention to Nappy.

But it was Dorothea who answered. "The holdup is that my brother should be in school. You want somebody to spar with your man, you find somebody else."

Duke held out his gloved hand. "And you are?"

The young woman didn't so much as look down at the hand. "Dorothea McBricker. Teddy's my brother."

"Thea! My name is T-Bird! How many times I gotta tell you that? T-Bird!"

"And Teddy should be in school. And as long as he lives with me he will be going to school."

"Yeah, well once I start workin' for Mr. Williamson for real, I'll get my own place! Ain't that right, Mr. Williamson?"

"You're not working for anybody until after you finish school!"

"Before we start planning out the future, can we deal with today?" Duke said smoothly. "Such as, I paid your brother fifty dollars to give my boy Billy a good workout and I intend to get my money's worth."

"I'll give you your money back," Dorothea insisted.

"Fine." Duke again held out his hand. "Fifty bucks, if you please."

Dorothea's eyes narrowed in anger but her voice softened. "You know good and well I don't have fifty dollars on me. Working folks don't walk around with that kind of money."

Duke turned away from her. "Go on back to sparring, boys. And don't take it easy on each other."

"Wait a minute!" Dorothea laid a hand on Duke's arm. Calvin Ballantine growled like an angry Doberman and took a couple of steps forward. Curtis Sapp waved him back. Sapp hadn't yet seen the woman Duke Williamson couldn't charm.

"I said my brother isn't going to spar with your man!"

"Miss McBricker, your brother and I entered into a business arraignment that we shook hands on. He agreed to spar with Billy for fifty dollars. Now unless you or somebody else is going to give me my money, T-Bird is going to spar. And I don't intend to stand here all day long and argue about it either." Using the brass head of his walking stick, Duke lightly brushed Dorothea's hand off his arm with a look that communicated better than words that it would be best for her if she not do that again.

Dorothea turned to Nappy. "Can you give him fifty dollars? I'll pay you back next week, I promise."

Nappy spoke around the cigar stub in his mouth. "Baby sister, either you're crazy or you think I am. I don't know you from Bathsheba. How do I know you'll come back with my money?"

"I give you my word!"

Nappy snorted and rolled his eyes.

In desperation Dorothea stepped over to Levi and looked up at him with pleading eyes as she said, "Can't you do something? Please? Can you lend me the money or talk to this man? I don't want Teddy getting mixed up with these people!"

Normally Levi would have followed Nappy's example and minded his own business. Especially when it came to anything having to do with Duke. But there was something about this firecracker of a girl that had affected him the minute he laid eyes on her. And he had to admit, he admired her for the way she'd stood up to Duke. She had steel in her spine for sure. Father Tim would have liked her.

"Duke."

Duke half-turned. "What's up, Dancer?"

"How about I spar with your boy?"

Now he had Duke's full attention. The gangster's eyes glittered warily as he walked over to Levi. "You? Why would you want to do that?"

"Because I don't have fifty dollars on me. Otherwise I'd give it to you so we could stop wasting the morning with all this here jaw-jackin.' Nappy's got a gym to run, this young lady has got to get her brother to school and then I'm sure she has her job to get to. You're a busy man. I'm a busy man. Seems to me the best way to settle this is for me to go a couple rounds with your boy. It's just sparring, right?"

Duke cocked his head to the side, looking at Levi with eyes that seemed to be dissecting the thoughts in his brain, so intensely were they looking at Levi's eyes. No, not just at his eyes. Into them. Finally, Duke said, "Get on out of there, T-Bird. Go on with your sister."

"That ain't fair, Mr. Williamson! That ain't fair at all!"

The honey and velvet left Duke's voice to be replaced by an ugly whip crack of pure rage; "Boy, you make me repeat myself I'm gonna make you wish you hadn't! Now getcher tail outta that ring, put your clothes on and go with your sister! And mind what she tells you, hear?"

Everybody went silent, startled by the sudden change in Duke's attitude and voice. It was as if he'd opened up a private cage somewhere in his soul and let a snarling beast out to romp just for a bit. And just as suddenly, he smiled and his honey velvet voice came back. "T-Bird, if you want to work for me there's certain things you have to learn. One of those is that you can't be a leader until you learn how to follow orders. Another is not to disrespect your own family. Now you get out of there, get dressed and go on to school like your sister says. Come by the liquor store and see me after school is out. We'll talk then."

Dorothea looked as if she were going to object to that but Levi caught her eyes and with a tiny shake of his head indicated that she should let it alone.

Duke nodded at Levi. "Okay, Dancer. Climb on up in there and give my boy a real workout, then. And thanks."

Dorothea smiled gratefully at Levi. "Thank you, Mr. Kimbro. I really appreciate this."

"You want to thank me, have dinner with me later on at Smackey's Diner."

"Oh. I...I...look, I'm not that kind of girl..."

"Damn, woman, I'm not asking you to run off with me to Tijuana and get married. You do eat dinner, don't you?"

Dorothea smiled. "Yes. Yes, I do. Very well. I'll meet you for dinner at Smackey's. Six-thirty?"

"I'll have a booth ready for us. Best go on now and take your brother to school."

Said brother was not in a good mood at all. He gave Levi a look of undiluted death. Levi had the feeling he and T-Bird were not destined to be the best of friends.

Nappy said to Levi, "You sure you know what you're doing, man?"

"What's the harm, Nappy? We're just sparring, is all. We go around three, four rounds and I give the kid a love tap, knock him on his ass just enough to give him the idea that maybe he should call it a day. And I get a date with a pretty girl out of it. What could go wrong?"

ROUND FOUR

It didn't take long for Levi to change into the appropriate gear. Nappy put a sparring helmet on his head. Made sure it was comfortable there. "I think you're crazy to do this, man."

"You worry too much. This will all be over in 'bout a half hour." But Levi had to admit that he didn't like how Duke was whispering to Billy Rico. The young man threw a look at Levi over his shoulder that wasn't at all friendly.

Levi called across the ring; "You know this is just some friendly sparring, right, Duke?"

Duke flashed a brilliant grin full of beautiful teeth he'd no doubt spent a fortune on. "Yeah, Dancer, yeah! I'm just telling Billy here that he's getting in the ring with a real pro, is all." Duke slapped Billy on the shoulder and stepped off the ring to take a seat on a nearby bench to watch.

Nappy himself rang the bell and Levi headed out to the center of the ring. Billy Rico went right to work on his midsection, which wasn't bad. Most inexperienced young guys concentrated on the head, trying for that one big shot that would seriously stun or even knock out an opponent. They didn't appreciate the value of laying the foundation for a later round knockout by working those ribs, taking the air out of an opponent.

Levi pulled his elbows in and let the boy have his fun so that he could look good in front of Duke. Billy had some power there, no doubt but he'd have more if he had that extra muscle on him. Billy kept on hooking in those rights and left to his ribs.

"Don't be afraid to mix it up, kid. Throw some jabs at my head just to keep me guessing," Levi said before he could stop himself. He hadn't meant to give out free advice, but what the hell. Long as he was in here, might as well.

But Billy didn't see it that way. "Tend to your fightin' an' I'll tend to mine!" And then he did let rip with four quick southpaw jabs that did indeed make Levi guess that maybe he was underestimating this kid. Levi went to the left, then to the right, demonstrating that light footwork that had earned him his nickname. Billy bobbed and weaved, trying to target someplace on Levi to hit. But suddenly, Levi had become as elusive as a shadow on a mirror.

Billy did the wrong thing then and pursued Levi instead of just hanging back and forcing Levi to come to him. Levi send him some strong jabs to remind him to keep his distance. Not strong enough to really give him pause but just enough to let him know he should respect the length of Levi's arms.

Billy banged his gloves together, decided to step up his game a bit and go right for Levi's head in a flurry of straight punches that Levi blocked with his forearms.

Nappy rang the bell and the fighters returned to their respective corners. Nappy gave Levi a drink of water. He rinsed, spat and said, "That wasn't a three-minute round, Nappy."

"So? Besides, I thought the kid could take a minute to cool off. He's takin' this a little too serious. You should teach him some respect."

"Nah. Let him have his fun. He ain't hurtin' me none and I'm trying to make him look good for Duke."

Nappy grunted and gave Levi a strange look but he let it go. He climbed down from Levi's corner and rang the bell for the second round.

And just like that, Billy came across the ring like a heatseeking missile and threw a solid roundhouse right at Levi's head that connected before he knew what was up. Levi stumbled backwards, almost went down before catching himself, managed to stay on his feet. That blow had caught him totally by surprise and Billy had put everything behind it. If Levi didn't have the helmet on and if Billy had that extra thirty pounds behind it, that would have knocked Levi out for sure.

"C'mon, punk! I got more for you!" Billy waded in with body blows that had real anger-fueled heat behind them. "Tryin' to make me look bad in front'a Mr. Duke? I'll bust yo' ass!"

Levi pushed the younger man away. "Man, you done gone crazy? We just sparrin' here!"

"Mr. Duke told me you think you such a big man! Get your jollies outta makin' people look stupid! I got your stupid right here!" And Billy Rico gave him another smashing roundhouse right and Levi tasted blood. And that's when he had enough.

He stepped in and slammed his right fist square into the younger man's breadbasket. Billy staggered backwards, spitting out his mouthpiece. One hand went to wrap around his stomach while the other went out to try and get some support from the ropes. But it was no use. Billy Rico went down like The Titanic, desperately gasping for air and wondering why he had no feeling in his entire body.

Nappy was already in the ring, turning Billy Rico on his side. "Just breathe easy, son. You just got the wind knocked outta you. Feels worse

Billy threw a solid roundhouse right at Levi's head that connected...

than it actually is. You just gotta get some air back in. Breathe, now. Breathe."

Levi stalked over to the side of the ring where Duke Williamson sat on the bench, smiling slightly, removing a cigar from a platinum cigar case. Levi yelled down at him, "What kinda games you playing at, Duke? What did you tell that boy that craziness for and get him all worked up?"

"I don't have the slightest idea what you're talking about, Dancer," Duke answered smoothly. "All I saw…all anybody here saw was you lose your temper at a kid just trying to get some expert practice from a so-called professional who damn near sent him to the hospital."

"The wind's just knocked outta him and you know it!"

Duke shrugged. "Damn shame, man…he's just a kid. Wasn't no threat to you. Kid had family down in Florida he was going to send money to."

Nappy spoke up from where he still knelt by Billy, who now sat up, looking much better for having gotten in some good air. "The boy's fine, Duke. No need on building this up into more than what it is."

Duke got up, his cigar in his dazzling white teeth. "Like I said, Nappy…" and here, Duke raised his voice so that everybody could in the gym could hear him clearly… "everybody here in your gym saw what happened." And with that, Duke breezed out just as regally as he breezed in.

Levi went back over to Nappy and Billy and they both helped Billy to his feet. "Look here, kid, Duke's playing with both of us. I dunno what game he's got going on…"

"Mr. Duke told me that you liked to embarrass other fighters, make 'em look stupid. He said I couldn't fight for him 'less I took your head off."

Nappy nodded at some of the other guys in the gym who had been training. Some of them were huddled in corners, talking quietly. "Duke knowed what he was doin'. Some of these cats in here gossip worse than old ladies sittin' in the windows."

Levi shook his head. "I'm not worried about that. I just don't want to get mixed up in Duke's games." He turned to Billy. "Hey, we cool?"

"Man, I just want to fight. I don't want to get in no trouble and I don't want to end up broke and on the street."

"Nappy?"

"You want me to look out for the kid? Sure. I can make some calls. Line him up with some legit fights. What you gonna do?"

"Take me a shower, change and then go have me a nice long chat with Mr. Duke Williamson."

ROUND FIVE

Duke Williamson had a whole bunch of "offices" where he conducted his business. But the one place he spent most of his time was a liquor store on Tompkins Ave. The store itself was totally legit. Duke only used the place to hold meeting and coordinate his number runners as well as the myriad other illegal operations he had fingers in.

Levi nodded at the crowd of retirees who always hung outside the liquor store no matter how cold or how hot it was. Inside, the owner/manager who everybody called 'Horse' even though Levi had never found out why raised his hand in greeting. "Duke said you might be along, Dancer." Horse pressed a button on the underside of the counter and buzzed Levi through to the back. He navigated a short hallway and knocked on the door at the end.

"Come on in, Dancer," Duke's jovial voice said. Levi went on into a moderate-sized room with comfortable furniture, a small bar and a TV set in the corner. The set was off but a radio perched on the windowsill tuned to an all jazz station played softly. Duke sat behind a battered classic office desk that was plainly only there to provide a place for him to set down his drinks and his newspapers. A stack of them occupied half of the desk's space. Lillian sat on the couch. Reclined would be a better word. But then again, Lillian was the type of woman who even when she sat in a straight-back chair gave the impression she reclined.

Levi looked around. "Where's the rest of your crew?"

Duke looked up from the *Daily News,* shrugging at the same time. "They're out working. What, you think I need Deathblow to stand over me all day long? Why? You planning on beating the tar out of me?" Duke chuckled. "I thought we were cool, Dancer."

"Dammit, Duke, what was all that back there about? Why'd you get that kid all riled up?"

"I wanted to see what he could do against a real fighter. Wanted to see if he had some heart."

"You could have spoken to me. I know how to push a fighter so he'll show his stuff. You didn't have to do that. The kid doesn't have the experience to know how to shrug that off. You could have gotten him hurt really bad."

Duke threw down his paper on the desk, sucked his teeth. "Man, I knew you wasn't gonna hurt that kid."

"Then what was all that nonsense you were throwing around back in the gym?"

"Nothing wrong with starting some rumors going around. Tends to make people get a little more creative with their bets come fight time." Duke waved at a leather armchair. "Sit down, man. Relax. Lillian, get my friend Dancer here a drink."

"Nah, nothing for me. I just wanted to let you know I didn't appreciate that, Duke. Play all the games you want but leave me outta them. We clear?"

Duke sat back, interlaced manicured fingers on his stomach. "I don't understand you at all, Dancer. What is it you want? It can't be money, otherwise you'd hook up with me and make a truckload."

"There's ways of making money, Duke. I'm not interested in your way is all. I make enough money for my needs and that's enough."

Duke shook his head. "That's a damn shame, man. I'm working on some deals that are going to put a whole lot of folding green in the pockets of my fighters. Me too. My boys are gonna take on fighters of the other boroughs. Have a kind of tournament. Then go on the road to other cities. Lot of money to be made. You throw in with me, you'll be a millionaire inside of two, three years. And that's a guarantee."

"And how much do you make?"

"What do you care as long as you get yours? Isn't that what this is all about?"

"No, it ain't. Like I said, there's ways of making money and then there are ways of making money."

"Oh, cut the baby bullshit!" Duke roared, slapping the desk with a wide hand. "You think you're some kind of hero who's gonna set the world on fire? Man, you beat the hell outta other men for M-O-N-E-Y and that's the bottom line. Don't come in my place of business trying to run me down and play at you're bein' so much better than the rest of us. When it comes down to it, you're just like us, Dancer. And you know what? I think *that's* what really bothers you."

"Whatever you say, Duke. Whatever you say," Levi turned to leave but Duke spoke up again.

"So how about this fight you owe me?"

Levi cocked his head in annoyance. "Now what are you talking about?"

"You put my newest fighter out of commission. I'd say that means you owe me a fight."

"I don't owe you a damn thing, Duke. Billy's fine. He just had the wind knocked out of him. He can fight."

"That's not what Deathblow is telling folks. Word on the street is that the boy has cracked ribs. You get funny looks the next couple of days, you'll know why."

"What is your problem, man? Why can't you just leave folks alone?"

"I do leave folks alone. Regular folks. But you and me, we're in the same game. And I just don't think it's fair you won't allow me to make some money. You're a selfish bastard, Dancer. You know you're one of the hottest tickets in town. It's not fair you don't let me get a taste now and then. Now, if you and Deathblow were to go at it…"

"I won't fight him."

Duke grinned. "You scared of him?"

Levi spat on the floor.

The grin left Duke's face. "You're lucky I'm in a good mood today."

"I won't fight Ballantine because he's not a fighter. He's a killer. And if you think I'm gonna give him the opportunity to kill or even worse, cripple me for life, you can just kiss my black…"

"You wanna watch it right there, boy!" Duke snarled, leaping to his feet. "And you might as well fight Deathblow right now 'cause it's gonna happen sooner or later!"

"You set me up with any of your other fighters and I'll meet 'em. But not Ballantine. You call Nappy and make the arraignments." And then Levi hurried up and left because he knew that if he didn't, either he or Duke would end up killing each other right then and there. Maybe they still would. But not now. And not today. Not when he had something else to look forward to.

As he hit the sidewalk and the cold air smacked him in the face he knew that the smart thing to do would be was to turn right back around, go back to Duke and tell him he wasn't fighting any of his people under any circumstances, period. But he wasn't in a smart mood. He had allowed Duke to play him and that stung. Stung enough that he intended to take it out on whoever Duke put up against him. And maybe then Duke would have sense enough to back off and leave him alone.

And Levi knew full well there was about as much chance of that happening as there was of him getting free food from a Chinese restaurant.

ROUND SIX

Smackey's Diner over on Myrtle Avenue was well known for its good, solid food at a reasonable price. You got a lot of food on your plate and depending on what you ordered, sometimes more than what you could eat right there. Smackey's was a family owned and run business. The cooks in the kitchen were all Smackey's aunts he'd brought up from North Carolina to work for him.

Levi sat where he could see the front door and tried not to seem anxious when it opened, which was every seven seconds. He pretended to read his *Daily News* but he had a twisty feeling in his gut he was being stood up. Dorothea was fifteen minutes late and Levi was getting the stink-eye from his favorite waitress, Glodean. The dinnertime crowd was coming in which meant that Levi couldn't tie up a table without ordering something. Glodean stomped on over on size twelve feet, cracking her plum-sized wad of gum she'd been chewing on for ten hours straight. "You gots to order something, baby. An' not just another cup a'coffee, either."

"Guess she's not coming. Might as well have my..." and that's when a breathless Dorothea ran through the door and wriggled her way around patrons leaving and up to the booth, touching Glodean lightly on the shoulder, indicating she should move aside and let Dorothea slide into the seat.

"I'm sorry I'm late. Missed the bus and had to wait for the next one, which of course was packed."

"Y'all want a menu?" Glodean asked.

"What's the special today?" Levi asked.

"Stewed turkey wings with two sides."

"Give me that with collards and corn." Levi said.

"That sounds good. I'll have that as well," Dorothea said. When their waitress moved off, Dorothea said as she shrugged out of her coat. "Well, my momma always said that first impressions could be deceiving and she was so right."

"How so?"

"You didn't wait for me to order first and you didn't help me off with my coat. Earlier today when you stuck up for me I thought you were a gentleman. Guess I was wrong."

"First off, you were late. I like to eat on time. Second, you sat down so fast I didn't have a chance to help you off with your coat. You want to go on back outside, I'll get Glodean back here and we can do this all over again right this time."

Surprisingly, Dorothea giggled. "I am sorry about being late. And I'm used to doing most things for myself. It *would* be nice if you remembered in future to help me off with my coat, though."

"I take it that means we'll have another date?"

"Is this a date? I thought we were just having dinner. I don't know you well enough to know if I want to date you formally, Mr. Kimbro."

"Ask me anything you want." Levi sat back in his seat, stretched out his arms to rest on the back cushion of his side of the booth. He grinned with easy amiability. "I'm an open book, Miss McBricker."

"Ah, I know something about you, Mr. Kimbro. When I could get my brother to stop yelling and cursing long enough to speak he told me about you. You've got quite the reputation, he says."

"How come I've never seen your brother around the gym before?"

"He just got here a few months ago. He's been bouncing around other gyms here in Brooklyn, a couple in Manhattan. Our family is down in Fincastle, Virginia. Most of them, anyway. Teddy just shows up at my door one day at Blip A.M. and says he's going to stay with me until he can get a job and get his own place."

"You didn't send him back?"

"He said he'd just leave home again if I did that. I spoke to my mother on the phone. Her and my father are just about exhausted from trying to deal with Teddy's nonsense. He wants big money and fast women. I figured that at least if he stayed with me I could keep him in line, make him go to school and at least get a high school diploma." Dorothea sipped water before continuing. "Teddy always did hate living in Virginia. Said he was tired of being country."

"What made you come up here?"

Dorothea shrugged. "The same thing, I suppose. Oh, I didn't hate it like Teddy but I knew that there wasn't much future down there. And besides, everybody my age leaves as soon as they can put enough nickels together for bus fare. And it's not that I don't mind Teddy staying with me but he wants that fast life and he's not fast enough to deal with the crowd he wants to run with."

"You said your father and uncles boxed."

Dorothea nodded. "Taught me, Teddy and my other two brothers and sisters how to box. One of my brothers is out in Los Angeles boxing. Mark's doing real well out there."

"Then how come Teddy didn't go stay with him, then?"

Dorothea laughed and shook her head. "Ever since they were kids Teddy and Mark fought like cat and dog. Folks in our town couldn't believe they were brothers, that's how much they disliked each other. Teddy wouldn't go stay with Mark if his life depended on it. But Teddy and I always got along. That's why he came behind me." Dorothea's face became serious. "Let's get something straight right off. I won't have you thinking he's some country roughneck."

"He just needs a firm hand is all. And from what I saw of you this morning, I think you've got that hand. You dealt with him just fine. And Duke as well."

Dorothea frowned. "And that's just the type of man I don't want my brother getting mixed up with! I know men like that. Soon as I came to Brooklyn they were on me like white on rice, trying to get me to…well, you know."

"Yeah…"

"But you seem like you're a cut above that sort. Why are you mixed up with them?"

"Fighting is what I do best." Levi shrugged. "And it's only something I'm doing until I get to where I want. It's a stepping stone, is all. If I were going to box professionally I'd be doing it already." Levi cocked his head as a sudden thought came to him. "You don't seem to be much surprised by my fighting in the backrooms."

"Please! Do you think Brooklyn is the only place that has backroom fighting? What else do you think was the big thing to do on Friday and Saturday nights where I come from? I saw many nights when my father needed extra money for something and he came home with his knuckles bloody and his face looking like he fell out an ugly tree and hit every branch on the way down." Dorothea shrugged. "He did what he had to do to get by. I'm sure you do the same."

Glodean returned with their food and they dug in with a will and for about five minutes there was no sound other than the clinking of their knives and forks on the china plates. Then Dorothea came up for air and said, "What do your folks think about your fighting?"

"I don't have any folks."

"Everybody's got folks, Mr. Kimbro."

Levi held up a hand for a pause as he took a drink of water to wash down his food before continuing. "I was raised in an orphanage. I don't even remember who my folks were. Supposedly they died in a car crash in Chicago. Nobody knew what they were doing in Chicago, why they were there, anything like that. I was about nine, ten years old and I was in the back seat of the car when it crashed. But I don't remember anything before waking up in the hospital. They say I was in a coma for three days. Father Tim told me years later that the doctors told him that I had some kind of brain injury, that's why I was in the coma. Guess it wiped out some of my memory."

"Father Tim?"

"Father Tim Brophy. He ran the orphanage I lived in, St. Vincent's. He was the one the hospital called because they didn't know what to do with me and apparently my parents had no information on them that indicated any next of kin. And honestly, the authorities weren't all that interested in trying to find any." Levi shrugged. "They were colored and nobody cared. Father Tim came and got me and took me to the orphanage. Father Tim didn't see color when it came to us boys. I slept and ate right along with the white boys."

"Were you the only colored boy there?"

Levi shook his head. "There were three or four of us. But Father Tim didn't treat us any differently from the white boys. And he taught us how to box right along with them so we could defend ourselves from the neighborhood kids. The orphanage was smack dab in-between Italian and Irish neighborhoods. Most of the time we were left alone. Most folks in both neighborhoods knew Father Tim and knew he didn't put up with no foolishness or messing around with his boys. But he couldn't watch us all the time so he made sure we knew how to use these." Here Levi grinned and held up his fists.

"It sounds horrible."

Levi shrugged. "It could've been worse. I'm not saying it was Heaven but it wasn't exactly Hell either. I did okay. I hung out a lot with Cholly and he helped."

"Cholly?"

"He was the handyman at St. Vincent's. Did the repairs, kept the boiler running. He had more books than anybody I've ever known and he lent them out to any boy who wanted to read 'em. Cholly also taught me carpentry, electrical work, plumbing…"

"If you know how to do all that then why are you working in a gym, fighting in barrooms?"

Levi waggled a finger. "Hey, can't tell you everything all at one time. Got to leave something for our next date."

"You seem awfully certain that there is going to be a next date, Mr. Kimbro."

"I feel fairly positive that there will be, Miss McBricker."

And then she gave Levi the best smile he'd seen in many a year. "You always this positive about everything you do, Mr. Kimbro?'

"Just about, Miss McBricker. Just about."

ROUND SEVEN

Levi continually moved away from the straight punches thrown at him by Shock Bronson. Shock had got his nickname because supposedly when he hit you with one of those flesh and bone mallets he called fists it felt like an electric shock. Levi intended to keep away from him this first round, see what kind of footwork he had, what kind of speed.

They fought in the backroom of an after-hours club on DeKalb Avenue. Unlike a lot of backrooms, this one had a makeshift ring. Not regulation at all. But then again, nobody wanted to see a regulation fight. That was not what they were here for. Levi got out of the way of a looping right cross with an almost dainty ease and the mob surrounding the ring yelled. They might have been glad Levi got out of the way but it was more likely they were disappointed.

Levi stayed on his toes, getting out of the way of Shock's straight punches, relying on his agility to keep him out of range of those long arms while delivering those double jabs of his that he liked to work behind. Shock plainly liked to be the aggressor, coming on in and catching Levi a good one right under the heart. Levi continued moving backwards, continued throwing double jabs and then suddenly stopping, planting his feet and delivering two solid left-right jabs that made Shock back up, blinking in surprise. Unlike the previous punches, these jabs hurt.

"Get in there an' fight!" Somebody howled and the rest of the crowd added their profane agreement. Shock came on in again, slamming his fists into Levi's side. Levi pulled his elbows into his sides and clinched, letting himself fall back against the ropes. Bendigo Cribb immediately jammed his muscular, meaty arms in between them. "C'mon, boys, break it up, break it up."

They broke cleanly. Shock tried a lunging jab that missed, following it up with a roundhouse right that Levi ducked under and drew screams of delight from the crowd. Backs were slapped. Money changed hands. A pair of purple panties were thrown into the ring which added to the profane merriment.

Levi sent a series of solid left jabs Shock's way. Shock didn't like that. His perfectly round eyes never left Levi's calm, unreadable face that showed no more emotion than a brick wall. One of Bendigo's people whacked the bell to signal the end of the round and that's when Shock went berserk, slamming his shoulder into Levi's chest, pounding his ribs with both hands, muttering curses under his breath.

Bendigo once again, got in there, pulling Shock off of Levi, yelling, "Gowan! Git ta yer corner! Git, I says!"

Shock stalked to his corner, kicking his stool aside, refusing to sit down. His corner man worked on his cuts and bruises while he stood glaring hate at Levi, who smiled back as though he and Shock were best friends.

"How you feel?" Nappy's voice was right in Levi's ear, which was the only way Levi would be able to hear him, so loud was the screaming and yelling of the half-drunken crowd who were about ready for their taste of blood.

"Good, good. That boy don't waste no time losin' his temper, do he?" Levi pursued his lips, blowing a kiss across the ring. Shock spat in Levi's direction. Levi grinned back.

"Don't you go makin' him crazy, now." Nappy warned. "You want him mad enough to be stupid and forget how to fight but not so mad he wants to kill you, hear?"

The bell rang again and Levi came out of his corner, straight at Shock. He threw several jabs at Shock's chin, taking Shock by surprise. The man hadn't expected Levi to come right at him all full of fire.

"Dancer! Dancer! Dancer!" The crowd bellowed as Levi circled to Shock's left, seemingly to glide backwards as he did so. Levi blocked Shock's jabs. Jabs that really stung. But Shock wasn't following up and going in after those jabs. He had decided to lay back a bit.

But when the punch came it came straight and fast. Levi let the punch slip and came in with a flurry of rights against his ribs. Shock recovered quick and slung a hook just below Levi's left ear.

Levi stumbled back but stayed on his feet. That had been a pretty good shot, one that made Levi see bright flashes in front of his eyes. He continued to jab, keeping Shock back.

And then Levi saw something out of the corner of his eye he couldn't believe. And he paid for it when Shock let him have a haymaker that ended up right in the pit of Levi's stomach. Levi covered up his face and head as best he could as Shock came at him, seemingly having grown another four or five arms in five seconds. Shock went to work on Levi's mid-section, a wide grin on his face. "You not dancin' so pretty now, is you, nigger?"

Indeed, Levi was not dancing at all anymore. His sole concern now was stay on his feet long enough to survive the round. Shock's sledgehammer fists banged away at his ribs as Levi kept covered up, the screaming of the crowd seeming to get louder but not as loud as the intimate grunting of Shock Bronson in his ears.

Shock went to work on Levi's mid-section…

And then the bell rang and Levi staggered away to his corner. He fell onto his stool and glared up at Nappy. "Hey, man, you know that girl's here?"

"That Dorothea chick? Yeah, I knew she was here. She asked me to get her in."

"Why the hell didn't you tell me she'd be here?"

"Because your mind is supposed to be on the fight, not tail!"

"And you didn't think me seein' her in the crowd alla sudden would throw me off? Dammit, Nappy, if we weren't friends I would think you an' Duke…" Levi stopped when he saw the look in Nappy's eyes and realized he was about to step way over a line he didn't want to cross. Napoleon Johnson had done some pretty underhanded stuff in his day. But backstabbing a friend wasn't one of them. And Levi damn well knew that.

"Shut your mouth. We got us a fight to win. We can argue afterwards. Let me work on that swelling a bit. Then you get back in there and kick his ass. He's mean, sure. And he's tough as old shoe leather. But he don't think. And that's how you beat him, man. *You* think. And you use your skills! He wants ta get rough? Then make sure he pays the cost! Now git in there!"

The bell rang again and Levi came up off his stool, looking at the grinning Shock Bronson through the thick haze of grayish smoke courtesy of the numerous cigarettes and cigars being smoked. An empty liquor bottle flew at Levi's head and he ducked to one side. It went on by, smashed on the floor outside the ring. "Fight, dammit! I got five hundred bucks on your black ass!"

Levi went at Shock as hard as he knew how, just trying to batter through the man's defense. Shock backed up, letting Levi throw everything at him, figuring that Levi would soon exhaust himself. But that was exactly what Levi wanted him to think. He abruptly circled, once again demonstrating that nimble footwork that had earned his name. Shock, taken off balance, tried to get some distance between them until he knew what was what and that's when Levi caught him with a roundhouse right.

Levi followed it up by pounding lefts and rights into Shock. Shock got in there, tried to tie Levi up. Levi shoved him away and sent a sizzling right into Shock's jaw with speed and precision. Shock's head snapped around and he stumbled to the side. He shook it off, snarling in rage as he waded back in. They stood toe-to-toe, trading blows with savage intensity, the tape on their hands turning red as Levi and Shock banged away at each other. Shock yelled through bloody teeth, "C'mon! C'mon!" Shock forgot all about fighting and simply lost himself in his rage to batter Levi to death with his fists.

And that's when Levi stepped in and made Shock pay.

The uppercut lifted Shock a full three inches up off his feet. He crashed to the canvas. Shock wasn't out of it but he was so close as to make no difference. Bendigo ambled over to Shock and bent down. After five seconds of examination he straightened up and waved his arms, signaling the fight was over. The room exploded into pandemonium as men and women screeched for joy at the amount of money they'd won or cursed at the loss of same.

From where he sat, Duke Williamson nodded at the heavily breathing Levi who stood over his defeated fighter, looking at Duke with open defiance. Deathblow stood just behind his boss, glaring at Levi with equal defiance.

Levi turned away and looked for Dorothea in the crowd and he saw her. And she was smiling. Levi strode back to his corner, held out his hands to Nappy. "Get this damn tape off of me then you and Dorothea got some explainin' to do."

ROUND EIGHT

"Why didn't you tell me you were coming to the fight? I just saw you last night." Levi demanded. He had found a secluded corner where he corralled both Dorothea and Nappy side by side. He glared at the both of them. "I don't like it when my friends play games with me."

"What games? I wanted to see the fight so I asked Mr. Johnson to get me in, that's all." Dorothea's voice may have been serious but there was a twinkle in her eye that was at the same time so cute and so infuriating Levi didn't know whether to kiss her or give her a clout upside the head. "I've heard so much about the great Dancer I wanted to see you fight. What's so bad about that?"

"Nothing! It's just that I don't like surprises is all. Dammit, Nappy, I wish you'd told me!"

"Now don't go blaming Mr. Johnson. I made him promise not to tell you I was going to be here. I wanted to see how you fight, not have you showing off for me or worse yet, not fighting how you usually fight." Dorothea paused for a few seconds before continuing; "You're an awfully private man, Levi Kimbro. This is a side of you I wanted to see without you trying to hide it or soften it for me. If we're going to be…friends then you have to show me what your life is like and this is part of your life. Maybe a bigger part than you want yourself to believe."

"That's the same reason she gave me for wanting to come see you fight, Levi. You ask me, the girl's got more sense than you do," Nappy grinned.

"You go on and get outta here before I remember I'm supposed to be mad at you." Levi gently punched the older man in the arm. "And thanks."

"Yeah, yeah, yeah. I'll see you in the morning." Nappy left them to find himself a drink and Levi finished buttoning his shirt.

"So, you want to know all about me, do you?" Levi asked. "Can I ask why?"

Dorothea shrugged. "I think I do like you, Mr. Kimbro. There's a lot to like. But there's a whole lot you don't let anybody see. I heard about what you did for the Allen boy."

Levi waved that away. "Don't make more out of it than what it is."

"Did it have anything to do with you and his mother?"

Levi's eyes snapped around in surprise so fast it was almost comical. "Look here, I don't know what you been told but it—"

Dorothea giggled. "You ought to see your face right now. You look like you've been caught stealing chickens. And people talk, Levi. You know that. And even more, people like to talk about other people and you're a grown man, Levi. Your business is your business. You don't owe me an explanation about anything. Unless you want to explain."

Levi shrugged into his coat. "C'mon."

"Where are we going?"

"My apartment. I want to show you something."

Dorothea stepped back, her eyes narrowing as she spat out, "I thought I made it plain and clear to you what kind of woman I am!"

"And I'm not proposing nothing disrespectful to you. I really want to show you something. Something I haven't shown anybody. Not even Nappy. But I'd like to show you and when I do then you'll understand everything about me you need to."

"Such as?"

"That I'm serious as cancer about what I want to do with my life."

Dorothea sized him up carefully. "No funny business? You promise?"

"You got my word."

Dorothea nodded firmly. "Let's go."

ROUND NINE

"It's just plain crazy keeping that much money here." Dorothea spoke in a hushed, reverential whisper as if she were in church. And with good reason.

Levi grinned up at her from where he squatted next to his hidey-hole filled with rubber-banded folded hunks of money. "You ever see the like?"

Dorothea shook her head slowly. "Levi, you've got a fortune in there. Are you out of your mind? Why don't you put it in a bank?"

"Naw. I don't like banks. Don't trust 'em. And you know there ain't a bank that's going to take all this money from a colored man without asking a whole lot of questions. Questions I can't answer. Next thing I know I'm down in the precinct house with a bunch of cops asking me where did I get the money, who did I rob to get it. And if I tell 'em I got it backroom fightin' they'll just take it for themselves with a kick in my ass for thanks."

"You could put that money in a colored bank, Levi."

"You think they're not gonna ask questions just 'cause I'm colored? Dorothea, I'm not putting my money in a bank and that's all there is to it."

Dorothea pulled her eyes from the money hidden in the floor to let her eyes roam around Levi's small, functional studio apartment. "Your place is small. But I like it. Are you sure your money is safe here?"

"I changed the locks on the door so my landlady doesn't have a key. And not even Nappy Johnson knows I keep my money here. There's only one person besides me who knows about this money. And that's you."

Dorothea gulped. "I don't know if I'm comfortable with you telling me this. We've only known each other a couple of weeks."

"You know what this money is for?"

Dorothea shook her head in a negative.

"I'm taking Business Administration courses at L.I.U. I want to own my own business. Boiler maintenance and repair to start with. Later on, when I can hire some men then we'll do electrical work, carpentry, plumbing. It'll be rough at first because I'll be doing the work myself until I can build up a steady clientele and afford to hire some help. But it won't be as hard as fighting in those backrooms, lemme tell you."

Dorothea's eyes were shining with understanding. "Why, I think that's grand, Levi! And now I do understand! That's why you got the Allen boy a job at Mr. Johnson's gym!"

Levi nodded as he replaced the floorboard. "Nappy's gonna need somebody to be there to do the maintenance work. I mean, if he needs me for anything, I'm there. But he's going to need somebody there all the time, on a regular basis. I can teach the Allen boy what he needs to know. And with what I teach him, he can get work anywhere."

"I guess I was right about you, Mr. Kimbro. You are a cut above."

Levi grunted as he moved the bed back into place. "Anyway, now you know everything about me you need to know." He turned around to look seriously at Dorothea. "As for me and Rose Allen, I'd like to clear that up."

"I told you that you don't need to."

"Hush up and let me finish. Yeah, me and her had us a couple good times. And that's all they were. She's a good woman who got a bad break and I may have taken advantage of that. But just like I'm a grown man, she's a grown woman. Nobody did anything they didn't want to do."

"Levi, I know you're not a saint. I don't expect you to be."

"You're the one who said that people like to talk about people. I'm just trying to let you know that if you want to know anything about me, just ask. I don't make excuses for my life or for what I do or have done. But from here on out, you want to know anything about me you ask me. And we'll deal with it from there. Fair enough?"

Dorothea smiled and nodded. "Fair enough."

"So, is there anything else you want to know about me?"

Dorothea's eyes looked down at Levi's bed as she said coyly, "Well… there are a few more things I would like to know…"

Levi got the distinct feeling he was being tested here. He folded his arms across his chest as he replied; "You said no funny business and I gave my word there wouldn't be."

He saw by the look on her face that he indeed had just been tested and that he'd passed that test. Dorothea said, "Thank you, Mr. Kimbro."

"You're quite welcome, Miss McBricker. And now, considering how late the hour is, may I escort you to your home and see that you get there safely?"

"You certainly may, Mr. Kimbro. You certainly may."

ROUND TEN

Dorothea unlocked the door to her Nostrand Avenue three-floor walkup apartment. Her lips still tingled deliciously from the kiss she had shared with Levi downstairs. It hadn't been a long kiss but it had been a telling one. And it had stirred feelings inside of her. But it was too soon to let him know about those feelings. She'd seen a lot about Levi Kimbro tonight. Enough to impress her. But enough to make her wary as well. She had not only been there to look at him fight to see how he interacted with that world. And she knew that he didn't like to admit it, but he was more at home in that world than he would ever admit to her. Or even worse, to himself.

The lights were still on despite the lateness of the hour and Dorothea knew why. Her brother Teddy sat at the kitchen table, the portable radio quietly playing. Somethin' Smith and The Redheads singing "It's A Sin to Tell A Lie." Teddy paused in his game of solitaire. That and the half empty pint of gin immediately told Dorothea how he had spent his night. "Why aren't you in bed?" she demanded. "It's late."

"Tomorrow's Saturday, remember? No school. And what about you? Whatchoo doing out so late?" Teddy took a swig from the bottle. "Hangin' out in the street ain't you. You bein' all respectable and shit."

"I've told you I don't like you swearing, Teddy. And I don't want you drinking in my house." Dorothea angrily took off her coat and threw it into a chair along with her purse. She walked through the apartment, turning off lights. "And until you start paying the electric bill, I'll thank you not to burn every light in my house."

"Oh, I'll have me some money. Soon. Soon. I'ma gonna start working for The Duke soon. And then I'll get my own place." Teddy went back to his solitaire game. "Get outcher hair and I won't haveta listen to your mouth alla time."

"I'm sick and tired of having this argument with you, Teddy. You're going to school. You're not working for Duke. He's a pimp and a hustler and I will not have you getting involved with him!"

"You think everybody should be a goody-goody like you, huh?" Teddy took another hit from the bottle. "Miss Prim-N-Proper. Walking the straight line. Goin' to church and living a clean life."

"What is wrong with you, Teddy? Why are you so mad all the time?" Dorothea sat down next to him, placed a hand on his forearm. It was hot and trembling.

"I ain't mad! I just want to get my own place is all! And make some real money! That's what I came to the city for! Not to go to school and sit around in this house all damn night long! That's why I left from down south! I coulda stayed down there and done this!"

"But you didn't. You came up here and asked to stay with me and I said you could stay with me as long as you went to school and respected my house. And you're not doing any of that. I know you haven't been to school in the past two days."

"Spyin' on me, huh?" Teddy's eyes narrowed as he shuffled his cards sullenly. "Well, I know a couple of things about you, too, Little Miss Prim-N-Proper who lives to pretend she's all high siddity."

Dorothea removed her hand. "What are you talking about?"

"You think I don't know you went to see that punk Levi Kimbro fight? You think I don't know you two been goin' out? You think I'm stupid?" Teddy slammed the deck of cards down on the table. "You won't let me work for Duke but you spend your nights with that chump! He ain't no better than Duke, lemme tell you!"

"Don't talk about Levi like that, Teddy. You don't know a thing about him."

"Bullshit! I done heard all I need to know about your boyfriend! You ain't nowhere near as smart as you think you are! And you ain't got all that class you think you got, neither! You know what kind of people go to them fights and you went anyway! Know why? 'cause you wanted to see the same damn thing they do!"

"You don't know what you're talking about, Teddy. You're drunk. Levi's a good man."

"Good man, my black ass! Stupid man is more like it! You know how much money he could be making fighting for Duke? But he won't do it? He won't fight for Duke! How stupid is that? Everybody knows they fight for Duke they can make a fortune!"

"Levi doesn't need a fortune! He's already got his own—" Dorothea bit her lower lip so hard she tasted blood. She hadn't meant to blurt that out. But Teddy had made her so mad…

With that unusual cunning that only the intoxicated possess, Teddy pounced on the statement she had cut off. "Already got his own what? What Levi already got?"

"Nothing!" Dorothea shoved away from the table and stood up. "You just got me mad is all. You're making me say things I shouldn't be saying."

Teddy's eyes glittered shrewdly. "Naw. You know something. What Levi already got? He got money?"

"I'm going to bed," Dorothea snapped and stomped out of the kitchen. She went to the bathroom to inspect the inside of her lip where she had bit herself. And she needed time to compose herself, bitterly cursing herself for allowing Teddy to get her so mad that she had almost blurted out that Levi had all that money in his apartment. She closed the door firmly and stood with her back leaning against the door, her body shuddering as she took deep breaths to get herself under control. She went over to the sink, rinsed out her mouth and was pleased to see that the cut wasn't as bad as she had first thought. Still hurt, though.

She opened the door and went back to the kitchen, her intention being to try and talk to Teddy again. But he was gone. The pint of gin was still there. Drained dry. The cards were still on the table as well. Dorothea went over to the chair where she had thrown her coat and purse. The purse was open and it only took a few seconds to verify that Teddy had indeed taken the fifteen dollars she had in her wallet and left the apartment.

For a few seconds Dorothea wondered if she should call Levi. But if she did, what would she tell him? Even if Teddy thought Levi had money, there was no way he could get to it. And Teddy was drunk anyway and with the money he'd just stolen he'd go out and get drunker and by morning he would have forgotten what he and Dorothea had been arguing about anyway. No need to call up Levi at this time of night and get him all excited over nothing. Teddy wouldn't do anything stupid. He'd just been mad and drunk. Everything would be okay in the morning.

Of course it would.

ROUND ELEVEN

"Mr. Levi? Can I ask you something?"

"You can if you can help me put away these tools at the same time." Levi smiled to show he was having some fun with Michael Allen. The boy grinned back with a set of amazingly strong looking teeth and bent to help Levi replace tools neatly into Levi's biggest toolbox. He had three of them and this one held the most tools. A split-top steel box, Michael could barely lift it as high as his knees with both hands. Levi picked it up with one hand and carried it as easily as if it were a loaf of Wonder Bread. "What you want to know?"

Michael lowered his voice. Voices tended to echo and carry down here in the basement. They'd just finished a minor repair of the boiler's feedwater tank pump and Levi had taken the opportunity to give Michael some lessons in boiler maintenance. "Mr. Levi, do you know what happened to my daddy? Does anybody know? Really?"

Levi said nothing for a few minutes. Michael had been working here in Nappy's gym for two weeks now and Levi knew full well that sooner or later the boy would get around to asking that question and Levi knew equally well that he had no answer for him.

"Mikey…'scuse me…*Michael*…you know your daddy was mixed up with some cats he had no business being with, right?"

"I guess so."

"You know so. Look, you're old enough to know the deal. Your daddy went out to rob and steal and he got caught. Them that get caught…well… they got to take what they got coming."

"Cops didn't do nothing about it."

"Yeah." They finished putting away the tools in silence and Levi latched up the big steel box. "What else you got to do today?"

"Empty out all the garbage cans, sweep and mop the staircase."

Levi grunted, reached into his pocket for his wallet and removed a ten-dollar bill from it. Held it out for Michael to take. "Go on and knock off early."

Michael blinked as he looked at the crisp bill in Levi's hand. "You don't pay me until Friday. What's this for?"

"Call it a bonus."

"Nossir." Michael shook his head in a firm negative. "You don't have to do that, Mr. Levi. I didn't mean no harm asking you about my daddy. I just thought that…what with me and you workin' together and all…"

Levi sighed and took the money back and replaced it in his wallet. He knew full well what he should have done in the first place because he could hear Father Tim's voice in his head just as clear as if he'd been standing right there telling him what to do.

"Sit down, Michael."

The boy sat down on the floor cross-legged and Levi sat across from him, letting his big hands rest on his knees. "Michael, there's no easy way to say this. But it's the truth. Your daddy's dead."

"You really think so?"

"I think that if he were still alive after all this time he'd have found a way to contact your momma. Or even if he didn't, he'd have called or come by somebody's house. You got family in Brooklyn, right?"

"Yeah. Plenty of 'em over on Marcy Avenue and some on Tompkins."

"And I think you know that he's dead. I think you just needed to hear somebody say it out loud. Am I wrong?"

"No, Mr. Levi. You ain't wrong. And you're right. I guess I do know he's dead. Or if he ain't he took the opportunity to run off. Which amounts to the same thing, don't it?"

"I guess I do know he's dead."

"Look here, Michael. I grew up in an orphanage so believe me when I say I understand what you're thinking and feeling. But you got to put that aside and be a help to your momma and be a man if for no other reason than to give your brothers something to look up to, be an example for them."

Michael's face had a grimness that no boy his age should have. "I understand what you're saying, Mr. Levi. That why you give me this job?"

"I gave you this job because you needed it. You've been doing fine so far. I don't think you're cut out for the stick-up kid life. I think you just went along with your boys that night you tried to rob me. I think you like to work. And I think you're trying to make a decision."

"What kind of decision?"

"You're trying to decide if you want to be a better man than your father. I think he would want you to be."

Michael nodded slowly and stood up. "I do appreciate the job and you talkin' to me, Mr. Levi. I'd better go on back upstairs and finish up. You need any more help down here?"

"No. Go on with your business. We'll talk more later." Levi watched the boy go and it seemed as if he walked lighter, as if he had put down an unwanted burden he'd carried for far too long. The amazing thing was that Levi himself felt lighter. Unburdening himself of the thoughts he'd been having helped him as well.

He went back upstairs to the gym, nodding at acquaintances as they passed him on the staircase and inside the gym proper. The place was busier than usual. All three rings were being used and the air smelled musky with the fresh sweat of the day. It was perfume to Levi's nose. He headed to Nappy's office. The door was open and Nappy hung up the phone as Levi walked in.

"I think I'm going to have to put in some overtime on that feedwater tank pump. It's okay for now but it's going to need some more work."

"So go ahead and work. What do you need to put in overtime for?"

"'Cause I don't feel like doing it now," Levi laughed, leaning easily against the door frame.

"Man, if this is what you're gonna be like now that you got a steady woman, do me a favor an' get rid of her."

"Weren't you the one telling me a couple of weeks ago about how I needed a woman?"

"Yeah, but I meant just for the night, not for life. You and that Dorothea seem to be getting along real good, though."

"Yeah. She's a girl with brains and class, Nappy. And she gets me, y'know?"

"You ahead of me, then. I had two wives an' ain't a one'a them under-stood what made me tick." Nappy reached for his ashtray and the unlit cigar resting in it, stuck the cigar in his mouth as he continued talking. "They just didn't have a head for the fight game and what it was all about. But as long as I paid the rent and there was food on the table they didn't much care what I did. But I 'spect most women are like that. You lucked out."

"Don't I know it." Levi was interrupted by the ringing of Nappy's phone.

Nappy picked up the receiver and said, "Johnson's Gym, what can I-oh, hey, Morgan. What's up? What? This again? I just got off the phone with Dusty. You know him, he runs that bar over on Utica. He wanted to know was his backroom going to be used. What? Naw, man...I tell you same I told him. I ain't heard nothing, I don't know nothing. What? Aw, man, why would I shit you? Yeah, yeah. If I hear anything I'll give you a call. What? No, man...I don't care what Billy says. I'm telling you I ain't heard nothing. That don't mean something ain't happening but...yeah, yeah...okay, man. Later." Nappy banged down the receiver, shaking his head.

"What's that all about?" Levi asked.

Nappy shook his head. "I been getting phone calls from folks asking about an upcoming fight. Supposedly there's a big one coming up. At least that's what people keep telling me. I dunno...I ain't heard nothing. But folks wanted to know if it were you fighting."

"Me? Why would they think it's me?"

"Why not you? There's only maybe two or three fighters in this part of Brooklyn that can fire up that much heat." Nappy leaned forward on his desk, meaty arms folded. "Speakin' of which, we oughta think about lining you up for another fight real soon."

"What's the rush?"

"The rush is because that girl is going to make you real soft real soon. I gotta get a couple more paydays outta you before she ties you down for good."

"Aw, man...it ain't like that. Neither one of us is even thinking like that. I know I ain't ready to get married and she ain't either. She knows I got a business I want to start up. I can't juggle that and a wife at the same time."

"That's what you say. Take from me as gospel; whenever you got a woman who acts like she ain't interested in getting married, that's when you got to watch out. Trust me, women are thinking 'bout getting married all the time."

"You crazy, you know that?"

"Watch what I say now. See, that's the plan...make you think that she ain't thinking about it and sooner or later that gets you to thinkin' of why she ain't thinking about it. Then one day you say to her; 'Hey, honey, how come you haven't never mentioned nothin' about us getting' married?' That's when she turns them big brown eyes on you all innocent like and WHAM! That's your ass."

"I'm going to leave you to your craziness, Nappy. I got to go downtown and pay some bills. Mikey's taking care of the garbage and he's going to sweep and mop the stairs before he leaves. I'll come back later on tonight to finish up on that tank."

"That reminds me...good call on that boy, Levi."

"Yeah?"

"Yeah. He's a good worker. He's been a real help around here since you brought him on."

"I've been showing him some things about the boiler. Couple more weeks I'm going to buckle down and really start to show him the nuts and bolts. He wants to learn." Levi frowned slightly. "Wish we had some more to do around here. Dorothea's brother could use a job."

"That T-Bird punk? He's workin' for Duke Williamson. Didn't you know?"

"That's the point, Nappy. Dorothea don't want her brother running around with Duke and his crowd. She already asked me if I could find him a job somewhere."

"Man, that punk don't wanna work. Waste of time trying to make a Joe Punchclock outta that cat. He don't want no parts of a nine-to-five."

"You know that. I know that. Try telling that to Dorothea."

"I seen plenty of boys like T-Bird. Come up here from down south green as a Christmas tree. Want to be big men, make big money and have women come runnin' when they snap their finger. They see a guy like Duke. He's got fine threads, nice ride, plenty of women and folks cross the street when they see him comin' an' they think, 'Yeah, that's what I to be like.' They don't understand that there's some cats that can learn the streets and some that were born for 'em. T-Bird ain't neither one and Duke is both." Nappy shook his head. "Sad, man. Sad"

"Yeah. Like I said, I'll be back later on tonight."

"So what about another fight? I can set one up for Saturday."

Levi nodded. "Sure, why not? Folks are talking about a fight already. Let's go ahead and give them one."

ROUND TWELVE

As soon as Levi turned the corner on his block he could tell that something was wrong. His landlady, Mrs. Jenkins was leaning out of her window so far it was a miracle she didn't fall out. Upon seeing him, she pulled back inside and shut the window. Obviously, she had been waiting for him to come on the block. Levi had no idea why. He'd already paid his rent for the month.

He unlocked the front door and stepped into the hallway. Mrs. Jenkins opened the door of her apartment. Mrs. Jenkins was the roundest woman Levi had ever met in his life. Her large, perfectly round head sat on top of an equally round body. She had no neck. Her arms were lumpy tubes of fat. Her legs stubby and lousy with varicose veins. Her feet so swollen that she hadn't been able to wear proper shoes for going on two years now and she got around in floppy slippers all the time.

"I'll be expecting you to move by the end of the month, Mr. Kimbro. I don't put up with no vandalism in my house."

"I'm sure I don't know what you're talking about, Mrs. Jenkins. What seems to be the problem?"

"I didn't say nothin' when you changed the locks on your door and didn't give me no key. I'm in my legal rights to have keys to all my tenants' apartments in case of an emergency. I could have evicted you then."

"Mrs. Jenkins, I think we both know why I changed the locks and didn't give you no key."

"I got a right to inspect the apartments, make sure nobody isn't having somebody live with them that don't pay no rent. I got a legal right."

"Mrs. Jenkins, just tell me what the problem is."

"It ain't my problem, Mr. Kimbro. It's yours. Now, I know all about you fighting and hanging out with hoodlums and I never said nothing 'cause that's your bizness and you kept it out in the street where it belongs. But when you bring it in my house, then it's my bizness. You got your friends tearing up your apartment…" Mrs. Jenkins broke off with a small squeal as Levi took a step forward, his face having gone from aggravated puzzlement to pure rage in nothing flat.

"What friends? What are you talkin' about?"

"Them friends of yours said they were going up to your place to get something! They asked me for a key and I told them you didn't gimme one! Then one of them laughed and said that it was okay, they didn't need a key! And then all that noise…"

Mrs. Jenkins was left talking to herself. Levi bounded up the stairs as if he were weightless, his heart pounding hard against his ribs.

The door had been taken completely off the hinges. Inside it looked as if madmen had a party. His mattress cut to shreds. All the food in the refrigerator dumped on the floor. His books ripped apart. His clothes cut up with knives or straight razors. The strong smell of urine filled the apartment. Cabinet doors torn off, holes knocked in the wall. Everything Levi owned savagely destroyed.

And the gaping empty hole in the floor where his money had been was the worst of all.

ROUND THIRTEEN

Dorothea's first act as soon as she stepped in the foyer of her building was to kick off her shoes. They were brand new and wearing them to work hadn't been the smartest idea. She worked the perfume counter at Woolworth's and as such was on her feet for most of the day. But the shoes were so cute and such a pretty tan color she couldn't resist. She walked on stocking feet up the stairs three flights to her apartment, fumbling inside her purse for her keys as she did so. Two of the keys were brand shiny new. She'd changed the locks three days ago. She hadn't seen Teddy for three days prior to that. No telling where he was or what he had been doing. And Dorothea didn't want to come back home and find her apartment cleaned out.

She gained the landing and walked over to her door, keys in hand. Suddenly she was grabbed from behind and a firm hand clamped over her mouth. A familiar voice whispered in her ear; "Open the door. Now."

Dorothea did as she was told. Once she and her assailant were inside, he slammed the door shut and locked it in one smooth motion. He then shoved Dorothea in a chair. "You stay right there and don't you move."

Dorothea looked up at him in utter disbelief. "Levi, have you lost your mind? What do you think you're doing? You almost gave me a heart attack!"

Levi Kimbro stood over her, breathing hard. Not from exertion but from the effort of trying to keep his volcanic rage under control. "You're lucky. I started to come down to your job and drag you outta there by your neck. But Father Tim always used to say; 'act in haste, repent at leisure.' And besides, the last thing I need right now is cops on my back. That's why I just waited here for you."

"Levi, what's wrong?" Dorothea dropped her purse to the floor and got out of her coat. But she didn't dare stand up. She had seen that look in Levi's eyes before. It was the same look he had that night when she had seen him fight.

"You know what's wrong. You give me my money back, we shake hands, say goodbye and that's the end of it."

"I don't know what you're talking about! You...your money? You mean it's gone? Your money is gone? All of it?"

And now Levi's eyes narrowed, even as the anger started to leave them. He trusted his gut, had to in order to survive the orphanage and the war. And now his gut was telling him that Dorothea honestly didn't know what he was talking about. But he had to be sure.

"You know full well my money's gone, woman. You're the only one you knew where it was! I didn't tell anybody about it except you! Now a week later I get to my place and it's been all torn up, my clothes cut up, everything been pissed on and every dollar I had stolen! I paid for that money with my blood and I'm gonna get it back!"

"Levi, my right hand to God...I did not tell anybody about your money! Do you really think that I would tell anybody about your money?" Dorothea stopped, her eyes opening wider as the thought hit her.

Levi saw her expression change and he jumped on it. "You know something." It was not a question.

"Teddy," Dorothea said in a voice suddenly gone hoarse with fear.

"Your brother? What's he got to do with this? You told him about my money?"

"The night...the night you showed me where your money was. I came home. Teddy was drunk and we argued. He was mad because I went to see you fight. He said some things about you. That you were a bum; that you were a fool because you wouldn't fight for Duke Williamson. We were yelling back and forth and I started to say that you didn't need Duke's money because you had your own money. I cut myself off before I said that, though!"

"No, you didn't! You said enough! Where is your brother?"

"I don't know! He hasn't been home in a week!"

"Don't lie to me, Dorothea! Where is he?"

"Here!" Dorothea flung her keys at him. They bounced off his chest and jingled when they hit the floor. "Look! You'll see that the keys for my apartment are brand new! I changed the locks because I didn't want Teddy coming in here and robbing me while I was at work!"

Levi bent down and picked up the keys, examined the new ones. He looked up at her. "Nappy told me today that Teddy's working for Duke now. That's why he hasn't been back. Duke owns a house over on Vernon Avenue. That's where his boys who don't have their own cribs lay-up. Teddy's probably there."

"Which one? Can we go there now?"

"Hell no. You don't want to go fooling around over there. And we don't know for sure he's there. He ain't the one I need to speak to anyway. He told Duke about my money and Duke sent some of his people to my place. Duke's got my money. Teddy used my money to buy his way into Duke's crowd."

"Levi, you have to believe me…I didn't mean for this to happen."

"Don't really matter, does it? I blame myself. When I kept my mouth shut, everything was fine. First person I tell about my money, it gets stolen."

"You wait just a damn minute, mister!" Dorothea leaped to her feet, her eyes flashing just as much wrathful anger as Levi's. "Don't go to blaming this all on me! You're the damn fool for leaving fifty thousand dollars in his apartment when anybody with any sense would have put it in a bank where it belongs! And I don't want to hear any more of that stupidity about you don't trust banks! That's where that money belonged, Levi! And you don't have anybody to blame for that except you!"

"My money was fine where it was. If I'm to be blamed for anything, it's for trusting anybody. Even you." Levi turned away but stopped when Dorothea laid a hand on his elbow.

"Wait! Where are you going?"

"Where do you think? I'm going to see Duke and get my money back, what else?"

"You think that Duke is just going to hand you back fifty thousand dollars with a 'I'm sorry, Mr. Kimbro. It won't happen again?' He'll kill you, Levi!"

"Not if I kill him first. And if he doesn't give me my money back that's exactly what I'm going to do! I'll twist his goddamn head off and flush it down the toilet!"

"No, wait! Let's think about this some more! We could call the police!"

"Even you ain't that naïve, Dorothea, so if you're gonna talk to me, talk like you got some sense. Duke pays off the cops. They're not going to listen to me. I got to handle this myself."

"And all you're going to do is get yourself killed! Call Nappy! Maybe there's something he can do!"

Levi yanked his arm loose. "This ain't Nappy's problem. I can take care of my own business. You stay here. Stay by the phone. If Teddy comes back, don't let on you know what's going on. Keep him here if you can. Once I finish my business with Duke, I'll come back on by through here."

"No, you won't," Dorothea said in a voice heavy as lead. "Because you'll be dead. Duke Williamson will kill you and throw your body in the gutter so that everybody will know what happened."

"What do you expect me to do, Dorothea? Let him keep my money?"

"Yes!"

"And then what do I do? I wouldn't even be able to get a fight because no man would consider me worth fighting."

"You could go legitimate. Nappy says you're good enough to be a professional boxer."

"There's no difference between a colored man stealing my money all at once or a white man stealing it a little at a time. And if I boxed professionally that's what would happen." Levi shook his head violently, as if trying to shake loose evil thoughts trying to dig rusty claws into his brain. "I got to do this the best way I know how, Dorothea."

"Levi, I truly am sorry."

"I know." Impulsively, Levi bent down and kissed her swiftly on the lips. "Stay here. Stay by the phone. If I can't come, I'll call." Levi went out the door before Dorothea could say another word.

Her legs suddenly went weak and she lowered herself back into the chair, her arms trembling. Fear had such a hold of her that she had trouble breathing. Levi was going to get himself killed, she just knew it. But what could she do? She couldn't call the police. Levi would know she had done it and that would be it for sure. Levi would never speak to her again. But wouldn't that be worth it as long as he were alive? If he went to confront Duke, he'd get nothing but a bullet in the head.

And what about Teddy? What if Levi got a hold of him? He might hurt Teddy. Not that Teddy didn't deserve a good beating but Levi's anger was so great he might not stop pounding on Teddy until he was nothing but a bloody lump.

Dorothea placed her hands on her shaking knees and looked at the phone, the thoughts chasing themselves around and around in her brain like a dog chasing a cat chasing a mouse. And she truly did not know what it was she should do.

ROUND FOURTEEN

Levi entered the liquor store, glaring at Horse who stood in his usual spot behind the counter. Without a word he buzzed Levi in.

Levi stomped down the hallway and kicked open the door to Duke's office. He stepped inside. Duke sat behind his desk, sipping from a chunky square glass full of ice and J&B scotch. Lillian occupied the couch as always while two of Duke's boys, who had been sitting in straight backed chairs in front of Duke's desk leaped to their feet.

Levi popped the first one right in his left eye. The man howled, hands going to his outraged organ. Levi followed it up with a vicious punch dead in the gut. Even while he dropped to the floor, Levi delivered a sizzling roundhouse that broke the jaw of the second thug. He hit the floor next to his partner, unconscious before he was halfway there.

"That's enough, big man," Lillian said coolly. Levi froze when he heard the cocking of a gun and turned his head to see her still in her reclining position. The only thing different was the silver .38 revolver she pointed at him in her exquisitely manicured right hand. "Just take it easy and be cool, baby." She smiled sweetly at him.

Duke calmly finished sipping his drink and put it down on the table. "What the hell is wrong with you, Dancer? You know better than to come bustin' up in here like you some kinda go-rilla. You tryin' to get yourself shot?"

"I want my money, Duke."

Duke Williamson leaned forward and cupped his hand behind his right ear, cocking his head to the side as if trying to hear better. "Eh? What's that you say? You want your money? What money? We don't do any business together. What money you talking about?"

"You know full well what I'm talking about, Duke. I ain't up for playing games with you. You gimme my money right *now* or I'm gonna come over there and pop your head like it was a pimple."

"You take one step toward Duke and you'll be dead as Julius Caesar, big boy," Lillian promised. "You need to sit down and relax."

"Then you best go ahead and shoot me 'cause I ain't sitting down." Levi turned back to Duke. "Dorothea's brother T-Bird told you I had money so you sent some'a your boys to look for it. Dammit, Duke, why'd they have to tear up my place like that? Maybe me an' you don't get along but I took you for a better man than that."

"I still don't know what you're talking about. You want a drink?"

"Stop playing with me, Duke."

Duke raised a hand. "How much we talking about here?"

"A little over fifty thousand dollars! You know how much it is!"

"Surely you don't expect me to just hand you fifty thousand dollars just like that?" Duke snapped his fingers.

"You stole my money, Duke. One way or another I'm going to get it back. I'm not leaving here until I get my money!"

"Man, you don't start acting like somebody what got good sense, you won't be leaving here at all!" Duke's voice turned ugly. He wasn't enjoying himself any longer. "And I'm telling you for the last time I don't know nothin' about no money of yours. But I'm willing to make a deal with you. You wanna listen?"

"No, but I ain't got much of a choice, do I?"

"Here it is. You say I stole fifty thousand dollars of your money. I don't have the slightest clue as to what you're talking about. But here's what I'm willing to do: I'll pay you fifty thousand cash money to fight my boy Deathblow a week from this Saturday night."

Levi's hands slowly curled into fists so tight that the tendons could clearly be heard cracking. "Duke, there ain't words low enough to describe what you are. You expect me to climb into the ring with your killer to be paid back my own money?"

"Hey, take the deal or take your black ass on outta here. But I ain't giving you no money. You want it, you got to earn it."

Levi's entire body trembled with the effort of keeping himself under control. He wanted nothing more than to throw himself across the desk and choke Duke to death. And if it hadn't been for that gun he would have. Levi was certain that Lillian had shot men before, just by the confident way she held the gun on him. It hadn't moved so much as a millimeter since she had pulled it on Levi. He couldn't see any way out of this. Either he had to take the deal or walk out of here empty handed. But that didn't mean he couldn't get a little something extra out of it.

"You got to come better than that, Duke. Throw in another twenty-thousand and you've got yourself a deal."

"What!"

"C'mon, man. Don't even try to jive me. You're gonna make two, three, maybe even four times that much. You want me to fight just for my own money? You got to sweeten the pot some."

Duke got a crafty look on his face. "Sure, Dancer. Sure. Let's shake on it."

Levi snorted. "If I ever shook hands with you I'd count my fingers to make sure all five were there. Your word and your handshake don't mean shit to me, Duke. Here's what we're gonna do. You show up at Nappy's gym with half the money tomorrow. I'll be there with Bendigo Cribb and a couple of his boys. You give Bendigo the money and he'll hold onto it for me until after the fight. You'll give your word to Bendigo you'll pay me the rest."

Duke plainly didn't like that. As powerful and as influential as he was, he still didn't have the heart or the muscle to cross Bendigo Cribb. Bendigo was just that bad. And he had friends just as bad in Richmond, Charleston and Atlanta. Friends who would not be pleased if Bendigo had beef with Duke. Friends who would come to Brooklyn on the first thing smoking to insure that Bendigo did not have any beef with Duke. If Duke gave his word to Bendigo that he would pay Levi, Bendigo would make sure Levi got paid. By the same token, once Bendigo had the money and instructions not to pay off Levi until after the fight, he wouldn't and there would be nothing on God's green earth that would make him do so before the fight was over and done.

"Okay, Dancer. If that's the way you want to play it, so be it. Let's say around six in the evening?"

"Yeah. See you tomorrow." Levi abruptly spun about on his heel and left without another word. Lillian uncocked her piece. "Thought I was going to have to shoot that boy for a minute there." She said quietly.

"I did too. Hey, T-Bird, c'mon outta there!"

Teddy emerged from the small bathroom where he had been hiding ever since Levi had been buzzed in. Duke had ordered him to go in there and not to make a sound or come out until Duke gave him the all clear.

Teddy had definitely come up a bit in the world. He'd gotten his hair conked and it gleamed in the fluorescent light as if polished. He wore a blue pin-striped suit. No off-the-rack, either. Duke had paid for it all as well as the new shoes and the gold watch and rings Teddy now sported. But for all that, he still looked like a little boy playing grown-up.

He gawped at the men lying on the floor. "You shoulda let me stay, Duke. I'd'a handled that punk."

Duke stood up slowly. "You couldn't handle The Dancer if he had both arms and legs broken." Duke came around the desk. "Dancer said his place was all tore up. What's that all about?"

Teddy grinned. "Me an' my boys just had some fun, Duke. Y'know… just to show him who he was messin' with."

Duke's hand whipped out in a blur, backhanding Teddy so hard it sounded like a gunshot. Teddy flew backwards to hit the nearest wall. He slid down to the floor with a thump so loud and so comical that Lillian laughed.

Duke yanked Teddy to his feet with one hand. "I told you to just find the money! Who told you to tear that man's place up?"

"I-I-I just thought- "

"Boy, once you started working for me you stopped doing your own thinking! Don't you get that?" Duke slapped him again. "How dare you disrespect a man's home like that?" Duke slapped him again. Teddy started crying, howling in pain and anguish. Duke slapped him a fourth time. "There's three things you don't touch when you work for me: a man's home, his wife and his kids. You got that?"

Teddy blubbered miserably.

Duke shook him so hard his teeth clattered together. "You got THAT?"

"Yes! Yes! Sweet Jesus, YES!"

Duke let go of Teddy. The boy dropped to the floor, snot dripping from his nose, a long drool of saliva hanging from his lower lip. Duke adjusted his own suit and said in a quiet voice, "Go on back in that bathroom and get yourself cleaned up. And then get out of here. Go on back over to Vernon Avenue and stay in the house until you hear different from me. I don't want you anywhere on the street where Dancer can get his hands on you. You want something, tell one of the boys to get it for you, booze, women, food, whatever."

Teddy got to his feet like an old, tired man. "Stay in the house? I can't go out at all, Duke?"

"No."

"Duke, I can't sit in no house all day and all night not doing nothing. I got to go out."

"Boy, if I hear of you so much as going to the curb to put the trash out, I'll cut your goddamn head off. You hear what I'm saying?"

Teddy nodded wordlessly and shuffled into the bathroom. Duke waited until the door closed before speaking again. He said to Lillian, "Get Horse in here to get these clowns up on their feet. Little Willie's gonna need to go to the hospital, I think. You make sure that knucklehead in there gets back to Vernon Avenue like I said and tell the boys to keep an eye on him. You tell them from me that if he gets away from them and goes outside, it's their asses."

Lillian nodded and watched him get his long leather coat. "Where are you going to be?"

"Who told you to tear that man's place up?"

Duke flashed that wonderfully engaging smile at her. "Didn't you hear Dancer, baby? We got a fight to get ready for!"

ROUND FIFTEEN

Dorothea opened the door of Nappy's gym timidly. While walking up the stairs she could hear the sound of Levi punching the heavy bag like he meant to knock it off the chain. And if what Nappy had told her about the mood Levi had been in the past three days was true then he probably was trying to do that. She looked inside the gym. Levi indeed was working the heavy bag. The gym was empty, most of the lights cut off. Levi circled the bag with that uncanny lightness of foot that had given his nickname. His feet were bare but he had training gloves on his hands. As he danced around the bag, Dorothea came into his line of sight. He stopped, reached out both hands to stop the bag as well. He just stood there for about a minute, catching his breath, enjoying the familiar pain in his arms and legs. Finally, he said, "Hey."

Dorothea managed a small smile. "Hey yourself. I saw Nappy. He told me you were here."

Levi nodded. "Yeah. Wasn't any point in going back to my place. Nothing left for me there. Nappy's letting me stay here until I win the fight and get my money back."

"Here? In the gym?"

"No, no. Downstairs in the boiler room. There's a couple of storage rooms down there. I got a cot, a hotplate." Levi laughed and shook his head. "Y'know, I always swore to myself I wasn't going to end up like Cholly. Living in a basement with nothing but the wheezing of a boiler for company. And that's exactly where I am now."

"I hadn't heard from you for three days. Not since you came to my apartment that night. But everybody on the street is talking about the fight you and Deathblow are going to have so I knew you must have gotten out of Duke's liquor store alive." Dorothea took a deep breath before asking the next question as she had no idea how Levi was going to react to it. But she had to ask. "Levi…did you see my brother there? Did you see Teddy?"

Levi waved her to come on over and have a seat on a bench while he took off his gloves. "Nah. Teddy wasn't there. I haven't seen him at all. He never came home?"

"No. And I'm worried near to death! He hasn't called, hasn't come by the house. And his so-called friends won't even talk to me! They see me coming they cross the street or turn around and head in the opposite direction as if I had the pox or something!" Dorothea sat down on the bench and watched as Levi flexed his aching fingers. "I just want to know if he's okay. Isn't there somebody you could ask? Maybe Nappy knows somebody?"

"Look, Dorothea, nobody in Duke's camp is going to talk to me or Nappy right now. And I don't want to get anybody mixed up in my mess. Duke's got Teddy. You got to understand that. Believe me, if Teddy were hurt, you'd have heard about it. Bad news travels the fastest. In a situation like this, no news is good news, believe me."

"You really think so?"

"Teddy's somewhere with one arm wrapped around some chick and the other arm wrapped around a bottle. He's partying or playing cards and not thinking 'bout you. That's hard to hear, I know. But it's the truth. Teddy's where he wants to be."

"You don't understand, Levi. I'm responsible for him! What am I supposed to tell my mother when she calls up here asking how her son is?"

Levi shrugged. "Tell her the truth. From what you told me 'bout the way he was acting before he come up here, I don't think she'll be all that surprised to hear that."

Dorothea dropped her head and Levi couldn't tell if she were hiding her anger or her sorrow. She abruptly reached for the thick gold tone clasp of her shiny black vinyl purse and snapped it open. She removed a white envelope from the purse and placed on the bench in the space between her and Levi.

"What's that all about?" Levi wanted to know.

"There's two thousand dollars in there. That's all the money in the world I have. I want you to have it."

Slowly, Levi reached for the envelope and picked it up. He hefted it in his hand. "Why you want to give me your money, Dorothea? You must have eaten a lot of bag lunches to have saved this up. You ain't making no fortune working at Woolworth's, I know that."

"I want you to take it. I feel responsible for your money being stolen. If I hadn't opened up my big mouth to Teddy, you wouldn't be in this mess."

Levi hefted the envelope again. "Or maybe you just don't want me to hurt Teddy if I run up on him."

"You want to hurt somebody, hurt me. I'm the one who opened my big mouth."

Levi sighed and leaned over, thrusting the envelope back into her still open purse. "Maybe you did run off at the mouth but it was still Teddy's decision to act on that. I can't hold you responsible for that."

"That's pretty thin thinking, Levi."

"Maybe so. But I can't be mad at you, Dorothea. I start thinking that way it'll wind up with me never wanting to see you again and I don't want that." Levi sighed again, leaned forward, elbows resting on his knees, looking at nothing. "I still got a whole lotta mad and hurt but I'm going to take it out on Deathblow. That's better than taking it out on you or Teddy, wouldn't you agree?"

"Can you beat him, Levi?" Dorothea slid closer to him, placed a small hand on his muscular shoulder.

"I got no choice but to beat him, baby. Duke is going to tell him to kill me."

"Why would he do that?"

"Because if I beat Deathblow, Duke has got to hand me over another thirty-five thousand dollars to go along with the thirty-five he done already give me. And men like Duke, if there's one thing they hate, it's to give over money. Deathblow kills me in the fight, Duke gets all his money back."

"Levi, if you know that then you can't get into the ring with Deathblow! That's just crazy!"

"No, it's not. It's not like I don't know what I'm doing, Dorothea. I wouldn't have lasted this long in the backrooms if I didn't." Levi finally turned to look at her. "Look, the whole thing with the money…you were right. I shouldn't have had it there in the first place. I could have put it in a bank a little at a time. Or spread it out over half a dozen banks. Plenty of ways I coulda done it. Truth to tell is that I just liked having all that money where I could look at it anytime I wanted. I committed sins of pride, greed and avarice. Father Tim would say I got what I deserved and he would be right."

Dorothea leaned over and kissed Levi lightly on the lips. "The more I hear about your Father Tim, the more I like him."

Levi kissed her back. "He would like you, too. When we put all this behind us I'll take you to Chicago to meet him."

"You promise?"

"Sure." Levi kissed her again. Not so lightly this time.

"No, I don't mean going to Chicago. I mean putting this behind us. Is that actually going to happen?"

Levi wrapped his arms around her shoulders and drew her closer, held her tightly and said nothing. Dorothea understood without a word being said and hugged him close, inhaling deeply of his scent, closing her eyes and enjoying the sensation of his hard, still sweaty muscles under her hands and then she lifted her head to accept his kiss and willed her misgivings away. She let herself feel nothing else except the roaring emotions flooding her senses. That was all there was now and all that she cared about.

ROUND SIXTEEN

So publicized was the fight and so many people wanted to see it that there was no way it could be held in the usual backrooms. So a suitable place had been found, a warehouse on Lorraine Avenue over in Red Hook. Owned by some guys Duke knew who used it from time to time for various illegal activities. Duke had even sprung to have a real regulation ring set up. And why not? The money he was going to make off this fight was going to be the biggest payday he'd seen in ten years.

The warehouse filled up quick with men and women eager to see what promised to be one of the most savage and brutal fights ever. Men in suits and broad-brimmed fedoras escorting elegant women in evening gowns and fur wraps around their slim shoulders. Working men still wearing their factory clothes and busted boots held together with duct tape. Hustlers worked the crowd, taking bets. Dealers sold joints, pills and coke. Bootleggers with milk crates containing pints and fifths of liquor. The echoes of their voices bouncing from the concrete walls of the warehouse. Those who could found someplace to sit down wherever they could find a space wide enough to accommodate their behinds.

Levi and Nappy stood maybe some twenty feet from the ring. Levi had removed his clothes and held out his hands for Nappy to tape them up. "How you feel, man?" Nappy asked.

"Mad."

"Make that work for you. Stay mad but stay in control." Nappy's wrinkled hands moved swiftly. They looked like the hands of an old man but they moved with the surety of a much younger man. "Deathblow ain't no fighter. He's just one big slab of muscle. But he's a dangerous slab of muscle. An' you know full well that Duke done told him to make sure you don't walk outta that ring alive." And now, Nappy stopped and looked directly into his friend's eyes. "Now you listen to me good, y'hear? You do whatever you gotta do, you hear? This is as real as it gets, Levi."

"Nappy..."

"Shut up. I'm talking. I got four sons and ain't a one of them turned out to be even a quarter of the man you are. I care about you more than I ever did those ungrateful layabout nogood rascals. I don't want to have to bury you, son. You understand what I'm saying here?"

Levi reached out a hand to cup the back of the older man's head, drew it closer so that their foreheads touched. "Yeah, I understand. I feel the same, Nappy." Levi let go of his head and stood up straight. "Now finish wrapping up my hands and let's get this thing done."

The cheering and yelling from the far side of the warehouse signified that Duke and Deathblow Ballantine had entered the warehouse. Time for the fight to begin. Nappy finished taping Levi's hands and nodded. They walked to the ring through the mob that parted for Levi as if he were Moses. Hands slapping in on his back, his shoulders. But he barely felt that. Levi was narrowing his focus, pushing everything else aside and concentrating on what he had to do. He climbed into the ring, lifted his hands above his head and the crowd bellowed their approval.

Deathblow climbed in the ring, wearing a sparkly purple robe. He loved to show off at a fight. Duke stood outside the ring, in Deathblow's corner. He tipped his sky-blue homburg in Levi's direction, smiling like a benevolent uncle. Deathblow shadowboxed in his corner, his eyes never leaving Levi's. His hands were already taped up but that didn't bother Levi. Bendigo Cribb was even now climbing into the ring to check them both out and make sure that their hands had been taped up fair and square. No hidden flat pieces of metal lying flat along the knuckles. No razor blades. No substance rubbed on the knuckles that could cause the eyes to tear excessively or swell up. Bendigo knew all the tricks and none of them got by him.

He finished over at Deathblow's corner, was satisfied that there was no chicanery there and came over to Levi's corner. His hands probed and squeezed the tape on Levi's hands and wrists and he nodded. He took out a small brown bottle from a pocket of his vest, tipped a couple of drops of the liquid contained within on the tape. He lifted Levi's hands and sniffed them both loudly. Again, he nodded in satisfaction. "Okay, come on to the center of the ring."

Levi followed him. Deathblow joined them and the two men stared at each other as Bendigo went over the rules. "We gonna fight this one Bennettsville style, which you both done agreed to. The round ends when one of you is knocked down. You return to your corners if you're able. If you're not, I count you out and the fight is over. If you are able, you got one minute to recover before I ring the bell for the next round. You do what I say at all times. The man don't do what I say, first time's a warning. Second time…" and here Bendigo Cribb produced his cosh and slapped the weighted end into a meaty palm. It sounded like a baseball bat hitting a side of beef. "Hattie here reminds you. Third time…" Bendigo put away the cosh and produced his gold plated .45 automatic. "…her sister Pearlie Mae stops the fight. No hitting below the belt, no eye gouging, no kicking and no biting. Outside a'that, whatever you do is whatever you do. We good?"

Levi merely nodded. Deathblow growled.

"Gowan back to your corners, now. Fight starts in one minnit."

Scattered applause and piercing whistles accompanied the fighters as they withdrew to their respective corners.

Dorothea slipped into the warehouse. Bendigo's men watching the door motioned for her to open up her purse and her coat. After the cursory examination, they let on her on. After some maneuvering she found a spot where she could see the ring. She found a large, rusty washtub and turned it over so she could stand on it. She was able to see the fight but she was confident she was far enough away so that Levi couldn't spot her. She had promised him she wasn't going to come to the fight but there was no way she could stay away. And not just because she was worried for Levi. She was hoping that since Duke was here, Teddy would be here as well.

Levi rolled his shoulders as Nappy put the black mouth guard in. "Remember what I said! He ain't no fighter but he's pure mean. And whatever you do, don't get in there tryin' to go toe to toe with him!"

The women in the crowd sent up a single lingering "ooh-ahhh!" offering to the God of Lust as Deathblow threw off his robe and stretched his arms wide. He turned in a full circle, letting the women see his magnificently muscled body, gleaming with oil. Deathblow Ballantine looked like some ancient ebony statue brought to life, every sharply defined muscle standing out in relief, throbbing with life and power.

Bendigo shouted; "Center of the ring!"

Levi and Deathblow walked to the center of the ring. Deathblow's face had twisted into a dark mask of pure rage. He was allowing his temper to run free, to fill every nerve, every atom of his being with nothing but a thirst for blood. Levi's face had no emotion on it whatsoever. He might as well be sitting in a movie theater, watching something taking place on a screen.

Bendigo looked at Deathblow. "Ready?"

Deathblow growled deep in his throat. It didn't sound human.

Bendigo looked at Levi. "Ready?"

Levi merely nodded.

"God be with the both of you, then. FIGHT!"

ROUND SEVENTEEN

Levi stepped back out of the way of Deathblow's looping right and came back in. Despite Nappy's advice he intended to get in there fast and start banging Deathblow's body. His arms pistoned in and out, hitting against a torso that felt like solid steel, so hard were the muscles. Deathblow snorted and shoved against Levi, making him stumble back.

The crowd stamped their feet and screamed, believing they had seen a near knockdown. But Bendigo waved his arms above his head and yelled loud enough to be heard; "That wasn't no knockdown! He slipped, he slipped!"

Levi circled Deathblow, pounding a series of lefts into his rib cage on that side. Deathblow ignored that and returned a solid shot to Levi's chest which he barely managed to deflect. He continued dancing around in a circle while Deathblow came after him slowly, growling and grinning as if he intended to enjoy this for as long as it lasted.

Deathblow threw a left that just missed Levi's head. He couldn't completely block the right that caught him in the jaw. Deathblow didn't stop there and with a speed that took Levi completely by surprise let him have an uppercut. Levi got some distance between them and then came back with a precise and accurate combination of right, left, right left. If Levi was going to do any damage he'd have to get in there but as soon as he did he got another uppercut for it. Nothing that hurt but like the first one it gave him something to think about.

Unlike Levi, Deathblow had no interest in working the body. He threw a right hook at Levi's head that didn't connect but sure didn't miss by much. Deathblow tended to leave himself open a bit when he threw that right hook, Levi could tell but his gut was telling him not to fall for that. There was something about the way Deathblow kept that left cocked when he threw the right hook Levi didn't like at all.

Levi sent in another series of body blows so fast and so hard that any other boxer would have at least showed some discomfort on his face. Deathblow seemed to barely notice. He cut off the ring, maneuvering Levi back into a corner but Levi nimbly danced out of the way. He'd seen

Deathblow do that very same thing to other fighters. Deathblow simply got them in a corner and battered them into submission. He could take their shots, absorb that punishment but they couldn't take his.

Levi gave him a four-punch combination, giving it all he had. Deathblow broke off growling, grunted and threw an elbow at Levi's head that connected. Levi stumbled to the left, trying to keep his balance. And then Deathblow was there, throwing looping punches that connected, one after the other. The first one straightened Levi up. The second sent him stumbling to the right. The third stood him up again and the fourth again sent him floundering to the left.

Levi grabbed onto the top rope to regain his balance. The caterwauling of the crowd seemed to have gotten louder since he'd been hit. Probably had. Deathblow came back in and Levi arms went out to tie him up in a clinch.

"Cut that out!" Duke yelled from Deathblow's corner. "Let's go! Let's get to work!"

Before Bendigo could come over and break them up, Levi shoved away, delivering three short, stunning jabs as he did so.

"Keep your distance!" Nappy bawled. "And move your head! Move your head!"

Deathblow gave Levi a good pop to the right side of his head. As his head snapped around, Levi could briefly see fistfuls of money changing hands as men bet on his blood. And that reminded Levi what he was there for.

Levi delivered three hard rights directly to Deathblow's jaw, snapping his head back, the blows hard enough to draw blood that drooled from Deathblow's lip and dripped from his chin. Levi danced back and forth, side to side and gave him another right, left and right combination. Deathblow took his punches as if he liked it.

And then it hit Levi. And then Deathblow hit Levi and just that quick, Levi was on his back on the canvas.

"To your corner! To your corner!" Bendigo hollered at Deathblow, who backed away slowly, banging his fists together. Bendigo went over to Levi, who had gotten to his feet. "Round over! You still wanna fight, son?"

"Hell, yeah." Levi walked over to his corner, sat down on the stool as Nappy got to work on his bruises and swelling.

"Man, what did I tell you about tryin' to go toe to toe with him? That ain't gonna work with him! He can take it and when you're winded he'll pound you into paste."

"It just ain't that, Nappy," Levi gasped out, trying to get breath in his lungs. "Deathblow's a freak. He likes the pain. I seen it in his eyes. He likes bein' hurt."

Nappy groaned. "Yeah, I heard some talk that he's a freak for pain. God only knows what he does with women. Or have them do to him. You got to outbox him until you see a chance to put him down! Double up on your jabs and don't forget to work them combinations! And move your damn head more!"

The bell rang for the second round and Levi sprang out of his corner like a man possessed and went across the ring at the grinning Deathblow who looked as if he just couldn't wait.

ROUND EIGHTEEN

It took everything Dorothea had to force herself not to shove and batter her way through the boisterous crowd and make her way to the ring, to get to Levi and beg him to quit the fight, to get out of there before he got hurt. If he needed the money that bad she'd work two, three jobs for him. She just wanted Levi out of there. The ear-splitting roaring of the crowd made her ears throb and seemed to be inside of her head. The warehouse was suddenly too hot and too closed in. She wanted to leave, to run away from this blood madness but she couldn't leave Levi. If she ran now she'd never forgive herself.

Across the warehouse, coming into the entrance, Teddy nodded at Bendigo's men. They gave him a quick frisk and let him in. Due to the crowd, Teddy didn't see his sister and Dorothea was too intent on what was going on in the ring to see Teddy. Teddy spied Duke at Deathblow's corner and shouldered his way toward him.

Levi blasted punch after punch into Deathblow's ribs. He didn't care how hard those muscles were. If he just kept hitting long enough and hard enough, something had to break. It just had to.

Deathblow did something Levi didn't expect and didn't see coming; a backhand that set off an explosion of pain in his head. His vision vanished in a flash of white for a few seconds as he went backwards a dozen steps, shaking his head, clearing his vision. Deathblow came up with a brutal kidney punch that made Levi grunt. Deathblow threw a jab. Levi blocked, jabbed back, got some more room to continuing clearing his head. His eyes watered but he couldn't take the chance to wipe them.

She wanted to leave, to run away...

Deathblow sent a couple more jabs Levi's way. Levi thanked God that Deathblow didn't seem to know anything about combinations. Levi ducked another one of the devastating looping rights Deathblow tried every so often. Levi knew that if one of those landed square, he'd be out for the night. He faked to his left and Deathblow went for it. Levi slipped inside real close and gave Deathblow an uppercut that rocked him real good. Deathblow spat out an obscenity.

Levi gave him another combination in the ribs. All were solid blows and Levi could have sworn that he felt something give.

"His right! His right!" Nappy was yelling at Levi. Deathblow's corner man was yelling something as well but Levi couldn't make out what it was. Levi knew nothing except he had to keep pounding those combinations into Deathblow and not let up, not give him a chance to throw a punch back. The shrill shrieking of the crowd increased in volume if such a thing were possible. Levi knew that crowds at these things were noisy but he'd never heard a crowd wail and yell as long as this one had.

Deathblow roared and clasped both his hands together, brought them down on Levi's right shoulder with enough force to drive him to his knees. Levi hit the canvas, rolled away from Deathblow and scrambled to his feet, got his fists up just in time to counter the looping right Deathblow aimed at his head.

Teddy gained Duke's side and tapped him on the arm. "Hey, Duke."

Duke turned his head in annoyance and upon seeing Teddy, that annoyance quickly turned into outright anger. "What the hell you doing here? Didn't I tell you to stay in the house until you were told different?"

"Aw, c'mon, Duke. I didn't wanna miss the fight! Wanted to see that punk Kimbro finally get what's comin' to him."

"I don't care! I told you to stay in the house! Boy, why won't you do what you're told?"

Teddy's face fell for perhaps ten seconds before twisting into an ugly mask of hate. "Y'know, man, I'm just about sick'a takin' your shit. Why don't you just gimme my half of the money and I'll split."

Duke turned back to Teddy, not sure if he was hearing him right over the yelling of the crowd. "Boy, what did you say?"

"My money! My half of the money! Kimbro's money! You said you'd gimme half of it! I want my half now!"

Teddy never saw the fist that knocked him to his knees. Duke had popped him just that quick. "Boy, you just 'bout the stupidest country nigger I ever did see. You really think I was gonna give an ignorant geechee like you twenty-five thousand dollars? Really?"

Teddy got to his feet, trembling and shaking all over. "You said you were gonna gimme that money, Duke."

"Get on outta here, Teddy. An' don't go back to the house. In fact, don't go nowhere near nothin' that belongs to me. You and me is quits. Go on back home to your sister. You ain't ready for this life and you ain't never gonna be ready. 'Cause you're worse than stupid. You're just plain dumb." And with that, Duke contemptuously turned his back on Teddy.

Teddy wiped away tears of anger streaming down his face, turned and shouldered his way back through the crowd.

Deathblow shoved Levi up against the ropes, used his left forearm against Levi's throat to hold him tight up while his brought his right fist down again and again like a sledgehammer of flesh, battering Levi in the face. The forearm felt like a bar of iron, cutting off Levi's wind. Desperately he let go of Deathblow and brought his arms up and inside of Deathblow's arms, windmilling himself free just long enough for him to head butt Deathblow. Blood spurted from Deathblow's nostrils. He screamed shrilly, like a steam whistle and waded back into the attack.

Deathblow swung a left which Levi blocked. He then lightly twirled on his heels, gaining enough momentum so that when he finished his turn he had both hands locked together, smashing them into the small of Deathblow's back. Deathblow yelped, dropped to one knee and Levi let his have both hands once again in the same spot. Levi kicked Deathblow over onto his side.

"Back up, back up!" Bendigo ordered Levi who was grateful for the chance to catch his breath and wipe his streaming eyes. "That wasn't a knockdown," Bendigo ruled. "The round ain't over, boys! Fight!"

Deathblow threw away all strategy and just pounded away at Levi, muttering in low, panting voice, "You mine, you mine, you MINE," while all the time throwing rights and left with such fresh ferocity it was as if they'd just started the fight.

Levi backed up, catching most of the blows on his forearms as he covered up the best way he could, trying to find a way to throw something, anything back at the frenzy driven Deathblow. Levi threw a clumsy left cross, followed it up with two right jabs. Deathblow bobbed and weaved. The jabs had stung. Not enough to hurt but enough to remind him who he was fighting.

Levi's feet and legs were a blur as he danced around Deathblow, belted him with a right cross that started Deathblow's nose to bleeding again. He followed up with three right jabs that had nothing but pure heat.

Deathblow snorted like a hog and spat a huge gob of bloody snot at Levi which he tried to duck and failed. But it did its job which was to set Levi up for that big looping right which Deathblow had thrown a dozen times now but missed. He didn't miss with this one. It was as if a hand grenade went off in Levi's head and he felt that familiar warmth fill his mouth along with that tangy hot coppery taste. Levi lurched backwards, totally disoriented. Deathblow hit him again with that big looping right and this time Levi did go all the way down, crashing hard to the canvas.

Bendigo waved Deathblow away and he did so but not before hawking and spitting another wad of blood on his downed enemy. Bendigo hollered; "You don't git up I gots to start the count, son! Whatcha gonna do?"

Levi reached out, thankfully found the ropes, used them to haul himself to his feet. Half of the crowd screamed foul, that Levi should be able to get to his feet on his own and if he didn't the fight should be over. The other half screamed back for the first half to shut the hell up. That was the half that hadn't seen enough blood yet.

Levi barely made it back to his corner. Nappy went right to work, giving him water, seeing to the cuts, bruises and stopping the bleeding. "How we doing, Levi? Talk to me."

"Nothin' I'm hittin' him with works, Nappy. Guy's made outta iron, I swear."

"No, he ain't. He's made outta meat and muscle just like you are. He may like pain but he ain't gonna like the pain you're gonna lay down on him. Am I right?"

"Yeah, yeah," Levi breathed deeply, rhythmically as Nappy did his job. Deathblow sat on his stool in his corner across the ring. He looked as if he were having the time of his life.

"I gotta find a weakness in him, Nappy. I gotta."

"You will. Just take your time and peep him out. Take this round to look for it. It's there. Just stop tryin' to overpower him. You're not gonna do that."

"I can't just stand there and let him pound all over me!"

"And I'm not sayin' you should! What I'm sayin' is that you should start using more than your fists out there!"

Bendigo signaled that the bell was about to ring and Nappy replaced the mouth guard. The bell rang. This time there was no rushing at each other. The two men circled each other. Deathblow plainly looking for an opening he could take advantage of and get in that one really good punch that would take Levi down. Deathblow faked a right hook but Levi didn't go for it. He placed three jabs right in Deathblow's gut. Hard punches. He switched up and fired a pair of straight jabs at Deathblow's jaw. It was enough to send Deathblow back several steps. Deathblow could take a punch. Deathblow actually liked to take a punch so what Levi had to do was frustrate him, get him mad enough to get sloppy.

Deathblow seemed to remember that Levi had ribs just like him and started to sling short arcing lefts and rights into Levi's sides. But Levi kept his elbows in and they protected his sides. Deathblow snarled and Levi allowed himself a laugh. Deathblow didn't like that. He snarled louder as he continued to try and batter Levi into submission.

ROUND NINETEEN

Teddy left the warehouse and looked up and down the street until he found what he was looking for. Duke's vanilla Cadillac Eldorado parked just a few doors away from the warehouse. Teddy ambled over. The driver's side window was rolled up. Teddy tapped on it lightly. Curtis Sapp rolled down the window with his left hand. He held that month's *Jet* in the other hand. "Hey, Teddy…what you doing here? I thought you weren't supposed to leave Vernon Avenue."

"Duke said it was okay I come down to see Mr. High-and-Mighty get what's coming to him. How come you ain't inside watching the fight?"

Curtis shrugged. "Jackie couldn't drive Duke tonight. Dumb bastard smacked his old lady around and the old lady's brothers are looking for Jackie so he's hiding out at his girlfriend's house over in Brownsville."

"Why don't Duke squash that noise?"

"You know Duke don't get involved in family stuff. And anyway, this ain't the first time Jackie and his wife been fussin' and fightin.' After a couple of days, he'll go on back home. Until then I gotta drive Duke. I don't mind, really." Curtis looked at Teddy with some suspicion. "What are you doing out here? Why aren't you inside watching the fight?"

Teddy watched Curtis's eyes as he said, "Duke sent me out here to check on the money."

Curtis's eyes flickered toward the direction of the car's trunk and that's all Teddy needed. He reached in, seized Curtis by his necktie and yanked upwards, exposing Curtis's throat. Teddy whipped up the linoleum knife which he had been holding out of sight and in one swift sharp stroke, cut Curtis Sapp's throat. Blood gushed out of the gaping wound and filled his lap. Teddy let go of the tie. Curtis slumped over on the passenger side. His body twitched and a horrid gurgling sound came from his severed windpipe as he still tried to suck air in. Teddy reached inside Curtis's jacket and found what he was looking for; a .38 revolver. Teddy slipped it into his own jacket pocket. He wiped off the blade on the sleeve of the dead man's coat.

He removed the keys from the ignition and went around to the trunk of the Cadillac. He used the key, opened the trunk. There was nothing in the trunk but a black valise. Teddy opened it and grinned so wide and so hard his jaws ached. The valise was full of money. Banded stacks of bills. The other half of the prize money Duke had given his word to pay off.

Teddy closed up the valise, shut the lid of the Cadillac's trunk. He could just take the valise and disappear. With twenty-five thousand dollars he could go anywhere he liked in the country and start over again. But there was one more thing he had to do. And if he didn't do it would keep him up at night and eat away at him like a cancer.

Teddy moved into the shadows of the doorway of an abandoned building next to the warehouse and stood there, fingering the gun in his pocket.

Levi twisted, slipped out of the path of the punishing blows and then went wild. Levi wasn't playing with him, wasn't testing him anymore. The flurry of lefts and rights took Deathblow by surprise. He gave Deathblow a hard-left hook that snapped the bigger man's head around. Levi followed it up with a left, a right and another left.

The crowd whooped and hollered as if the world were coming to an end. Levi skipped and moved right then left, living up to his nickname, dancing out of the way of Deathblow's right hook.

Levi threw a left hook that finally hurt Deathblow for real. He could tell. It was in the eyes. Those eyes that had not long ago been encouraging the blows and the pain that went with them. But this was different. It wasn't fun anymore.

A fresh surge of adrenaline flooded Levi's system as he ruthlessly blasted straight right after straight right. Levi ignored the ache in his right arm and shoulder and continued targeting Deathblow's face. Deathblow backed up into the ropes and lay there as Levi went to work on his mid-section.

Duke Williamson clenched his cane so hard his hand ached. He had told Deathblow to take Levi down clean, fast and hard. Forget about giving the people their money's worth. Duke wanted Levi taken out. For good. But Levi had proven to be every pound the fighter he was. He was giving as good as he took and now it looked as if he were turning the tide of the fight.

Duke had given his word to Bendigo that he would pay Levi and had even brought the money, let Bendigo see it as an act of good faith. But that didn't mean that Duke had any intention of handing it over. Best to slip out now while everybody was concentrating on the fight. It was too damn cold in Brooklyn anyway. Six months in St. Thomas or Tortola sounded good right about now. Hell, why not take the whole year? He certainly had money enough. And that would be more than enough time for the heat to die down. It wasn't the first time Duke had taken a sabbatical when things got tight and it wouldn't be the last. And once he was safely out of the country, he could make arraignments for somebody to kill Levi. That would solve the problem once and for all. Bendigo Cribb couldn't exactly complain about keeping his word to Levi Kimbro when there was no Levi Kimbro alive, now could he?

Duke turned slowly so as not to draw attention to himself and leisurely made his way through the crowd. Nobody paid him a bit of attention, so intent were they on watching the war in the ring.

The right side of Levi's face looked as if he'd been hit repeatedly with a two by four. Those looping right hand punches did their work. It would be a long time for all that swelling to go down. But Levi still stayed on his feet, alternately slipping punches while getting in there and pounding away at Deathblow's ribs.

And then he did feel something break. A rib in Deathblow's left side snapped. Levi followed it up with a three-punch combination and then went upstairs with a head shot that rocked Deathblow back on his heels. More head shots, left, right, left, right. Deathblow's mouth guard flew up and away, arcing out into the crowd who stamped their feet, the clamor of individuals merged into one murderous, blood hungry wail of primitive lust.

"He can't keep up with your pace!" Nappy yelled. "Don't give him a chance to get back in the fight!"

Levi slammed home a right that landed solid, knocked Deathblow into the ropes. Then a hard left to the head. Followed it with another right to the head. Deathblow wasn't looking so good himself now. His right eye was almost completely closed. Levi kept hammering away, not letting up for a second. The tape on his fists were no longer white. They were dark red with blood.

Dorothea jumped up and down on her overturned washtub in pure delight. "Get him, Levi! Get him!" she screamed. She couldn't help herself. Before the fight, her mind's eye could only see Levi's broken body at Deathblow's feet. But here was Levi pounding the iron man of muscle into jelly. She clapped her hands excitedly. If he could keep this up, keep Deathblow on the offensive, Levi could win this thing and this terrible night would be over. If only she could find Teddy, it would be perfect....

Duke left from the warehouse, nodding at Bendigo's boys who unlocked the door and let him out. Duke rapidly walked over to his car and reached for the handle of the back seat. "C'mon, Curtis, get this thing moving. I need to stop a couple of places and then..." Duke had the door halfway open before he realized two things: Curtis wasn't answering him back and the car wasn't running. Duke had one standing order for whoever drove him to keep the car running at all times.

"Dammit, Curt...if you been shootin' up in my car..." Duke came around to the driver's side of the Cadillac and his eyes opened wide. Curtis Sapp lay across the passenger's side. The gold leather seat was now soaked with Curtis's blood. The open eyes of the dead man looked directly into Duke's.

The first bullet took Duke right in the small of his back. He cursed and whirled around just in time to catch the next bullet in his stomach. Duke's hands scrabbled on the Cadillac's fender and door, scratching the paint off as Duke slumped to the sidewalk, his back up against the car. Anther bullet joined the one already in his stomach.

Teddy slowly walked from his hiding place in the doorway and stood over Duke, the smoking .38 in his right hand, the valise in his left. "Ain't so tough, are you, Duke?"

"You done gone crazy!"

"Nah. I ain't crazy, Duke. I just finally learned what you been tryin' to teach me. And I thank you for bringin' me into myself at last."

Duke reached for his shoulder holster and yanked out his snub nosed .44 Magnum. "Go to hell!" He squeezed off two shots. The first one took Teddy in the stomach. The second smashed into his right shoulder. Teddy dropped the valise, screaming in pain and rage. He fired back, but his shots went wide. Even with his fading vision and three bullets in him, Duke was still a better shot than Teddy. Two more of Duke's heavy Magnum slugs slammed into Teddy's torso, kicking him up and back. Teddy fell to the already bloody pavement, his .38 clattering away.

Now there were no sounds, just the ragged breathing of two dying men. Teddy looked up into the night sky and the stars suddenly seemed so much brighter. "Why'd you treat me so bad, man?" Duke couldn't answer. He was dead. His eyes still open, looking at Teddy with something like satisfaction.

Teddy heard footsteps approaching. They sounded like high heels. He turned his head. It was such an effort. His whole body felt both heavy and light at the same time. He saw a slim hand reach down and pick up the valise. Lillian stood over Teddy, the valise in her hand. She looked over at the once elegant body of Duke Williamson. He was elegant no longer. Then she looked back to Teddy.

"You know your problem, Teddy? You're only bad on the surface. Duke and me, we're bad all the way through. On the inside, you just stupid."

Teddy tried to tell Lillian she was wrong. He was supposed to be a big man on the streets, with a big car and fine threads. Women lined up outside his door every night. Fat rolls of money in his pocket. He wasn't supposed to be lying on a cold Brooklyn street with half his insides shot out. And then Teddy closed his eyes and died.

Lillian turned away and started walking, the valise held tightly in her hand. Already detached from the scene, she wondered calmly where she might go. Maybe New Orleans. Or Tampa. Or Miami. One thing was sure. There was enough money in the valise to buy her a new life, and that was enough for now. She'd decide where she was going when she got to the train depot.

ROUND TWENTY

Levi caught Deathblow's desperate uppercut but managed to get out of the way of the wild follow up right that found nothing but air. They circled each other, the tape on their hands ragged shreds of bloody cloth.

Sweat thickly coated their faces, their torso, their legs. It dripped from their chins in thick drops, soaking into the canvas under their feet.

Deathblow pumped two fast left jabs at Levi. He blocked one, took the other. Levi pushed him away and delivered a haymaker with his left that sent Deathblow spinning into the ropes. He hit the ropes, bounced off of them and right into Levi's wicked right cross. Deathblow's legs visibly wobbled. Levi pounded solid body shots into Deathblow's gut. Deathblow bent over, trying to catch his breath.

Levi gave it all he had. First a left uppercut that snapped Deathblow's head up and back. Deathblow stumbled back and forth like a man on the worst drunk of his life. Levi delivered the right uppercut. Deathblow dropped to his knees and as he did so, the crowd went wild. Levi took his time, drew his arm back slowly and with a speed that made the air hum, delivered a straight right to Deathblow's jaw.

Deathblow hit the canvas, completely out cold. Pandemonium took over completely and the next day people for blocks around would say that it sounded like New Year's Eve in a nuthouse over on Lorraine Street that night.

Levi could barely stand but he did so, lifting his arms high above his head as he received his due from the mob. Twenty and fifty-dollar bills were thrown into the ring by jubilant and appreciative big winners who'd be going home with fat wallets thanks to Levi. The money would be gathered up by Bendigo's boys and given to Levi. Minus ten percent for Bendigo's trouble, of course.

Nappy wrapped his arm around Levi's torso, helping him stand up. "You okay, son?"

"I will be once I take a shower and go to bed. We won, Nappy!"

"You sure did. You beat that boy into bad health for sure."

"Let's go find Duke and get my money," Levi said. He watched as a couple of Duke's boys lifted Deathblow from the canvas and carried him from the ring. Levi wasn't surprised that he didn't care one little bit if he had severely hurt Deathblow or not.

Nappy was already cutting the tattered tape off of his hands. "You know there's only one reason you beat him, right?"

"I got a harder head?"

"Nah. You's a fighter, Levi. With a fighter's heart. A fighter's soul. Deathblow, he ain't nothing but a vicious animal who was told he could fight. That makes all the difference in the world."

And listening to the cheers of the crowd, Levi couldn't help but agree with him.

"Levi! Levi!"

He turned to see Dorothea climbing through the ropes. She ran to embrace him tightly. "Oh, thank GOD! I thought that thug was going to kill you!"

"Dorothea, I thought I told you I didn't want you coming to this fight!"

Dorothea looked at Levi with firm determination. "Get used to it, Mr. Kimbro. Because I'm going to be in your corner for every fight you have from now on. And not just the ones in the ring." She took his swollen, battered face gently in her hands. "You understand what I'm saying?"

Levi smiled as best he could. It hurt even to smile but it was a good, honest hurt. "Yeah, Dorothea. I understand."

FINAL BELL

Levi heard the door of the rooftop kiosk open behind him and he turned slightly to see Dorothea coming towards him. "Hey," he said, delighted to see her. It had been a week since the fight. Duke's dead body had been left where it was after the fight as everybody in the warehouse had taken off in different directions as if the body had the plague.

Levi had been with Dorothea through the painful process of shipping Teddy's body down south for the funeral. Levi had slipped a few extra dollars to Bob Drake at the funeral home to go through extra effort to clean up the body and make Teddy look presentable. Levi had assumed Dorothea would be going down south as well, but she didn't. He wondered if she felt she had failed her brother and simply couldn't face her family. Or maybe she had done all the mourning for her poor lost brother even before he was dead. It was pretty clear what had happened in the parking lot on the night of the fight, but that didn't stop the police from rousting everyone they could for a whole week. It was a week where everybody had kept their heads down and spoke softly. Levi had been hauled into the local precinct to answer questions about Duke Williamson's death along with a bunch of others. Naturally the police knew that Levi was a backroom fighter and they heard about the fight. They'd kept Levi for half a day before turning him loose.

"We know about the money Duke stole from you, Kimbro," one of the investigating detectives said to Levi just before the police turned him loose "And just because you were getting your brains beaten to pulp in the ring doesn't mean you didn't have somebody else kill him for you. You don't leave town for any reason until we tell you different. And we'll be keeping an eye on you."

"Nappy told me you were up here. Whatcha doin'? Contemplating the mysteries of the universe?"

"Nah. Not really. Just come up here to think a bit. Come on over and cop a squat." Levi waved. She walked over to where he sat on a folding wooden chair. He got up and let her sit down. He went over to a rude shed and got himself another chair, opened it up and returned to sit back down next to her, thrusting his hands in his jacket pockets.

"You keep chairs up here?" Dorothea asked.

"Got a grill in there, too," Levi said, jerking his head toward the shed. "Summertime come, me, Nappy and some of the boys like to hang out up here. Grill some burgers, franks, steaks. Drink beers and just enjoy ourselves."

"Little too cold for all that," Dorothea said. And she was right. It was the last week of March and even though it was a little milder than one would have expected for this time of year, it still wasn't nowhere near spring.

"I was just looking and thinking."

"At what?"

"That." Levi again jerked his chin. This time in the direction of the island of Manhattan. Dusk tickled the sky and Manhattan was beginning to light up for the night. Levi loved to look at Manhattan at night. At night the city seemed to transform into a magical city of light. It looked like a wonderland where a man could make anything of himself he wanted. Manhattan was a city of promise. Which ones you chose to believe was up to you. "Nappy says we can make a lot of money over there."

Dorothea shook her head. "Levi, you got thirty-five thousand. Isn't that enough?"

"No. It's not. And we done been through this, Dorothea. I got to fight. Once Duke's people heard he was dead they divvied up his money and booked. There's nobody to get the money that's owed to me from. I got to fight. Nappy says that all I need is a couple of big paydays and I can get them over there in the city." Levi took his hands out of his pockets, wrapped her small hands in his as he continued. "Once the cops found out there was an illegal fight that night and that Duke was involved, they cracked down hard. I won't be able to get a fight in Brooklyn for the next six months. I can't wait that long."

Dorothea sighed. "I'm not the kind of woman to cry and whine and beg, Levi. I'm in your corner, just like I said. But that doesn't mean I'm not going to speak my mind."

"I wouldn't give a damn for a woman who wouldn't. So, you on board with me, Dorothea? All the way?"

Dorothea scooted her chair closer until they were side by side. "Let's just sit here for a while and look at Manhattan, Levi. It's so pretty. Let's leave all this talk of fighting until tomorrow. Okay?"

Levi's reply was wordless but spoke volumes. He wrapped one muscular arm around Dorothea's slim shoulders and the both of them sat on that Brooklyn rooftop, enjoying the comfortable silence, not minding the chill wind that blew around them. They shared an inner warmth. And as the night came on, they watched the lights of Manhattan blaze brighter and brighter, illuminating the night sky as if lighting the way for Levi Kimbro to come and try his luck.

THE END

Writer-

DERRICK FERGUSON - was born and raised in Brooklyn, NY, which as most right-thinking people know is The Center of The Known Universe. After a diverse and somewhat infamous career in the security field working for various employers such as the NY Board of Education and Home Depot he retired early to take care of his health and dedicate his life to the one overwhelming passion of his life: the telling of stories that he hopes entertain and excites those who read them.

"I've been telling stories and writing them for as long as I can remember. Mostly retelling stories that I read in comic books, saw on TV or just heard from others verbally. My first crack at true creative innovation came from when I was seized with an inexplicable obsession with Mad magazine's "Spy Vs. Spy." I filled up whole spiral notebooks writing two and three-page stories about those characters. From then on I just wrote whatever struck my fancy. I wrote stories about my favorite superheroes such as Thor, The Black Panther and Iron Man. You could say I was ahead of my time as I was writing fan fiction before I knew what fan fiction was. I would also write Edgar Rice Burroughs influenced stories about my classmates. When I was supposed to be doing my schoolwork I was making up stories with my classmates as the characters. I would write on both sides of a sheet of loose leaf notepaper and that was a chapter that ended on a cliffhanger. Once it made the rounds of the classroom, I'd start on the next chapter."

Derrick wrote mostly for his own enjoyment during the 1970s and 1980s. During this time, he submitted manuscripts to various publishers who sent them back as fast as he sent them out. New opportunities came about with the advent of The Internet. Derrick quickly became involved in Star Trek fan fiction communities as well as Marvel and DC fan fiction. It wasn't long before Derrick and a number of his fellow fan fiction writers joined together to create Frontier Publishing, a fiction website devoted to publishing serialized novels. At the site's hey-day there were at least half a dozen serialized novels going strong at one time. Derrick's first Dillon novel, **_Dillon and The Voice of Odin_** was presented first at Frontier.

Unfortunately, Frontier Publishing had to close up shop after a couple of years, and that may have been the end for Derrick's writing career and his now-beloved character Dillon if Derrick's friend and fellow writer Russ Anderson hadn't cajoled him into sending the completed serial off to a publishing house for one last shot at getting his writing into print.

"If anybody has read and enjoyed my Dillon stories then they should go right now and send Russ a thank you email. If I'm Dillon's daddy then Russ is his granddaddy," Derrick said. "If it hadn't been for Russ kicking me in the ass and throwing considerable support behind me to get that book published, you might not still be reading Dillon adventures today."

Thanks to Russ, **Dillon and the Voice of Odin** was finally published in 2003 in paperback—or "dead tree format" as Derrick facetiously calls it—, Derrick's professional writing career began in earnest.

Like many writers, Derrick is a voracious reader, and it was quite difficult for him to narrow down the list of writers who have influenced him over the years. "That would be a really long list if I had to name all the writers who have influenced me," he said. "But I'll just give you The Dirty Dozen of the writers I love the most and who I feel have influenced me the most: Robert E. Howard, Chester Himes, Roger Zelazny, Ishmael Reed, Mike Resnick, Jim Steranko, Ian Fleming, Larry McMurtry, Robert R. McCammon, Lester Dent, Charles Saunders, and George C. Chesbro."

What drives Derrick in his career as a writer? "I like telling stories," he said. "It is no deeper than that. For some reason God gave me the gift of making up outrageous stories and the ability to communicate them in an entertaining manner through prose . . . What do I hope to achieve? That my stories can entertain and maybe make somebody's day a little easier and maybe make them forget their troubles for a couple of hours."

BASEBALL IN DECEMBER

Dexter Fabi

Ronan was both certain and uncertain if he was going to make it to the majors. At times he felt an absolute guarantee because of his rigid work ethic, where he proved to others that he would do a task a hundred times if it took a hundred times to get it right. His Iowa Cubs teammates curiously pondered what he was still doing on the field after the lights had gone down, why he was still swatting in the cage after all his teammates had called it a night, and why he was always the first to get up and run five miles.

It was sophomore year of high school when scouts from the majors had first come to watch Ronan's batting skills, and even more came in his junior year and senior year. They were so taken with his abilities that he was signed to the Minnesota Twins organization and scheduled to play his first season in the bush leagues with the Cedar Rapids Kernels, a Class A team. He knew he had to work his way to the next level, a Double AA team with the Twins, and it could have been due to nervousness, but he did not do well in Cedar Rapids for his first year in the minors. His second year with them showed him much improved with the power back in his hitting and his infield statistics impressive, the Twins association reassured that they were correct in taking him on. As all ballplayers, he did have his slumps, but on the whole his second and third years were consistent and on an incline.

The Minnesota Twins themselves were involved in an unpredictable shakeup and a trade happened where the Twins acquired one of the Chicago Cubs' star players in a three-person deal including Ronan, another Twins busher, and a closer in the Twins' bullpen, along with some money. Both sides agreed that it was a fair-minded deal. Cubs management had recognized the potential Ronan Kiley had, having led the Cedar Rapids Kernels and the Double-A Pensacola Blue Wahoos to regional success owing to his prowess at the plate and his near impeccable infielding at second. They were so confident in Ronan that after a three-month stint with the Double-A Tennessee Smokies, they had bumped him up to the

Triple-A Iowa Cubs. The hits were coming and his name was already being floated around as a future phenom. In the rundown locker rooms, seedy hotel rooms shared with three other minor leaguers, fields barely lit for night games, and sweltering bus rides without air conditioning, he started to feel a sense that maybe he'd make it up. His perception anguished him at times, that if he stayed a minor leaguer he felt he would just disappear. Now that he was with Iowa, he knew that mistakes were fatal, that he had to be in the best physical shape of his entire career if he was going to gleam in the bright lights.

Ronan was popular with the Iowa Cubs, both as a teammate and as an Iowa fan favorite. Local stories were written about his work ethic and questions appeared in interviews about his relentless need to drive himself to the point of almost having no personal time. He would respond that "life is work," and that was all that he said in response. Then he would go dependably to the cages at night as if there were an hourglass marking his time.

During one particular game as an Iowa Cub against, coincidentally, the Triple-A Twins affiliate Rochester Red Wings, the Iowa Cubs were down 3-0 in the eighth inning. The Iowa bats were dry and a local Triple-A Championship on the line as this game was the last of a seven-game contest. The Red Wings had called in their best closer on scarcely one day rest to finish out the game. It was the top of the Iowa Cubs order with Kiley in the third at-bat. The first in the top of the Iowa order was Buster Niemczyk who had struck out from a high and tight fastball. Next was Olen Fisher, the other power hitter of the Fisher and Kiley hitting duo. Fisher had squeezed a desperately needed bouncing grounder that swept past the first baseman and went through the hole into right field, allowing him to reach first base.

Ronan was at the plate and ready to get the game into the stratosphere for the Iowa Cubs when he realized that they were intentionally walking him. Ronan was a professional by this time, not showing aggression at their decision.

With Iowa Cubs now on first and second, another strikeout happened, leaving the Iowa Cubs down to their last out in the eighth. The next batter was walked unintentionally, loading the bases for the next at-bat, the Iowa Cubs' starting pitcher. People in the stands considered the inning over and the three players stranded on base since traditionally pitchers did not focus on their hitting skills. Incongruously, on a second pitch, the Iowa Cubs pitcher had managed an accidental line drive into an unprotected area in center field. This had scored two easily and Ronan was being signaled to hold up at third base but his instincts had told him to go all the way home. He plowed at his topmost speed, barreling into the Red Wings' catcher. The catcher had caught the ball and tagged Ronan, but the force of Ronan's charge had caused the catcher to loosen his grip on his glove, the ball spilling out and tying the game.

The score being even, the Red Wings were unable to put up any more runs, sending the tie to the ninth where Ronan was able to swat in Olen Fisher with a confident double where he wanted it, in a deep angle of right field. The Iowa Cubs captured the championship from the Red Wings due to the Kiley and Fisher combination.

Kiley continued with the Iowa Cubs the next season with the feeling that he would get the call up. His time with the Iowa Cubs was flourishing—he had great friends in Buster Niemczyk and Olen Fisher, they were practically his brothers, and the tattered conditions of the minor leagues no longer bothered him. Rather, he indulged in everything that the minor leagues held, for he had a new gut feeling that it was soon to be a part of his past and that he would never look on it again. It was only when something was walking away into the distance that he realized how much vastness it held, how much it had meant.

That year there was a new addition to the Iowa Cubs roster, a bigshot from the majors who was rehabbing a knee injury he had incurred with the Chicago Cubs during the current season. Cervantes was in the gallery of ace pitchers at Wrigley Field, nearly the National League Rookie of the Year three years back and already had an expected seven shutout games a year with a career earned run average of 3.04. Timothy Cervantes was elected to the All-Star Game two times in his young career.

Often when a major leaguer of Cervantes's caliber comes down to the bush leagues for a rehabilitation stint, the crowds thicken for a minor league game. What was interesting about Cervantes that Ronan had discovered was that he had no ego—he had arrived with his agent to Des Moines, Iowa, not with a sense of royalty arriving among peasants but as a team player ready to do his job. Like Ronan, Cervantes had been traded during his early professional baseball career in the minors, being traded far more times than Ronan before finding himself on the Iowa Cubs. In some ways, Cervantes returning to the Iowa Cubs was a homecoming.

Ronan Kiley and the returned Iowa Cub had gotten along incredibly well—they were always talking, and they had become immediate friends. They trained together regularly, with Kiley greatly effective at hitting Cervantes's palmball and practicing pick offs for would-be stealers at second base. Ronan's other good friends on the team, Fisher and Niemczyk, felt themselves being dissociated by Ronan and reasoned that it was Ronan's ambition to get to the major leagues that had so fascinated him with the major league pitcher. Ronan noticed this and made efforts to reassure them that their friendships had not changed, even going so far as sacrificing his own self-punishing practices to spend more time with them. Still, it was evident that Kiley and Cervantes appeared to be relatives or blood brothers after two weeks into the Iowa Cubs season.

There was already talk floating that Olen Fisher, along with Kiley, were going to be brought up to Wrigley Field during this season. Anyone watching them would be assured that they were poised for major league glory. Fisher was a built-in hitter and right fielder and the practices that he had to go through with the team looked in a way superfluous to him since he already had an inborn ability—just an innate all-around hitter, strategist, and fielder who knew what to do among many possibilities in any given instance.

The season went along well, with Cervantes providing an occasional shutout during the seven innings he pitched, giving a panoply of split fingers and cut fastballs. Sometimes Cervantes pitched for only five innings in the beginning of his rehabilitation with the Iowa Cubs, a prosperous five innings that displayed a peek of the majors in the minors. As his injury healed, he ingratiated himself to the fans of years ago who welcomed him back warmly. He remembered the first names of many of the Iowa fans after three years of being in the big leagues, addressing them on a first name basis that reassured them that he had not forgotten them.

Tickets for the Iowa Cubs were sold out now that Cervantes was back, in addition to the dual hitting and fielding threat of Kiley and Fisher who were practically confirmed to be with the Cubs in Wrigley before the season was out.

In fact, it was earlier than Kiley and Fisher had expected. They both had the news from their agents, who had mysteriously remained silent while negotiations with the directors occurred in Chicago, that they were both to have their major league debuts: in a week for Fisher, and in two weeks for Kiley. They each took the news differently, with a look of savoring delight on Fisher's face and a feeling of attainment emanating from Kiley. They both wanted to celebrate their graduating upward and invited Niemczyk and of course, Cervantes. They had more occasion to celebrate since they had also won a four-game series against another Triple-A team with a sweep.

Ronan Kiley was so rigorous with himself that he never drank, but this time was an exception where he relaxed his own relentlessness. All four were drinking in Cervantes's fancy hotel room, the expected place for such a celebration, and at one point Niemczyk had felt so out of place after numerous rounds of imbibing that he had left the room. Niemczyk had taken a huge hit to his self-esteem, knowing that he wasn't going to make it to the majors and that he'd be a minor leaguer who stayed a minor leaguer—making a less than modest living and always on the road, a vagabond, and playing in his later years for professional leagues not even in the country. He would remain a player who wouldn't merit a footnote.

Cervantes was the first to notice that Niemczyk was gone. Cervantes was as inebriated as Ronan and Olen were. Ronan had completely let go of his normally iron clad self-control as the guys drank to the good news.

On his search as the noisy Olen followed behind Cervantes, he swayed a bit through the hush hallways way after midnight, the silence far and wide in the hotel. An introverted effect had descended on Ronan as he followed the two. Olen was taking his celebration of being a Chicago Cub too far this evening, so much so that guests in their hotel rooms were disturbed enough to call the front desk.

It was Cervantes who had found Niemczyk in the parking lot behind the wheel of the car that Ronan and Olen had driven to Cervantes's hotel.

The paltry middle of the night lights of Des Moines barely illuminated Niemczyk's streaked face as he berated himself for not being as good as the other three were. Cervantes did what he could with trying to pull him back to a more optimistic reframe of Niemczyk's thoughts, Cervantes telling him how frankly happy he was to be back with the Iowa Cubs. This didn't affect low-spirited Niemczyk at all and he had slurred out poignantly in response, starkly: "You know what I amount to? Categorically zilch."

Once he had said this, Cervantes, Kiley, and Fisher, all four not quite sober, decided to take a drive to clear Niemczyk's head. They had taken a drive to cheer themselves as well, for Niemczyk was a friend they were leaving behind.

Olen was behind the wheel since Cervantes still attempted to talk Niemczyk into a restored mind and Kiley wanted to be present with Niemczyk, a stalwart comrade through his time with the Iowa Cubs. Behind Olen's driving, Cervantes and Kiley were making concerted efforts to get Niemczyk back from his self-imposed humiliation.

The streets of Des Moines at this hour were surprisingly busy as it was a Saturday night, and in Des Moines, all hell usually breaks loose every Saturday night.

They didn't notice Olen's excessive speeding as their whole focus in the back seat was on sobering up Niemczyk to return to reason. The three in the back seat of the beat-up car that only a minor leaguer could afford didn't notice as Olen nodded his head at times as if on the cusp of waking and dreaming. They didn't notice, so focused they were on the agonized Niemczyk as Olen completely passed out at the wheel and the car ran 95 miles per hour through a wooden fence and into the thick barrel trunk of an oak tree more than a hundred years old.

Cervantes had been thrown from the car, the only one of the four who was catapulted from the vehicle that wrapped contortedly around the massive trunk. Regaining his senses, he immediately looked up, wincing in pain as his knee injury had returned, all the progress of healing while with the Iowa Cubs made futile. He looked to see the car steaming and glass shards splayed all around, the inferno of the car starting minutely and crawlingly as he picked himself up and started to yell their names. To his alarm, no one had responded. Through the distorted windshield, he had seen the bloodied face of Olen, and could see him still breathing.

"Kiley! Niemczyk!" Cervantes yelled hoarsely, his eyes ablaze as the front of the car started to catch fire, the engine looking as if it was about to set off.

Cervantes roared once more, face contorted with pain as he continued around the car, searching for his two other Iowa teammates.

He heard a faint "Cervantes" but couldn't be sure. Cervantes inspected the back of the car and saw that Niemczyk was covered in blood while Ronan was mouthing words that Cervantes couldn't distinguish.

He went to check to see if Niemczyk was alive by shaking him. Cervantes could not tell if Niemczyk was still alive but knew he had to do something for Kiley who had confirmed that he was alive with his narrowly audible voice. The heat of the fire had inched closer to Olen, signaling to Cervantes that he had to make a quick decision and save at least one life before the car overheated and all four of them were dead.

It was not difficult for Cervantes to get Kiley out of his seatbelt but the door wouldn't budge as he tried with all of his strength, wincing in agony as his relapsed injury felt as if somebody was stabbing his kneecap.

The glass of the window near Kiley was sharpened apart, and small as it was, it possibly could fit Kiley out of the devastation. The quarter glass window was still intact and if Cervantes smashed this, it would create a larger space to get Kiley out before it was too late.

He neglected to tell Kiley to get back to avoid the harmful effects of the shattered glass as he wrapped his hand in his Iowa Cubs jersey and punched determinedly into the quarter window. His first impact shattered the glass, so wired with adrenaline that he felt for a moment impervious to pain, keyed into panic.

Kiley was fully alert now as Cervantes helped him out of the wider aperture. With a bit of adjusting, Cervantes was able to struggle him through, Kiley exhibiting blood from the shattered glass and the jagged edges.

Kiley and Cervantes saw the flames engulf the front of the car as they both ran clear, their eyes in absolute dread as they saw the explosion that had happened mere seconds after they reached safety.

They would never know if Niemczyk was still alive when the explosion of the car happened or if he was beyond rescue. Olen would never have a day of the dream that he already had in his grasp.

The Iowa Cubs had done all the necessary commemoration of the two on their roster. Black armbands were worn by the team as Cervantes had to start over the rehabilitation of his knee.

Cervantes was hailed as the hero of the incident, with many journalists and sportscasters stating that Kiley would have also been dead if Cervantes had not extricated him. Kiley knew that he owed Cervantes his life, his best friend on the team now that the other two, Niemczyk and Olen, were gone. Cervantes and Kiley were assailed by thoughts of Niemczyk and Olen, hunted down by Olen's dream burnt and the unknown of Niemczyk.

The Cubs organization had the best psychologists to counsel them through such a time of ordeal as they continued with their professional ballplaying. Cervantes had grappled with the thought that had he the chance, he could have saved all three of them. He was tormented that Olen was still alive yet he had no time to save him. He looked to time to heal.

Though the other Iowa Cubs had removed their black armbands weeks ago, Kiley and Cervantes had kept theirs on their uniforms for weeks more.

It was an odd feeling for Kiley as he was called up during the regular major league baseball season to Wrigley Field for his debut. Cervantes was still recovering his knee with Iowa and was still indefinitely on the disabled list.

Suiting up in the home team locker room, Kiley felt a complex mixture of elation and mourning as he knew that Olen could have debuted with the Chicago Cubs around the same time as him.

As he ran onto the field and was introduced during the player introductions, he received a standing ovation from the sea of the crowd. Never had he seen so many people for a game he was about to play. He looked around him, at the Wrigley Field lights, at the scoreboard from another time, at the immortal ivy-covered walls and smiled for a second, for the first time in the weeks since the incident. Thoughts of his friends, Niemczyk and Olen, drifted wistfully in his mind as he doffed his cap and saluted the crowd. As the photographers hovered closer, the crowd cheered for Kiley, the newest teammate in Cubbie blue as all knew what had happened in Iowa.

Kiley's first at-bat as a major leaguer was encouraging as on the second pitch he had hit a line drive into left field, allowing him to reach first base. Kiley was pointing up to the sky at perhaps the forces that had smoothed the way for him or at the beauty of a Chicago sky on a summer day about to turn into natural owl-light as the strong electric lights started to permeate the stadium.

Ronan Kiley became a sensation in the major leagues, fast becoming a favorite with the Cubs. In his second year he was voted to the All-Star Game because of his exceptional batting and fielding record and driven personality. By this time, Cervantes was also back with the Chicago Cubs, and he too was again voted to be an All-Star, Cervantes and Kiley the lone two Cubs to represent the organization at the July All-Star Game. The major league crowd was intrigued that both had narrowly escaped death to return to the majors and it could be that this is what compelled those who voted for them. Cervantes's popularity in the media and among fans was at a peak, the same occurring for Kiley as each were featured prominently and regularly on cable sports networks, websites, and print media, both of them making the front covers of magazines with their bankable looks. They had requested before each media interview that questions about Niemczyk and Olen not be asked since they wanted their memories respected, but rather that questions about what they had learned from the accident were fair game for the interviewers.

Even in the aureole of success, Ronan still couldn't shake that night when he almost died. He would be eternally grateful to Cervantes and was glad he was back. There were angles to the journalistic news stories about a famous saying, "If you save someone's life, you are responsible for them forever." While reading up on these articles, Cervantes felt an obligation to protect Kiley. It was in every perspective logical for Cervantes to keep intact the life he had saved for as long as he could.

In his third season with the Chicago Cubs, Ronan Kiley's batting average and fielding percentages were prosperous, and he had become a famous second baseman in the National League Central. There was still a vulnerability within him, uncertain fear that he would be sent back to the minor leagues. He felt again that he would disappear and be neither here nor there if he wasn't a major leaguer. Ronan's all-or-nothing take on life, that baseball was a metaphor for existence in which you either make it or you don't, consumed him. He had taken up again his other passion besides baseball, that of drawing. He started drawing again in sketchbooks to ease his mind, his russet hair getting in the way as he concentrated on rendering anatomy and landscape.

"Think of our friends who are no longer with us—Niemczyk and Olen," Cervantes had said to him. "Are they nothing?"

Ronan looked up from his cup of strong coffee combined with black tea in the dugout, dawn light spreading across his features.

"Never will they be nothing."

"And they never made it to where you are now, Ronan."

"I see where I was heading with all of this. I need time to think, to rethink about all I'm putting myself through."

As the Cubs season went on, it had been weeks since Ronan had a chance to hang out with his buddy Cervantes, both of their schedules being so hectic with commercial spots, radio advertisements, and photo shoots for various media markets. It felt reassuring that Cervantes had scheduled an evening in the Rogers Park area of the city in a hidden spot where they wouldn't be intruded upon by fans and the media. It was a rare spot that allowed them to be human for an hour or two.

The Chicago Cubs were currently at the top of the National League Central and it was mid-August. At the beginning of the season the team was consistently third place in the division, but the Cubs had battled back to the number one spot. Pitching was top notch, fielding and on-base percentages were ideal, and the main lineup was producing well.

Though the Cubs were enjoying being on top at the moment, the other four teams in NL Central were gaining. St. Louis and the Brewers were just a half-game behind. The Reds were three games behind the Cubs while the Pirates were four games behind. The division was tight, and management knew it.

When Ronan arrived to Cervantes's table, there was a grim look on his face.

Ronan had thought he could always read Cervantes but this time he couldn't fathom what was going through Cervantes's head.

"Timothy," he saw as Cervantes was thumbing his soda and herbs. Since the accident, both of them had not touched alcohol again.

"Timmo, what? There something I should know?"

Cervantes couldn't answer yet with the news. He took more sips, wishing he could order a stiff liquid to go with what he was about to tell Ronan.

"I'm about to get traded," he said after minutes of stillness. Ronan could barely hear it, yet he knew what he heard.

The impact of it made him blink, as if he had just seen a shockingly rare triple play.

He wondered how it was possible that Cervantes could be traded since their media headline had caught the national imagination: star Cubs pitcher saves the life of future star major-leaguer in car accident and go on to be teammates in the Windy City. He hoped this wasn't true, that what Tim told him was just smoke, but he knew that what he heard was fact.

"Don't believe it. How the world are you ever being traded?" was all that Ronan could say, hoping he was being toyed with. He sank since he knew Tim's personality. He wouldn't be the kind of guy to make frivolous statements.

"Here I am, responsible for your life for the rest of mine," he said, evading the question at first. "I pulled you from the wreckage, only to be sent to another team after three years. I thought there was mercy and justice in this world. It looks like there isn't."

Cervantes then downed the entire contents of his soda, a reflex, as if its contents were a remedy. He looked around at the surroundings. Cervantes found this place comfortable. It wasn't an extravagant place, it was a regular neighborhood hole in the wall.

"Which team got you?" Ronan asked after they had both sat for a time.

"The Boston Red Sox. The same team that Olen was rumored to be traded to once he made it to the major leagues."

"Management thought up something, didn't they?"

"Apparently management came across a huge deal to get what they feel is a stronger pitcher than me from the Red Sox in a three-way trade for me and two top Cubs prospects in the farms. Along with money. Let's not forget about the money. The money that the Red Sox have been offered in the trade sweetened the deal so the Cubs could get Nick 'Crackerjack' Harrell. So named because batters can't seem to crack his pitches."

"I know the division is tight and the other four are gaining, but I don't see how this is this a good move? There are no guarantees that Crackerjack will get us to where we want to go."

"I knew that if things came to a head in the division like this and our top spot in the standings at the moment wasn't locked, the Cubs would do anything, including trading me, to get what they want."

"This is a surreal world, Tim. They think that trading you to the Red Sox because Olen was going to be on that team makes it okay, that it justifies this? This doesn't make sense to me. Your pitching is doing fine. You've had several shut-out games this season and haven't any slumps or injuries. You're also in your prime. How can you explain this? I mean, not with what the Cubs are trying to justify it with, but how do you reason this?"

Cervantes's glass was empty and so he ordered another soda, with bitters this time.

"Buddy, they want a pitcher better than me. Crackerjack is what they feel is the deal of a lifetime, what the owner and all involved think will get the team far."

…he ordered another soda, with bitters this time.

"You're better than Crackerjack any day. What did management tell you? Level with me, man."

"Okay, all right, okay!" he yelled, in spite of himself.

"Timmo," Ronan said, giving Cervantes a wounded look.

"I'll explain my own way, then. They won't say it, but they've believed that having that one ace pitcher, that one devil in the deck, would carry them where they want to go. They won't admit it, but I believe that it's the whole team as an entire equation that make or break them. I certainly don't think that one man can bring the Cubs out of this tight division, but they certainly think so."

"Did you try to negotiate out of it?" Kiley asked.

"My agent did all that he could. My agent knows me and knows that I have this obligation to protect you and be responsible for you for your entire life. Once I've saved your life, I have that obligation on my shoulders. He tried this with management but they wouldn't give. They were too blinded by Crackerjack."

There at that table, they arrived at the explanation that both sides, the Cubs and Red Sox, must think it's a fair deal. Cervantes the amazing pitcher and the Cubs coughing up two of their brightest prospects for a pitcher with one of the best ERAs in the entire league. It would generate even more press and word-of-mouth marketing for Cervantes and Kiley to be separated, thus making the Cubs, and now the Red Sox, even more money.

Ronan thought about money. Ronan thought about the ephemerality of fame, how a major leaguer's career was never forever.

"There's got to be a way," he said, though he knew that there wasn't.

"Look, we'll always be friends. We have to accept reality. Every chance I get I'll come and visit. Listen, I thought I would be a Cub in the beginning of my career, but the majors are so fluid. There is no such thing as spending your entire career with one team anymore. What rules are ticket sales and the filling of pockets of those that make the decisions."

Cervantes looked up determinedly.

"We're going to have to accept it and not fight it. There's the chance that you too will be traded from Chicago, that chance hanging over your head. Sure, they've kept former players for their whole careers on the Cubs, but I have hope from what I've seen in the past: they've traded away Cubs to other teams, popular ones, only to bring them back after four or five years and keep them almost permanently. I'm hoping that this will happen."

"The same crossed my mind too," replied Ronan.

Cervantes's head went back down trying again to completely accept the news.

Cervantes had gotten on the plane bound for Boston, having said at most brief farewells to Chicago and his teammates. He didn't want to make a big, strained overture about the whole deal and didn't want to prolong the inevitable. It was best to get to his new city and get along with his new life there.

He was leaving a whole universe behind, and thankfully there was not a member of the press in sight as he had made sure of taking a private flight in an undisclosed hour of the night.

Cervantes had taken out a sketchpad and pencils. This was an effective form of relaxation that his best friend Ronan had taught him, to sketch without worry or self-consciousness.

Cervantes let his hands and mind autopilot the drawing. He was sketching the fields of Iowa and what looked to be a baseball diamond.

The lines and perspective of the Iowa baseball field were getting clearer, almost on par with Kiley's skilled sketch work.

Deep in thought, part of his mind asked himself if he had ever done anything for himself, if he had sacrificed living his own life for others. The major league game was a business where they'll pay you two dollars for your soul, and millions for any other part of you. He wondered if it was all worth it.

The sole way forward was to let go. He had to give Boston a chance. Perhaps he'd be happier there. He couldn't see the sun now, felt that he was grappling his way through shadows on a wall. He had saved a life, that was it. Did he owe Kiley anything anymore? But who aside from them could say that he didn't owe Kiley protection? They weren't there at the accident to see the shattered glass lacerating into Kiley as he pulled him from the car.

He penciled in the uniform numbers of Niemczyk, Kiley, and Fisher on his drawing.

Cervantes suited up for the first time in a Red Sox uniform. Looking into the full-length mirror and seeing publicity shots of him as a Red Sox pitcher made it seem to him that he was born into a new existence. He was feted around, introduced, interviewed, made all of the press junkets and publicity requirements that his agent and the Red Sox wanted him to do.

Getting onto the new mound felt exciting and remote all at once, as if thrust into someone else's spotlight, an alternate life of another who had chosen differently. He warmed up and felt himself getting into his zone again, letting his muscle memory take hold. His pitches were on target in the strike zone and reaching into speeds of high 90s. He tuned out everything and everyone for a change, locating the sweet spot of the baseball, consciously deciding to allow himself time to adjust to a new team. He'd retreat inward and try not to be a team captain. Let anyone else be the team captain while he fused back into himself.

His debut with The Olde Towne Team, the Red Sox, as a starting pitcher was propitious, with seven innings pitched, four walks, three runs, and only one homerun given up. The win was credited to him, not to the closer, thus gathering his first win in the major leagues that wasn't for the Chicago Cubs. As he went to the dugout after his seven innings were complete, the crowd were on their feet with applause. He saluted warmly into the air, conscious this time of his acting.

That night, however, in his new home in Beacon Hill, he continued with his sketch of Iowa, the picture emitting warmth to him.

In September, the Red Sox were in first place in the American League East. The Yankees, their deep-seated rival, were a half game behind their cleats. Every game counted for the Red Sox and the Yankees, both teams fighting for the one playoff spot.

There was a three-game series of the Yankees versus the Red Sox, a certified gold mine for the American League and everyone who had a piece of the major league pie. The major sports networks carried any series between the Yankees and the Red Sox in prime-time slots as it drew out both the best from the players and the worst in the players, as it also drew out mostly the worst in the fans but also the best from them.

The Bronx Bombers took the first game due to an absolute blowout from their hitting lineup, making a lopsided score of 7-2. Cervantes didn't pitch that one but he was slated to pitch in the next game.

Before the game, he dedicated his start to Olen Fisher and Buster Niemczyk. The crowd cheered when Olen Fisher's name was said on the speakers during Cervantes's dedication. The Boston fans knew their stuff, knowing that Olen Fisher would have become one of the Red Sox had he lived to see another day.

To him, the crowd was deafening and raucous throughout his pitches. Cervantes kept breathing, calming himself as he pitched this one for his buddies departed to elsewhere, to the grand unknown. The game carried depth for him as he tried not to look at the fan-made signs with photographs of Olen Fisher. Cervantes was in professional rapport with the catcher and the pitching strategies of this team. He slipped in almost effortlessly as he grounded out some, issued a few walks, flied out some, and fanned many of them. Many of his fastballs went past the 100 miles per hour mark. He felt he could go further than the fastball barrier at certain points in the game.

The game was tied into the fifth, with the Yankees swapping out their starter for a reliever, one of their most dependable in the bullpen.

Into the sixth, it was a virtually superhuman performance between the two pitchers. The game remained tied into the ninth, with both teams stranding players in scoring position. It headed into the tenth and then the eleventh when a member of the Yankees baubled on an easy play, a potential groundout, advancing to third base a player who should have been out. Cervantes's opposing pitcher showed anger in his face, yet continued with his formidable pitching. Cervantes saw that the error from the Yankee had tilted this pitcher off his game. Extra innings were always intense because the stakes were multiplied. Maybe the eleventh inning would be lucky. Cervantes was still pitching and he was tired. His manager insisted that he be relieved, but Cervantes refused, knowing who this game was dedicated to.

The pitcher was so bothered by the groundout error that he had walked a batter after a full count, loading the bases. His manager and the infield had come to talk to him and it looked as if they were going to pull him out, but the pitcher convinced them to keep him in.

When Cervantes saw him walk the next batter, the crowd vented utter joy. Cervantes was shining as he could hardly contain his gratification that he had commemorated his two Iowa Cubs teammates this way. He was visibly glassy eyed as the camera zoomed closer to capture his features.

Cervantes knew that his former teammates in Chicago were watching, that Ronan was watching. He was going to phone Ronan that night if Ronan didn't call.

"Hey, congratulations, big guy."

Ronan's particular cadence reminded Cervantes of home, of friendship, of the gleaming fields in the summer sun of far-flung Chicago.

"I'm glad you called. I knew you'd call," he said back into his phone.

"Things aren't the same without you here. Crackerjack is no substitute at all. Not the same as before, man."

"Crackerjack's bringing in the wins for the Cubs, I hear. It gets so busy here in Boston that it's hard to keep track. I hope he won't replace me as your best friend?"

"What? Hope you're joking."

"I might think I'm joking, Rory," Cervantes replied.

"Anyhow, thanks for dedicating that game to Fisher and Niemczyk. What a game. Saw it all. Nothing better than that for our friends."

"They'll always haunt me. They'll always haunt us."

Cervantes couldn't see Kiley's nod of agreement.

"They'll be there," the second baseman responded, wistfully.

"Eternally," Cervantes said. They reflected on the devastation briefly.

"How are your new teammates?" Ronan asked, after a stretch.

"They're teammates, that's all. It feels more like a business transaction than a team with a sense of camaraderie at the moment."

"At the moment," repeated Ronan.

They talked more about the game dedicated to their Iowa teammates and how "epic" they both thought it was.

"Tim," Ronan said after a bit of a lull in their conversation. "Don't feel responsible for my life anymore. You don't have to anymore."

"But I have to. I saved your life. What would it mean if I let you slip, let you fall, or at worst, let you die like our buddies? What would saving a life mean?"

"Timmo, you no longer have to be a shield. How would it be even possible with our careers on different paths now? We're even in different leagues, you with the AL and me with the NL."

"It's still possible. There's the offseason, Rory."

Ronan had already put himself in Tim's shoes and imagined if he had saved a person from a car accident. He would do whatever it took to make sure that life stayed saved.

"Listen, I've got to go. I've got to take care of myself a bit more. Big game tomorrow, new series with the Angels here."

"Yeah, me too. Things are getting wild in the NL Central. September looks like it's going well. We hope to expand our magic number soon in the Cubs versus Cardinals four-game series this week. Hope we get to clinch the division."

"Keep working hard. Keep going no matter what."

"You got it royally, mister."

As he finally got to rest, Cervantes thought of himself as the Catcher in the Rye, saving children from falling. There in that heady field of rye, Kiley was on the cliff teetering, about to tumble. It was Cervantes's priority in any uniform to keep a life he had saved undamaged.

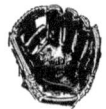

The next day on the field with the Red Sox, he started to assimilate with the team but for the first time in his life didn't bother with memorizing anyone's first name or being on a first name basis with fans. It could have been his way to ease the pain of being far from what he's known for so long or a conscious breakpoint from the past.

The Red Sox were first in the American League East and their magic number was down to three. As little as three more games and they were going to win the AL East pennant and be in the American League Division Series.

And they did so. There was just one loss before the Red Sox secured the pennant, and the city of Boston erupted in drunken revelry. "Southie," as the South End was known, was broadcast on the screens as being the rowdiest that evening. There were so many fans of the Red Sox around the country, for they were closely loved as they were formerly "cursed" to not have gone all the way to the World Series and won, magnificently having broken an interminable dry spell since the year 1918 to win the World Series title in 2004. Each chance at the big trophy was never taken for granted by the people of Boston and New England.

September was theirs. The manager was a skilled one, pushing them not with force but with a go-getting, believe-hard-to-win firmness of purpose. He valued every player on the team and geared them up for war similar to a general sighting through binoculars the nuances of a battlefield soon to be filled with his cavalry, his infantry.

Ronan didn't want to say this during the conversation with Cervantes, but the Crackerjack was doing as the Cubs organization predicted. He was leading the charge and bringing them forward. However, the Cubs had fallen out of first place in the division as September unfurled itself, and kept dwindling as the Cardinals were now in first place.

As NL Central division play went further, the Cubs had no chance to secure the NL Central pennant as it was now beyond their reach with barely a few games left. The Cardinals were going to coast easily to the pennant, and the Cubs' single hope to get an invitation to the postseason dance was to go for the NL Wild Card spot.

At the moment, the NL Wild Card competition consisted of six teams within striking distance: the Cubs, the Padres, the Phillies, the Reds, the Diamondbacks, and the Marlins.

The scents of September baseball wafted pleasantly as baseball executives for the Cubs team were in the grandstand. Now that he was a Cub for three seasons, Ronan wondered if he would make the postseason with them for the first time. It was a longshot, but a longshot that he was willing to work for.

The Diamondbacks were unable to keep up with the other five teams in the NL Wild Card chase while the St. Louis Cardinals got to their magic number and won the NL Central Pennant. Ronan couldn't watch the celebrations that St. Louis had on the television. He remained focused on the target ahead, which was helping his club get to the playoffs through the only way, the one Wild Card on offer in the whole league.

Cervantes was catapulting smoke, having struck out nine in a row in the American League Division Series against the Seattle Mariners. It was the first game of the series and he was on the hill, his mechanics precision sharp, though almost giving up a longball to the Green Monster. The home team uniform was beginning to feel like a second skin to him, a new vista, a Red Sox pitcher's life. The stands of Fenway were frenetic, inebriated, and solid fanaticism. They took Cervantes into their fold even though he was less open than usual. Possibly it was that inborn charisma of his that he could not stop, although he felt himself retreating within when he was not on the mound.

After that opener to the ALDS[1] against the Mariners where Cervantes received a close win of 3-2, he turned on his screen at home and stood up when he saw the news.

He was monitoring the Cubs and Ronan's chances of making the playoffs. He was melancholy to know that the Cardinals had beat the Cubs to get the pennant, but Cervantes thought the Cubs had a viable shot for the National League Wild Card, though that race was too close.

He felt a rush to the head when there, in the glow of the dark, sportscasters were proclaiming a situation that had never happened before in major league baseball history.

The NL Wild Card ended in a five-way tie for the first time since the establishing of a Wild Card spot. All five teams had the exact same win-loss record for the regular season. There were so many teams in the National League that a five-way tie was not impossible. The odds of it happening were so remote that no rules were made in the case that it ever happened, what with the Wild Card being created in 1994 in the NL.

All of major league baseball and those involved were watching and listening with a sense of wonder, awestruck as to what was going to happen next. The American League was on track already with the ALDS happening, and while Cervantes should rest up for the second game of this ALDS, he was glued to the news which kept spouting forth.

There was talk of how long this would delay the postseason, speculation as to how to break the five-way tie by the sportscasters, how the major leagues were going to sort this out, and if this would cancel the World Series because the delay would be too long.

---

1   American League Division Series— determines which two teams from the American League will advance to the American League Championship Series. The Division Series consists of two best-of-five series, featuring the three division winners and the winner of the wild-card play-off.— **editor**

As Cervantes continued with the Olde Towne Team in their charge through the ALDS, top major league baseball executives, owners, managers, lawyers, and representatives were meeting in rooms to agree on a way to break the five-way NL Wild Card tie between the Chicago Cubs, the Philadelphia Phillies, the San Diego Padres, the Cincinnati Reds, and the Florida Marlins. Similar to a diplomacy meeting, each of the five teams had come forth with their suggestions, their ideas, and they all knew that new rules had to be made that would stand the test of time and that they were charting new territory in professional baseball. Each person involved in the negotiations felt as if they were in an otherworldly place, that they thought they would never see a five-team NL tie in their lifetimes, much less six lifetimes.

Cervantes did find the time to call Ronan, whose amazement was tangible.

"Is there any news as to how they're going to figure this out? I try to sort the hearsay from the facts. There's so much information going around."

"Brass isn't spilling," Rory excitedly said. "They're trying to reach an agreement that will be fair to all five teams."

"Management must be about all of this. All the money coming in, all the press. It's made headlines around the world. It's brought almost constant media attention."

"Ride is just beginning. The Cubs have a one in five shot, the way people see it around the city."

They too made their theories as to how to sort through a five-team draw.

"If only Buster and Olen could have been around to see this," reflected the Cubs second baseman.

"They weren't so lucky as you and I. If I could have, I would have saved them too."

"Olen would have been on your team, I'm sure, all up thrilled about this five-way tie, Timmo. Made me realize that it's not about my ambition to go far, or else feel that I don't matter. It's about people. The four of us. When you were traded, it made me realize this even more."

"I'll be following everything when I can," the pitcher said, abstracted, inundated. "So much happening at once. It's a heated-up series here in our ALDS with the Mariners. Some of our pitchers are becoming balky."

"But you're doing well, I know it. On top of your game."

"I so wish I was with the Cubs at this moment. If you do find the time to visit me here while the rules are being hammered up, let me know. Maybe, if the White Sox win their ALDS, we'll be in the same city, my hometown, Chicago."

"You can bet on it. Or hope on it. It's been a while and I've got to see what became of your drawing skills."

Though the Red Sox pitchers were less controlled than usual, the Red Sox were able to win the ALDS against the Mariners in four games, sustaining just one loss. The people of New England fueled bacchanalias throughout the region and in every bend of the city Bostonians call The Hub.

The Yankees had lost to the Chicago White Sox in their ALDS, which caused even more of a stir in New England since the Yanks were the undisputed public enemy. The Yankees were the AL Wild Card and they had gone down to the Chicago White Sox with two games lost out of their five-game series.

Cervantes was looking forward to meeting up with his best friend in Chicago now that the Red Sox and White Sox would be fighting for the American League pennant. There was a heating up everywhere, even in countries around the world that were previously oblivious of baseball. The five-way tie the National League was disentangling held everything to a full stop in that league. Waiting in the wings was the winner of one of the two NLDS[2] series, the San Francisco Giants. Also waiting in the wings was the pennant winner of the NL East, the Washington Nationals, who were going to play the NL Wild Card winner if it was ever decided how they would go about breaking the five-way tie.

They were glad to see each other after a sailing of time, finding this irradiant pocket in the clock where they could catch up. They bantered and were serious, at times buoyant and contemplating ways to bring Cervantes back to the Cubs, the whole time mesmerized as the plans and designs came from the major league commissioner, legal counsels, umpires, historians of baseball, and the people as to how exactly a winner in a five-way tie was to be decided. A four-way tie would have been easy to decide, but how to create a structure where all five teams had an equal shot was bewildering.

They reminisced late into the evening of days of yore, halting away the flood of worries that the postseason brought. Traveling the pathways of

2   National League Division Series.

yesterdays, they couldn't help realize that a new kind of postseason was summoning them.

As Cervantes toed the rubber in Boston before his windup, he reflected on the ALCS[3] so far. The Red Sox were leading the series with three games to one, the series now being played in front of the Boston devotees. This was the third game in front of the Boston rooters, home field advantage on the team's side as Cervantes began the eighth inning. He was throwing with surgical dominion for the first six innings but his mechanics began to falter. Maybe there was no such thing as home field advantage after all as he felt the weight of all the expectations.

He let loose a screaming fastball to the White Sox cleanup hitter, Archer, to the inside right corner. That brought the count to two strikes and two balls. Cervantes was breathing deeply to calm himself down as the infield and the manager came to the mound to talk with him.

After the talk, which did calm his nerves to a certain degree, he launched a sinker. Archer connected, and sent it flying above the Green Monster.

The crowd seemed depressed as Archer rounded the bases. The White Sox were now one run ahead in the game, and the clinching game this evening may go down to the wire.

The manager had pulled him from the game for a reliever, and the regularly calm Cervantes walked to the dugout crestfallen.

He watched the rest of the game standing up against the fence with the rest of his teammates and saw the poetry in motion of their best reliever. He was able to keep the score the way it was until that gleaming instant when the Red Sox answered back with a two-run homer. The crowd exploded and when the Red Sox closer achieved the final out, Boston went consummately stratospheric. Cervantes was going to the World Series.

---

3   The American League Championship Series is a best-of-seven playoff and one of two League Championship Series comprising the penultimate round of Major League Baseball's postseason.

The rules for how to play the five-way tie for the NL Wild Card spot kept the National League in delay, all the way to mid-October. The media was rife with speculation and theories, so when the commissioner of baseball came to the cameras for a special press conference, all of America and parts of the world were glued.

Initially, Major League Baseball was going to resort to their already written rules of how to break a two-way tie for a Wild Card and the already written rules of how to break a three-way tie for a Wild Card and combine these two plans. That meant that there would be a Team A, B, C, D, and E to be decided to play it all out. The blend of the existing MLB rules proposed that there was going to be a Team A versus a Team B one-game decision, a Team D versus Team E one-game decision, and Team C would have the easiest path since they would only have to play one game: the winner of the Team A versus Team B game. The winner of the Team C versus the winner of the Team A versus B game would go on to the final game for the Wild Card, a one-game decision. This one game decision would be the winner of the A/B/C game versus the winner of the D/E game.

However, during the delay, many of the upper echelons in baseball thought about how unfair Team C had it. Team C only had one game to play and win it to get to the Wild Card Game while Teams A, B, D, and E have to win two games to get to the Wild Card Game.

To make it more even, instead of one-game decisions between the five teams, MLB decided that there would be multiple series to equalize the playing field. Team A and B would have a five-game series against each other and so would Team D and E. Team C would then play whichever team received three wins first, Team A, B, D, or E, and then play them in a seven-game series. The seven-game series would be played in the home stadium of Team A, B, D, or E. The winner of this series would then play for the Wild Card, which would be the winner of the Team C versus first-to-reach-three wins versus the winner of the A versus B game or the D versus E game. Home field advantage would be moot since play to determine the final Wild Card winner would be played in a neutral stadium in a warm state. This is how the five-way tie was going to be broken, with the two five-game series both starting simultaneously in a matter of days.

Most were confused when it was described but it when it was diagrammed, people began to understand:

To break a five-way tie of Team A, B, C, D, and E:
- Team A versus Team B (a five-game series)
- Team D versus Team E (a five-game series)
- Team C versus the first team to win three games (Team A, B, D, or E) in a seven-game series where Team C does not get home-field advantage
- For the Wild Card: the winner of the seven-game series versus the leftover team who won their five-game series (a seven-game series in a neutral stadium)

Kiley and Cervantes were in Chicago in the same secret place where Ronan had learned the news of Cervantes's trade earlier in the year. They were in windswept awe as they watched the television and thought what was decided was fair. After all, this was the best that all the team heads, directors, lawyers, and administrators could do. Primarily, though, Kiley and Cervantes knew that since this Wild Card five-way excitement was raking in a gold mine for major league baseball like never before, the one-game setup was less conducive to cashing in than the sequence of series setup. The whole situation sent an electromagnetic thrill throughout the baseball world and the major leagues knew that they were essentially giving the fans what they wanted. They knew that this whole structure would be talked about, and that was the reason why the National League put it in place. It would dominate the news cycles. It was far more exciting than one-game decisions, and it made things more even for all five teams.

Of importance was to decide who would be Team A, B, C, D, and E among the Chicago Cubs, the Philadelphia Phillies, the San Diego Padres, the Cincinnati Reds, and the Florida Marlins. There was talk of seeding each team to decide who would be A, B, C, D, or E, but this was decided as arbitrary. Since each team was indeed equal in the standings, then it would be fair to draw lots to decide who would be A, B, C, D, and E. Drawing lots was agreed upon by all involved, since each of the five teams had an identical win-loss record of 83-79 in the regular season.

The managers of each of the five teams would draw the lots in Cooperstown, New York, in the Baseball Hall of Fame. It was to be filmed closely to see that no cheating would be involved.

Cervantes couldn't be there at Kiley's apartment to watch since he was in the midst of the American League Division Series against the Chicago White Sox. Kiley watched with held breath as each team manager drew from a uniform cap once worn by Ty Cobb to decide Team A, B, C, D, and

They were in windswept awe as they watched the television ...

E. It was theatrical, cinematic in a way, and Kiley wished that Cervantes could also have seen this live. It was a dreamlike chord in sports history.

They each read the lots they drew and the teams were assigned this way: Team A was the San Diego Padres. Team B was the Chicago Cubs. Team C was the Philadelphia Phillies. Team D was the Cincinnati Reds. Team E was the Florida Marlins.

Therefore, the whole plan was:

- San Diego Padres versus the Chicago Cubs in a five-game series (home field advantage decided by coin toss)
- Cincinnati Reds versus the Florida Marlins in a five-game series (home field advantage decided by coin toss)
- Philadelphia Phillies versus the first of the other four teams to win three games (in a seven-game series where the Phillies don't have home advantage at all)
- The Wild Card Series: the winner of the seven-game series versus the other winner of their five-game series for the Wild Card spot (to be played in a seven-game series in a neutral stadium)

The newspapers proclaimed all of it and it was explained repeatedly so everyone soon saw daylight. Hearing on the radio or finding thoughts in the papers, it seemed that the Padres and the Cubs had the most difficult paths to the Wild Card since to get there they had to possibly play up to five games, and then after that possibly play up to seven games, and then possibly after that to play up to seven games for the Wild Card, making that a total of nineteen games. The same could also be said for the Reds and the Marlins. The Phillies, in contrast, had to possibly play up to seven games and then another seven games for the Wild Card win, making a total of fourteen possible games for the Phillies. Yet the Phillies would never have home advantage and a home crowd since they were Team C and had to sacrifice that to equalize the entire situation.

There was also another possibility that was widely talked about, something that would make everything even more sensational: the chance that the Padres or the Cubs and the Reds or the Marlins would each win three games at the same time. Major League Baseball saw this possibility looming, of course, and knew that it would draw even more spectators and fans to the whole phenomenon. If, for example, the Padres and the Marlins had each won three games in the same amount of time, then more rules would have to be drawn up to see which of them would play the

Phillies. The top decision makers were secretive about what they might have had in their sleeves in the event this happened. They reveled in the potentiality since it brought increasing suspense to the whole endeavor.

Timothy Cervantes's fate decided and with the National League about to resume, he had considerable time to breathe in October. The Red Sox fans had taken him in, though he still felt as if he was walking somebody else's life. Yet, he grew to love Boston, finding himself in the city's farmers markets, walking around the flat of the Hill and the Irish Riviera, and dining by himself in the North End. He visited the historic areas where events that gave birth to the country took place, the patriot within him momentarily giving him a well-needed diversion.

He saw the blur turn to focus in the National League. In the hunt to face the Red Sox for the big prize were the San Francisco Giants, who had won their NLDS, and the NL East Pennant Champion Washington Nationals, who would play in an NLDS with the Wild Card winner.

The Red Sox would be idle for weeks while the National League played out. He couldn't deny the excitement of this month, a mirage Wild Card October where major league baseball would be played against the autumnal ivy of Wrigley. People had sold out the tickets to the games and were zealots about the pleasant chaos and eventual order to emerge from the Wild Card five-way draw.

Practices in Boston were mandatory while the Red Sox were waiting, but Cervantes was able to find time to go to Ronan's games when he could.

The Cubs were the beneficiaries of the coin toss for home field advantage so they would host the Padres for the first and second game, and the fifth game if it came to a fifth game.

The same evening, the Reds were playing the Marlins in Cincinnati, with the Reds having won their coin toss.

Cervantes was there for the second game at Wrigley Field against the Padres. It was an added enjoyment to see Wrigley Field decorated with the red, white, and blue playoff buntings and to see in person his best friend play in the postseason. The Cubs had defeated the Padres in the first game, and the Cubs on the second night's game had won easily. He and Ronan did have a chance to speak on the phone for mere minutes before Ronan had to land in San Diego for the third game.

Cervantes watched the third game alone from his home in Boston, where the Cubs went down excruciatingly in an asymmetrical victory for the Padres.

The news that same night arrived that Cincinnati had defeated the Marlins in three consecutive games, a sweep. The Reds were therefore the first team to win three games, sending them to play the Philadelphia Phillies in a seven-game series.

The executives released a collective sigh of relief because they didn't have to draw up more rules if two teams had won three games in the same amount of time. The Reds were the one and only team of the four playing in the National League at the moment to get to the three wins to face Philadelphia.

The Cubs had cleared their first obstacle, the Padres, with their win of the fourth game in the series.

The Cubs now joined the other teams waiting as the only series being played in major league baseball was the Reds versus the Phillies in a seven-game sequence that was to be played entirely in Cincinnati. The Phillies were not to receive home field advantage once ever since that was what was decided on to make it all fair.

The Cubs, the Giants, the Nationals, and the Red Sox were all watching from the sidelines, as enthralled as the fans. Legions had descended on Cincinnati, a sudden baseball mecca for up to seven games.

The Reds were fluctuating in crescendo and decrescendo against a fully ruthless Philly team. It went to a game seven, which is exactly what the Major League bank accounts wanted, and the Reds came out on top, cleaning up the Phillies and sending them packing back to Pennsylvania.

It was now the second week of November when the Cubs had to face the Reds in a seven-game series for the Wild Card in a neutral stadium. The neutral stadium was decided to be Dodger Stadium since it had the highest seat capacity of all major league stadiums.

The legions of people were there in Los Angeles's Dodger Stadium when Cervantes had time away from the constant Red Sox practices that kept them ready for the World Series while waiting for the National League to play to a pennant champion.

The teams remaining in the hunt and watching the series in Dodger Stadium were the NLDS Champion San Francisco Giants, the Red Sox, and the Washington Nationals. The Nationals would play the Wild Card winner, the victor of this seven-game series, in an NLDS.

There was talk that whichever National League team made it through to the World Series that they would be too exhausted to continue to play.

There, in the neutral territory of colossal Dodger Stadium, fans were gathered from all places to witness the historical. There looked to be a predominance of Cubs fans, but they were submerged in the total crowd of all fans of baseball. The Reds were favored to win this seven-game series in L.A.

Though the Reds were favored, soon the Cubs were leading the seven-game series three to one, with the Reds having their fresh busher up at the plate in game five. The score was 4-3 Cubs in the sixth. There were no outs and the rookie had laced a triple into right field in the sixth inning. The power hitter for the Reds was in the hole, and the Cubs decided to intentionally walk him when he came to the plate. The batter that followed him was the starting Reds pitcher who was known for hitting in clutch situations. On the first pitch, the Reds pitcher had tried to lay down a bunt as the Cubs infield moved in closer. The bat didn't connect and it was now a count of two strikes and two balls to the Reds pitcher. He swatted his entire being at the next pitch and sent the ball into the right field corner as the two men on base rounded to home as the Reds fans in the stadium bubbled forth in ecstasy. The Reds were now ahead in game five at 6-4.

The Cubs were never able to come back in game five and the Chicago fans had left in a fugue of gloom. There was always the next game, game six, another elimination game for the Reds.

Cervantes was in Dodger Stadium to watch game six and he felt as if he could touch the excitement detectable in the air. The National League was right in stretching out the NL Wild Card fever. He felt that he had slipped into a degree detached from actuality where the most inaccessible of odds were also the likeliest of chances.

The game was scoreless after the ninth, forcing the game to extra innings. Both pitchers, Nick "Crackerjack" Harrell for the Cubs and Ari Calvaruso for the Reds were in textbook, almost flawless form. Crackerjack had allowed not more than four hits while Calvaruso allowed three hits. Watching this game, Cervantes recognized, was a master class in pitching. Both pitchers were not giving an inch to the other and both were fierce, dominant, and precision-focused, as if they more than owned the hill that they were perched on.

Dodger Stadium was gripped as the eleventh inning rolled by, still scoreless, and bound delightedly in fascination into the twelfth inning.

In the twelfth, the Reds had put one on the board at last. This drew long faces from everyone who were for the Cubs, including Cervantes, who did not want to see this series go to a game seven since the Reds planned on bringing out their ace pitcher and multiple Cy Young winner, John Schachter, on hardly two days rest, a significant risk to Schachter since he could incur injuries.

Kiley was up at bat and knew the pressure was on him. He kept adjusting his stance and felt that he couldn't get comfortable as he faced Calvaruso, the pitcher who had the whole Cubs dugout tied up in obscurities this evening because the team couldn't figure his pitches out.

Kiley dug in and told himself that he was a major leaguer who had what it takes, and summoned up his drive, his energy, calming himself and reaching a zonelike state. Kiley had a keen eye to the pitches now and kept deciphering Calvaruso, watching him and his moves, his windups. He was at a full count and the Cubs had a hope that he would be walked when Kiley swung at the next pitch and streamed the baseball into left-center field. He was able to reach first base easily as the Cubs fans in the crowd went soaring.

The next Cubs batter went down on a strikeout. Crackerjack would have been next batter but the Cubs decided to make a move—they would take Crackerjack out to bring in their clutch hitter. Crackerjack was not pleased with this decision but the skipper decided that he needed to rest, there was going to be a lot of baseball ahead and he had already given a hundred and dozens of pitches tonight.

Cleeve, all muscles and intimidation, was the clutch hitter that was at the plate for the seated Crackerjack. Calvaruso was ready and felt in control while absorbing the signals from his catcher and the coaches. Calvaruso couldn't trace the plate, pitching three balls. Cleeve had wisely kept from swinging. Calvaruso started to sweat and kept wiping his palms onto his pants, trying to recover his grip on the ball. The rosin bag wasn't drying his hands and the ball felt prone to sliding from his grip.

He gave his fourth pitch to Cleeve and it was declared a ball, having painted microscopically outside of the box.

The Reds manager, Calvaruso, and three other Reds were fuming at this call. There were no video reviews left as the Reds had used all of theirs earlier in the game. They ganged up on the home plate umpire, convinced that it was a strike. The whole confrontation had become so intense that the manager had used profanity that reached subcutaneously in a personal attack on the umpire, and the umpire had had it. He tossed the Reds manager and the three Reds besides Calvaruso out of the game.

Wondering who was right, Cervantes looked closer on his phone at the video review, which was available to everyone who wanted to look. He did see that the umpire's call was right and that the Calvaruso pitch was undeniably a ball, within a hair. The Reds would realize that they were in error later on when they had the benefit of seeing the video dissection.

With Cleeve at first and Kiley on second, Calvaruso had his eyes on them in case they were thinking of a double steal. Calvaruso felt himself pushed off his edge after his manager and three of the best Reds players on the team were tossed, and he anxiously toed the rubber and glared at the Cub runner on each bag.

He let loose a hard, high slider and the Cubs batter connected far more easily, as if Calvaruso had let his guard completely fall, the ball's trajectory from the bat deep into the hole between left and center field. Kiley was being waved around to go home, the wave that he wanted. The whole club knew Kiley was fast and could run like a stag. He ran, frantic to tie the game and keep it alive.

As he crossed homeplate, he was tagged too late by the catcher. The game was now tied.

There were no further runs by the Cubs in the game and this sent game five into the thirteenth inning. The reliever that replaced Crackerjack was Kweon, a pitcher renowned for his no-nonsense approach to the craft of pitching. He was able to keep the Reds in check, having them strand two players on base as the Cubs went up to bat. Crackerjack heaved a sigh of relief. His masterpiece was still intact.

Calvaruso was showing signs of tiredness as he was kept in the game. Still he attempted to recapture his zone. He couldn't find the plate as he walked the first two batters. The third batter was Kiley, and Kiley had connected and belted another single again, gleaming as he reached first base.

With the bases full of runners and no outs, the whole stadium had stood on their feet to expectantly see the final victor of the NL Wild Card, which the Cubs were poised to be.

After a talk by the infield to Calvaruso, Calvaruso managed to talk them and the pitching coach into keeping him in. Calvaruso was known as a player who could talk his way out of anything or into anything.

He showed signs of regaining his heat, but then let loose an unpredictably wild pitch which the Reds catcher couldn't see after it had bounced off of his left knee.

The Cubs had coasted to victory and sheer elation as they intersected home plate. Calvaruso was in tears as the rest of the Reds team looked on in green-eyed agony as the Cubs piled up and celebrated their hard-fought battle to the Wild Card spot, breaking the five-way tie that had captivated the imagination of the baseball world.

Kiley couldn't find Cervantes after he learned that Cervantes was at Dodger Stadium, but Cervantes was able to find him in the champagne-soaked locker room. For that moment, it seemed that all was coated golden in the world. The Cubs weren't thinking of their competition ahead, the Nationals, the Giants, and the Red Sox, all three teams waiting for their turn. The spotlight was on the Chicago team right now, having gone through an unprecedented Wild Card contest. Kiley wanted to bask in the luminosity and the grandeur as he put the future on hold. He wanted this sensation to be permanent. He was drenched in champagne and wanted to be soaked more. He and Cervantes let the inebriating champagne stream in rivulets on their faces but never opened their mouths to taste it, wiping it away each instance they could.

The Cubs were going on barely one day of rest as they flew to D.C. for their NLDS against the Washington Nationals. The Nationals had home field advantage since their record during the regular season was slightly better than the Cubs' regular season record, so the first two games were played in the nation's capital. The Cubs took these first two, ablaze and looking invulnerable, and Kiley thought it incredibly surreal to be back in Wrigley this late November, about to clinch it against the Nationals as he saw red ivy. The outfield bricks were in their autumn wardrobe.

The third game of the NLDS for the Cubs was taken by the Nationals and was a close one, 5-4 with bobbles that had cost the Cubs in the eighth inning.

The fourth game was a hitting extravaganza as the Nationals and the Cubs both came swinging, their bats alive against the most inscrutable of their pitchers. Crackerjack was on the mound and scratched his head as he normally kept his hits down to a minimum, but both sides were belting longballs, three-baggers, and even squeaking infield hits. In the ninth inning, Washington was behind by two runs and the bases were loaded with the Nationals on two outs. Crackerjack was kept in the game, and he looked weary. All the Cubs needed was one out to get past the Nationals and Crackerjack was able to seal it with the most unforgiving forkball in his array. Once the Nationals batter had swung and missed, the Cubs ran onto Wrigley and heaped up in exultation. They were advancing on to the National League Championship Series.

While he could sense that Tim's congratulatory effort on the phone was genuine, they both knew the amplified chances of them facing each other in the World Series now.

Tim was conflicted about the forging ahead of the Cubs since it was all so complex for him. He was more than enthusiastic for the Cubs push through the five-way NL Wild Card tie and was swept away along with everyone else who followed and loved baseball.

"I'm beyond the sun happy, Rory. This is what you've wanted."

"Luck seems to be on our side. With more of it, we'll clobber the Giants, hopefully."

"Obviously you will and then we'll face each other in the World Series. The thought makes me wish I was never traded. I could've done everything that Crackerjack did to get the Cubs to where they are right now. It should have been me, Rory, there to throw that forkball."

Soundlessness was on the line as they both knew what was likely to happen, both fathoming how they were going to react as best friends if they were against each other on opposite teams in the World Series.

"Vanquish the Giants for me," Cervantes ordered, almost militarily.

"Each time I hear you pushing me to be my best, I hope for a miracle to happen where you're back here on the Cubs."

"Unavoidable, isn't it, that thought. If only. We have to make the best of what will happen."

"Letting you know you don't have to feel you have to protect me anymore."

"I can't do that," he automatically replied.

"Let go, I'm giving you permission. We can play the what if game, can't we, all night? If I wasn't saved by you in that accident, if Fisher was the one who was alive instead of me? Niemczyk?"

"I can't not protect you," he said again, speedily. "You must understand that I saved your life and there is a duty that comes after that. It's not negotiable. It's irreversible."

Kiley knew in his gut that once a life is saved it had to remain saved. The media would seize on the possible Cubs versus Red Sox, or rather, the Kiley versus Cervantes story that would be milked as the deepest lode gold deposit found.

"Won't look at the media or even talk to the media if it comes to that," Kiley intoned.

"So don't I, without doubt. 'So don't I.' It's Boston speak for 'me too.' I'm learning the language here."

"So don't I," Kiley repeated.

Cervantes was both excited for himself, for the Red Sox, for Kiley, for the Cubs, but was so clashing internally that he needed time to gather his wits. He both wanted and didn't want the Cubs to advance to the World Series, and it was then that he decided to immerse himself in practices in Boston and with hope catch one or two games at Wrigley.

San Francisco had the opening game of the NLCS as they had the better regular season record and they took the first two games viciously, conveying the series to Chicago.

Cervantes was unavailable for the first five games of the NLCS as practice for the Red Sox had intensified since their opponent for the World Series would emerge soon.

He did have time to catch the sixth game of the NLCS in San Francisco, taking a red eye flight after a battery of hectic Red Sox practices.

Cervantes was incognito, hiding from the media and in a private box arranged by his agent. He sat hidden behind his agent and a thick group of people he knew from Boston in the box, watching the game live on a San Francisco night that brought winter to the bone.

If the Giants didn't win this game, then the Cubs would become the

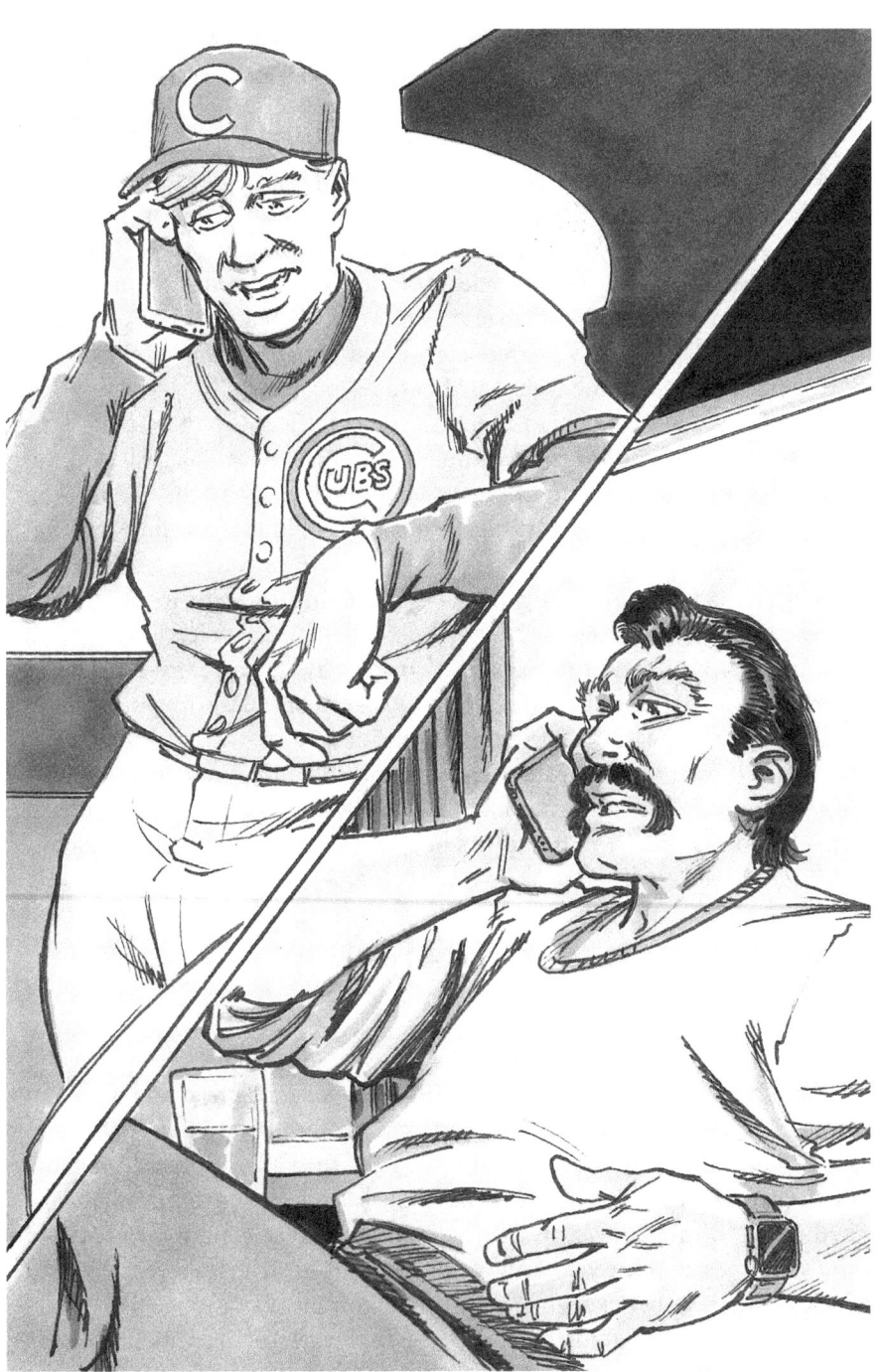

"Won't look at the media or even talk to the media if it comes to that."

National League Champions and go on to the World Series versus his team. He watched neutrally and grimly as he reasoned with himself that either outcome was good—Kiley would achieve his dream of making it to the World Series or, otherwise, Cervantes wouldn't face his best friend and possibly hurt him in a merciless series.

The sixth game that Cervantes was watching was no contest. The Cubs were the only ones on the board with six runs while the Giants had none into the seventh. The Giants had stranded many runners during the course of the game and had stranded more in the eighth. The Cubs had expanded their lead with a three-bagger and an RBI by Kiley followed by a solo homerun from the Cubs third baseman.

The Giants were down to their last out and already the Giants fans were starting to head for the parking lots as they knew what was coming. Some, however, were staying as they wanted to commend the Giants for a season well-fought and well-played, even if they didn't make it to the final showdown.

The NLCS was won handily in an embarrassing 9-0 score for the Giants.

He watched the screens as he saw the city of Chicago volcano-erupt and watched his best friend so exhausted from playing so many postseason games as he leapt into the air as if he was on top of the world, pure delight making way through the fatigue and weariness.

The Red Sox pitcher sat there as everyone, including his agent, filed out of the stadium. He sat in the box for a while, enigmatic, and then went directly to his hotel room and his bed in a daze, waiting till tomorrow morning to process it all.

The skipper for the Cubs saw that his team was energized and worn out from all of the games they had to play in the strenuously unique postseason. He had debated with himself whether to keep the Cubs' momentum going or to give his team rest. It was a hard decision for him to make, and he had come to the realization that he couldn't play a bone-weary team in the World Series. He requested five-day rest for his team before the World Series and the upper executives saw this as completely rational. The World Series was therefore going to start in the first week of December.

Boston was going to have the benefit of homefield advantage in the series. There was talk of "snow delays" instead of well-known "rain delays" and what the freezing temperatures of both cities would do to the pitchers' arms.

There wasn't much worry about having baseball in winter temperatures since other sports events were held in colder climates. Both the Chicago fans and Red Sox Nation were ready to see history unfold before their eyes no matter how below freezing it was.

Ronan, after the NL Pennant win, was himself too drained to think of anything but recuperating in Chicago. He took to bedrest and healing his body from the wear, storing himself up for an intense encounter with the Red Sox.

The teams were about equally on par with each other, according to the sports pundits, with no clear favorite to win the series. News, publishing, and radio made much of the core battle, which was between former teammates Cervantes and Kiley and their story from Iowa to the present.

Both were hounded with press calls and requests for interviews, but they had kept their mutual promise that they wouldn't give in to the media's attempt to exploit their situation.

During the third day of Ronan's complete self-imposed seclusion at home, he woke up one morning and the full brunt had hit him. How could he even think of defeating the guy who had rescued him? He would have been six feet under if it weren't for Tim. An inner skirmish began from that third day of rest. For the next two days of his deep rest, he distracted himself with his etchings and drawings while resting from bed. It served to take his mind off of the upcoming confrontation, and as a light snow fell outside his window, he wondered how Cervantes was coping with it.

Yet they had already talked about it. There was no rulebook for situations like these, and damn nothing that could have prepared them for what was coming.

He continued drawing the four of them, Kiley, Fisher, Cervantes, and Niemczyk in Chicago Cubs uniforms against radiant Midwest skies as he delved deep away from the here and now.

It felt soothing to get back to practice and to adapt to the freezing temperatures of Wrigley. The ivy on the bricks in front of the bleachers were all brown vines now, and instead of a rain crew there was a snow crew in case of snowfall.

This is sports, he reasoned, it's everyone for their team and their team exclusively. There's no way he can alter his performance or for Cervantes to alter his. He knew that the media and fans would be watching to see if they would water down their skills in favor of the other. They were both under microscopes as far as the public was concerned.

There in the batting cage, he wondered if he could live with a World Series win.

The Red Sox took advantage of the Cubs five-day recuperation and practiced tougher, raring to go, ready to conquer and inflict damage.

Cervantes occupied himself with honing his control, which was sharper than ever. He didn't want to think about Rory at the moment. He had made up his mind that he would face the situation when it happens. He thought there was no use in worrying about it for now.

Even so, entirely not on the surface was his wish that he would not face Rory at the plate, though it was fated. He was scheduled to start at least two of the games in a theoretical seven-game series. Their pitching rotation was already planned by the manager and with Cervantes starting two, and at most three, games, that meant that he'd be pitching to Rory about four to five times each game, making that a possible eight to fifteen meetings between him and Rory of pitcher and hitter during the entire series. There would be more meetings between them if the games went past nine innings.

He didn't hold back on his skills and pitched with determination.

The Boston crowd was pulsating as the World Series began, with the first two games on home turf. There were five starting pitchers in the rotation for them, with Cervantes scheduled to pitch the third game and the sixth game if it came to a sixth game.

The Cubs were in top form for the first game in spite of being halfway rested and dog tired. It looked as if adrenaline was propelling them, and they won the first game closely, with their bats thriving and their pitching full tank. Kiley's bat was finding its mark and his fielding at second base was impeccable.

Boston put up a challenge in the second game, with one of their ace pitchers, Sutton, serving up the heat. The Cubs were narrowly able to put up two runs to Boston's five, with an error from the Cubs' shortstop and an unintentional balk from Chicago's starting pitcher. Boston celebrated in all areas, from Southie to the Combat Zone to downtown. All of New England rejoiced the Cubs being beaten.

Tim and Ronan both were in their opposite dugouts, glad they hadn't faced each other on the mound and in the batter's box. They had to wait a day and contemplate now that the third game was going to be held in frosty Chicago.

It was torturous for both of them, and they felt that they had to, in some way, naturally sedate themselves because the situation was overwhelming. Time was solid while they faced each other for the first time in this series, both wearing the World Series patch on their upper arms but on different uniforms.

Cervantes had grounded out his best friend for the first edgy encounter, and then struck him out for their second meeting during the game. When it became apparent in the sixth inning that Cervantes was on the path to a no-hitter in the World Series, it made sense for his team to comply with the unstated rule in baseball that a no-hitter was not to be talked about while the pitcher and the game were in progress. There was just one no-hitter in all of World Series history and for it to happen tonight would just continue with the surrealism that was this postseason's middle name.

The Cubs couldn't figure out Cervantes's pitches and when it was time for Kiley to be up at the plate, the pressure between them appeared to be off since Cervantes was at this time beyond hitting. Kiley was hitting in the 300s for the postseason, but in this game, he couldn't recognize Tim in his no-hitter cloak. It was as if he was completely blind to who he was pitching to, some other no-hitter personality, treating batters as objects rather than as real people. Tim looked overtaken, his skills in pitching having subdued the rest of him to make way for a no-hitter.

Cervantes was on the way to the second no-hitter in World Series history when he gave up a single in the eighth inning to the Cubs. There was then a standing ovation from the Chicago Cubs and fans, with Kiley whistling loudly, simultaneously glad and mourning that it wasn't a no-hitter. Rory's was a tangled reaction to the near no-hitter. He saw Cervantes snap out of his no-hitter rush and he saw him looking for Kiley for the first time in the Cubs dugout.

Cervantes continued on in the eighth to other Cubs batters and gave no more hits besides the one. The Sox skipper decided to pull him since his pitch count was considerable, and again the Cubs crowd had stood on their feet in respect.

Into the ninth, Kiley faced a reliever, classified among the Red Sox's best, and hit a double-bagger. It was then that snow began to fall down lightly, then in sizable cascades, and the game had to be delayed due to snowfall.

The snow crews had drawn the tarp over the field while everyone waited for what felt to be hours even though the home crowd knew that this game was probably Boston's.

Through the snowfall, ethereal throughout Wrigley, people were taking photos and players all took to their locker rooms. The Cubs skipper and coaches were giving their vital rally and morale talks while the Red Sox were waiting for the snow to be cleared.

During the snow delay, Kiley was joyful that tonight it seemed he wasn't facing his best friend on the mound. Rather, he was facing a no-hitter machine with a no-hitter internal flood deluging him, so much so that he found it excusable and that they were both off the hook in the tense situation they were both in.

Approximately two hours later, seeing the snow had stopped, the crew made sure that the field was completely playable. The snow crew had used a ground cloth that covered the diamond from snow, with a separate one covering the areas of the outfield and the areas outside the foul lines. These were brought out and laid on the ground in the timeliest way so that when the umpires had called to play ball after the delay, the playing field was ready.

The Red Sox were able to close the game with a tortuously angled grounder that their third baseman had caught in a contortionist play, and hurled it to first for the force out.

The near no-hitter made headlines and still Cervantes wasn't able to be interviewed, having kept to his promise that both he and Kiley were not to be distracted by the press. He wanted the no-hitter so much that he couldn't remember facing Kiley. He knew that Kiley knew it too, that their friendship was still intact and that the possible no-hitter that was in progress had allayed their fears of one defeating the other or betraying the friendship of the other.

The grandstand was filled to the brim in the Friendly Confines with people in their bulky winter clothing. The weather forecasted no precipitation for the fourth game of the World Series, yet the snow crew was there obligatorily. The cold wind this evening was in the direction of the bleachers, making longballs carried on the winds even more probable.

On the hill was Crackerjack for the Cubs and another ace pitcher for the Red Sox, Clarke. This was Crackerjack's first start in a World Series. He nervously toed the rubber but then fell into concentration, sending the ball flying to where he wanted it. He used a nasty curve ball when batters least expected it and this kept him going, keeping the Red Sox blanked from the board. Clarke had previously been in a World Series with another team so he already had the experience. Even so, it still was the World Series, and it took him a few moments before he too found his command of the ball. Both pitchers were first-rate until the seventh inning, when Clarke gave up a homerun that was carried by the winds. Clarke threw his glove down in frustration, knowing this was strictly a pitcher's duel. If Clarke knew that Crackerjack would give up three homeruns in the next inning, he wouldn't have felt so pressured to throw his glove.

Both of them were kept on the mound while the bullpens for each team started warming up. The wind toward the ivy was a strong gust, and it carried baseballs into the bleachers and far onto Waveland Avenue. The score was tied up into the ninth until Kiley had lobbed a solo into the net in front of the bleachers, winning the game and sending Clarke misty-eyed from the mound and the Cubs rushing the field.

The Cubs and the Red Sox were now tied in the series two games apiece.

The last game for the year at Wrigley Field was to be played. The Cubs needed this win before going back to the Hub, back to Boston, in confidence.

The starting pitcher, appreciatively, was not his best friend. This pitcher was loose and couldn't control his mechanics, reminding him of certain pitchers he had seen in the minors who had given in to pressure. The Red Sox starter was removed after three innings, having given up six runs. They brought in a reliever who fared no better, giving the Cubs two more runs.

Boston wasn't shutout as they were close behind, with the score being 8-6 Cubs in the sixth inning. Boston soon took the lead, coming from behind with bases on balls from the Cubs relievers and runs batted in. There was a new reliever on the hill for Boston, what appeared to be the fifth reliever they used for this game, and he had struck out nine batters in a row and made the last out himself by bare-handing a line drive. The Cubs didn't get the win they needed before going back to New England.

Boston was now ahead in the series with three games to the Cubs two wins. The sixth game was an elimination game for the Cubs, and all of Boston was ready to seal the pact.

It was also the situation that Kiley and Cervantes both dreaded. Cervantes was the starting pitcher for this elimination game, and was also coming off a near no-hitter.

Fenway was as Siberian as Chicago, with a hint of snow to occur for the sixth game. Both teams were operating on one day's rest and all of the baseball world and the sports world was tuned in. They knew what was at stake, both the friendship of Kiley and Cervantes along with which team would be crowned champion.

It was now or not at all for Kiley's dream and it was time for Cervantes's dream of having a World Series ring on his hand and possibly being the World Series MVP. Cervantes could taste victory for his Red Sox. It would be picture-perfect for Red Sox Nation to have their World Series win at home.

Cervantes was different from his appearance previously in the near no-hitter. It looked as though his delivery had changed or that he was distracted. For the first two innings Cervantes couldn't paint the plate and filled up the sacks, only for the Cubs to leave them stranded. Cervantes kept breathing profoundly as the cameras all focused on both Kiley's and Cervantes's expressions, the both of them maintaining stoic poker faces.

Cervantes soon gained back his mastery in time as one of the power hitters was in the hole for the Cubs. The Cubs' clutch hitter came up to the plate with runners on first and second and only one out. Cervantes let loose an incalculable curve that had the batter swinging at air. The batter felt that he was going to curve him again but Cervantes had finished him with a circle changeup.

Kiley was up now, and he knew that his friend's arsenal was stocked full. He had shut out the Cubs and it was the bottom of the seventh. Cervantes had not shown invulnerability, though. He had shown that he could be figured out. It wasn't in the Cubs' cards this evening that they'd have their men on the bags make it to home plate. The Red Sox were two runs ahead to none. This was Kiley's opportunity at the plate, and the Cubs fans in the grandstand here at Fenway sat morbid as the Sox were about to win the series.

Cervantes didn't let up. He fired a two-seam fastball that got past Kiley looking. Cervantes was cold and in total grasp, cold in the coldest air that this series had ever been played in. He gave the expression of being elsewhere, avoiding Kiley's eyes.

He and the catcher agreed on a splitter, which again caught Kiley looking. This was the Cubs best chance this evening to get on the scoreboard, and it was up to Kiley to do so or not.

Cervantes next pitched on the line between the strike and ball area, and the manager had come out to the umpire after declaring it a ball. The Red Sox manager and the umpire had at it for a while, though civilly since the Red Sox skipper was wise enough to know that he shouldn't push getting tossed. While the manager and the umpire were arguing, Kiley again tried to search for eye contact from Cervantes. Tim was adrift in his own world, completely preoccupied by the prize of winning the series.

Cervantes had wanted to cannon a slider but changed his mind mid-windup to a curveball.

This was a surprise to Cervantes as he let the pressure of being so close to being the champions of the World Series get past his armor.

The ball had careened into the right side of Kiley as he stung over in pain.

It was an unwritten rule that a batter who gets hit by a pitch doesn't rub the area, giving the pitcher no satisfaction.

The doctors came out to check on him, and as Kiley was on the ground for an insufferable fifteen minutes being examined by team doctors, Cervantes could only stare, rooted to the mound.

Seeing this right before him, it was as if Cervantes had snapped out of his otherwhere state. He saw the pain that he had caused to Kiley, and could feel the warmth of Iowa looming and weaving in the December air around him.

The cameras had all captured the look of shock on Cervantes's face and the gasping pain that Kiley showed as he got up and hobbled his way to first base.

Cervantes had regained his control after unintentionally hitting Rory, though he felt that at any moment his pitches could become as wild as a firehose if he had again let his guard down. Hitting Rory was unraveling him.

Tim could see the cleanup hitter in the batter's circle and summoned himself to regain his abilities. He confirmed to himself that he was a bit unraveled as he thought the Cubs were attempting to steal and realized that the bases were already full.

He was able to get out of the inning with solely one run scored, a Cubs batter having lined into left field, allowing the player on third to tag home. He then struck out the next two batters and went to the Red Sox dugout shaken.

Kiley was going to be in extreme pain tomorrow as he saw how fast that ball was that went cruelly, unintentionally into him. For now, Kiley was allowed to play.

Cervantes hoped to close out the game without facing Kiley again, but the Cubs were gaining. They just needed one more run to tie the game, and it was too dangerously close. It was the Boston crowd's turn to feel morose.

He managed to keep them scoreless though he felt off as they entered the ninth inning. Cervantes was saved by a shoestring catch by his right fielder along the way to the ninth.

There was one out and only one on first base as the Cubs were down to their last two outs.

And it was Ronan Kiley who came up to the batter's box.

This time, Ronan could tell, Tim had come back to himself. He finally saw the Tim he knew. They did recognize each other for the first time in the series and it was an acknowledgement so subtle that the cameras couldn't detect it. There was an unstated statement, as if they could tell what the other was thinking.

Cervantes showed he had steam as he let loose a splitter that caught Kiley swinging.

He then threw a four-seam fastball that Kiley fouled back into the stands.

This was the moment, though, the moment where Cervantes had to prove his principles. This was the last chance and he knew which choice he was going to take.

He could still see that Rory was in pain from his pitch that had hit him, and he knew that Rory also knew what kind of ball was going to be thrown next.

Cervantes threw a palmball, and Kiley was so completely attuned to the timing of Cervantes's palmball that he swung accurate in time, connecting bat to ball and sending it to the bleachers, winning the game and sending the series to a winner-take-all seventh game.

Cervantes had his head down as he exited the mound, pretending melancholy at a game lost but inside he was all elation.

The last game of the World Series had both guys on the benches watching, seated for the whole game. It was discovered that Kiley on deeper examination by the medical staff had fine hairline fractures on his ribs from being hit by the pitch. Cervantes was done with pitching in the series. They watched their teammates as they were at their finest, with falling liners into right-center field, clutch hits by the cleanup guy for the Red Sox, scratch hits by the Cubs that got them on base, bunts beated out, and breathtaking and beautiful sliders.

The teams were tied into the ninth and headed into the tenth as Cervantes and Kiley tensed.

The snow began a light and gossamer fall, and it was decided that there was going to be no snow delay. The ground was still playable and the entire sight was beguiling. The breaths of the players were more visible through the snow as they steadily aimed for the title.

It was anyone's game still and the Cubs threatened with a double on two outs, merely to leave that player at sea. The Red Sox answered back with a three-bagger but they had stranded that player also.

It wasn't until the eleventh when the Cubs had two outs and one runner on second in scoring position. Up at bat was the Cubs' leadoff guy, who was one for four this night. The reliever on the mound had served up a four-seam which the leadoff guy didn't even swing at. Still, the reliever wasn't taking anything for granted. He wound up and threw a rare knuckleball, which was swung at and missed.

The next pitch was exactly what the Cub wanted, a bullseye in the center fastball. He linked with it, breaking his bat as he knocked it on wings into deep left field.

The Cub on second base was being waved around and he ran as if he was a greyhound unchained.

He rounded third and went for home, sliding around the catcher and hoping that his reach was far enough for his hand to touch home plate.

He tagged home with the outer contours of his hand a fraction of a second before he got tagged.

The umpire yelled him safe and the crowds in Chicago and the baseball realm were sent to directly to paradise.

Cervantes saw that a beaming Rory was kept from the field due to his injury while his teammates surged onto the diamond, world champions.

The rest of his teammates having gone back to the locker room, Timothy Cervantes saw before him the team that had went through the gauntlet to win the World Series and lived to tell.

He was appreciative of their victory and marched back to the Boston clubhouse, contemplative of the two Iowan Cubs on the roster elsewhere while musing on the warmth of winter, the vastnesses of the town of Chicago, the good sportsmanship of the city of Boston. And he knew that when he saw Rory in action next, he'd be with the Iowa Cubs recovering. Then eventually, with a bit of luck, Rory would be on the Red Sox. Time had its sudden whims and its skill to heal. Entering a muted locker room, thoughtful of how he would react if he ever had to face him in a World Series as opponents again, he thought of the evolution of baseball. In years to come, he knew this series among the snowfall would never thaw, would always be preserved.

THE END

"Baseball in December" Post-Essay

L et me declare, sports fan—I figured if I couldn't be a baseball player, I'd write about baseball players. I would get into the motivations of my athlete characters and act them in my mind's eye, and after fully rendering being a pitcher and a second baseman, have the plot issue forth.

Yet that's not how it happened, most faithful baseball reader—it started with a title. And it was a title that told me it was time to get up and swing in the batter's box.

The growth for this story stemmed from its title, which is unusual for me since most of the time when writing stories I create the characters beforehand. "Baseball in December" was a title that arrived, boltlike, to me and it sent my imagination soaring—how is major league baseball possible in December? How can I get the World Series to play in that month in a plausible way? After some two weeks of planning, looking up official major league baseball rules and reading major league baseball article writers, I devised a way to delay the World Series to the time of snowfall and holidays.

The most challenging portion of this story while writing it was drawing up the rules for a five-way National League Wild Card tie that would be fair-minded to all of the five teams, and since it took me a couple of weeks to solve this puzzle, I reflected this in the story. This disentangling from an unparalleled situation was my method for binding up the National League and placing them in a thrilling limbo delay to have the World Series play in December. A five-way tie is possible in either league but the chance is so remote that major league baseball hasn't written rules in the event it should happen. It was up to me, and I drew up a heap of rules, pondering them, arranging them, rearranging them, altering them, asking myself how to increase the volume of the excitement to maximum-level, how to stretch the postseason out to take advantage of a five-way tie and keep baseball fiction readers ecstatic.

Though set firmly in the world as we know it, I wanted to put a touch of "postseason unpredictability" in it, since we all know that when *every* baseball postseason happens, there are shocking unforeseeable occurrences, making us wonder if what we saw in October happened.

With "Baseball in December," I wanted to chart new land for the major league baseball story—instead of having one protagonist, let's have two protagonists. Let's also have at its central core a story of two best friends, a story of friendship surviving death, and the severities of being against each other on different teams. Would they set aside their professionalism or will they let their careers overrule their respect for each other? Who would the reader cheer for, Ronan Kiley or Timothy Cervantes? Would the reader be conflicted in who they want to "win," Tim or Rory? Would the reader be rooting for both of them and be happy with whomever wins the big series? Which team would you cheer for now that you know Kiley and Cervantes, what their fears are, what their likes are, what they want? Having the reader face an interrogation and declaring their allegiances was the fun part of the story to write, leading the reader to side with either or both of the main characters and to discover why they wanted their hero to win.

In a sense, "Baseball in December" is not a tale of one hero, but a tale of two heroes with two distinct narratives, a dual point-of-view story. Both of the two leading players experience their wins and losses, and if they were playing for any team, the actuality was that they were both on the Iowa Cubs team throughout the whole story. Of that, there was no doubt, and the irony—that with professional baseball pulling them in every direction, they still were both, without interruption, Iowa Cubs, even if they both get to the World Series; and along on the ride of this Iowa Cubs story were their other best friends in the roster beyond: Olen and Buster.

The original manuscript had Ronan Kiley's father as a major character. I realized after my first draft that Kiley's father was a residual character that was distracting and that it was essentially Cervantes who takes on the father figure role after the life or death incident in Iowa. The lines of dialogue that I had written for Ronan's father I altered and gave to Tim Cervantes to say.

There was another character that I removed from the original narrative, that of Cervantes's cousin, Ambrose, during his first flight to Boston right after he learns that he gets traded. Ambrose, in the first draft, was looking over Tim's shoulder on the flight and admiring Cervantes's sketch while trying to console his spirits about being sent away from Chicago. I found the scene far more effective when I wrote out the character of Ambrose and had Tim flying alone.

As the story progressed, characters were shaved off since I wanted to increase the suspense of the eventual showdown between Tim and Ronan. Live sports are the last real bastion where we can see actual, live emotion, and the best fictional sports stories are emotional stories. These characters were removed to sharpen the focus on the hard working, ambitious Ronan Kiley and the logical, dutiful Timothy Cervantes. Along the voyage, the two main characters learned volumes about themselves and what is important—people. People who weren't as lucky as they were and dreams realized through Pyrrhic victory—a victory that is so detrimental and emotionally costly that it doesn't seem like a victory. Yet, a win is a win, and wins are eternal.

I've always wanted to write about a non-mundane World Series; for example, a World Series where a brother faces his own brother but with far more at stake—how about one person who saved another person from death's door? What would that pitcher go through if having to face that kind of situation? There were layers of depth to this story because I wanted it to say something and I wanted to depict a deeper stratum of professional baseball that is behind the scenes—the concept that baseball players, no matter how much we idolize them as demigods, are human beings after all.

Being from Chicago, I am a Cubs fan. I am also a fan of Boston and New England. My American League team is fanatically the Boston Red Sox. Having visited both Wrigley Field and Fenway Park, I can vouch for the rip-roaring times to be had in each. What fascinates most people about both teams were their dry spells—the decades that went by without a World Series title. Sure, they came close, but never that World Series win, that Golden Fleece, leading both teams to be decidedly "cursed" with people wondering if their team would ever win the big series during their lifetimes. These former "curses" on both teams are what make both the Boston Red Sox and the Chicago Cubs so popular and celebrated. They're both among the most popular major league baseball clubs of the thirty teams in the majors. In the 21st century, both teams broke their curses in our world. In the fiction of this story, the World Series also can never end in a tie, but then I required the story to conclude with both chief characters attaining something for themselves and for their teams.

The astute reader may have been amused by the pulling of lots from the hat of Ty Cobb in Cooperstown to determine Teams A, B, C, D, and E, since "Ty" sounds exactly the same as "Tie." I did search the Baseball Hall of Fame database collection online and there is a uniform cap for Lou Gehrig in their holdings, but no Ty Cobb uniform cap, so the Ty Cobb uniform cap in the Baseball Hall of Fame is entirely fictional.

In preparation for this story, I consciously avoided looking at Bernard Malamud and W.P. Kinsella's works or watching *The Natural* and other well-known baseball movies because I didn't want what already has been done before to seep into my original story. What I did was read a book called *Baseball's Best Short Stories* and that influenced me about how to write action in a baseball story and conveyed to me what made these stories "the best." I always study from the best and form the foundation from there. Without doubt not an influence on this story but worth citing (or maybe it is an influence because of its surrealistic quality?) was *The Twilight Zone* episode "The Mighty Casey," which has surprises in it and, as mentioned earlier, like all memorable sports stories, has a hold on the emotions. Come to think of it, there is a tinge of Rod Serling in "Baseball in December," but I took the Serlingesque and recast it with a distortion of Sophocles, a dream fantasy Sophocles fond of optimistic endings.

I do think there is one unanswered question in the story, the part where Ronan wonders if he would be happy with winning the World Series. The answer to that is an obvious affirmative. Though with a bit of struggle, Rory would, in the end, be happy, as any baseball player would, with having that World Series ring. Every baseball player in the world wants that.

So there you have it—a "wild" postseason (you can say that again), friendships in peril, memories of sacrificed friends, and wintertime baseball. It's a portrait of two heroic characters who I hope the reader has come to be fans of (and want mint baseball cards of). It was the baseball story I was meant to write and I hope you enjoyed it immensely.

DEXTER FABI - Dexter Fabi is a visual artist and writer from the Chicago area. The many hats he has worn include teaching English as a second language in Japan, being a college teacher in California, maintaining an online store of rare and vintage books, and being an information technology administrator for a company in downtown Chicago. After receiving his Master of Science from DePaul University in computer technology, he worked in the industry for years until becoming an educator. Working in the mediums of digital and handmade art, he has exhibited his artwork in the Midwest and in Europe for the World Science Fiction Conventions in Kansas City and Helsinki. He has garnered awards for his art, including an award of First Place in The Waukegan Public Library's Ray Bradbury Creative Contest for Visual Art in June of 2015, held by the very same library that Bradbury himself visited and loved as a child growing up in Waukegan, Illinois. He continues creating for art shows every year. In the course of his writing, he is also the recipient of the literary award of Best Short Story for *The Royal Wedding of Oz* at the annual Winkie Convention presented by the International Wizard of Oz Club. Among his many hobbies are Egyptology, cinema, genealogy, languages, folklore, baseball cards, pulp fiction, listening to music, and reading, his eternal obsession. He lives in the suburbs of Chicago and is a full-time tutor. He can be found online and can be contacted via Etsy, www.etsy.com/shop/ FixedBeArt.

THE KICKER

Ron Fortier

Walter Reed Hospital 1968

Lucas Brown sat propped up in bed trying to read the latest issue of *Sport's Illustrated* without interruption. Unfortunately his left leg itched constantly which was a bitch as he had lost it back in Vietnam. Shrapnel from the mortar had ripped it apart beneath the knee and doctors in the emergency field hospital had amputated it in order to save his life.

Brown had been in a medically induced coma and by the time he'd come out of it, he was in an Army facility in Tokyo with one less leg than he'd come into the world with. The initial realization had been hard to accept. As he'd looked down at the stump where his left leg ended, all the hopes and dreams of his future evaporated like a wispy fog cloud in a cold wind.

There would be no college football for young Lucas Brown. No razzle dazzle record breaking stats for the NFL scouts to be awed by. No big recruiting contracts to sign. No Hall of Fame pro career awaiting his return to civilian life. No sirree, it was all gone. Just like his leg. Left behind in some stinking jungle where what was left of it had most likely become bug food that would end up fertilizing the ground beneath it.

He was only in Japan for a few weeks, then it was on a plane back to the World, or as it was better known, the USA, and Walter Reed Hospital in Washington, D.C.

And now he was having what the doctors had told him was known as a Phantom Itch. Somehow his brain refused to accept that there was nothing below the right knee and would create these faux feelings as if there was something real to scratch. Which made it all the more unbearable. How do you scratch what isn't there?

He tried to go back to the article about the Green Bay Packers only to have the itch persist. In frustration, he tossed the magazine onto the small lamp table to the right of bed.

"Aw...fu—" A nurse walked by with a young woman and two small children and Brown shut his mouth hard swallowing his curse. Along with dealing with his missing limb, he was also learning how to curb his language since returning to the World. Whereas the F-word had been a constant spice to his dialog while in Nam, it was no longer an acceptable utterance in his new, civilized surroundings.

Instead, he grabbed the bed sheet that covered him from the waist down and jerked back the fold to reveal the bandaged stump.

There! He told himself. *See! There's nothing there. There is NO ITCH!!* He swallowed hard, closed his eyes, put his head back and forced himself to breathe easy. Within minutes he'd calmed himself and the itch had abated. *Thank you, God.*

It was almost noon and Brown decided instead of getting served in bed, he'd use his crutches and go down to the cafeteria on the first floor for some lunch. As he turned his body around, he thought of how his physical therapist, Paul Rainer would be happy with him. The rehabilitation specialist was forever urging Brown to move; to get out of bed and stay active. Brown understood Rainer's attitude and for the most part agreed with it. There was no way he was going to let his handicap stop him from moving forward with his life.

Granted he would have to alter his goals, but Lucas Brown had been raised with a can-do philosophy. His parents had told him from the time he could actually get off the rug and walk on his own that no goal was beyond hard work and determination. As he stood up on his right leg and slipped on a blue cotton robe, he couldn't help but wonder where this new road would take him.

Next he grabbed his sturdy crutches, adjusted them under his arms and then with practiced motions propelled himself forward. He'd been using the crutches for almost three months and each new time he felt more confident in his ability to get around with them. It had been an awkward gait to master and the first few times he'd attempted to do so, his balance had deserted him completely. He fell to the floor, embarrassed and angry. For an athlete, it was the ultimate betrayal. His sense of self had been attuned to a lithe body able to twist, turn and run. All of that was gone. Now he was a one-legged freak and if he wanted to get somewhere, he would have learn to walk all over again.

Thanks to Rainer, and the dedicated nursing staff, he did just that. No one had laughed at him that first time. They had only helped get him back up, stepped out of the way and encouraged him to try again. The look in their anxious faces only reflected genuine faith and support. Brown vowed he wouldn't let them down. Or himself.

So here he was ambling down the center of the ward, his right leg stepping down first and then his crutches taking the lead in a steady rhythm that would reinforce the strength in his arms while his single leg established a strong balance that would carry him along without doubt or hesitation.

He exited the sleeping ward into the spacious Day Room lounge where other patients were either playing board games, watching TV or visiting with relatives. Beyond this room were the elevators. The lounge was brightly lit with sunshine streaming through giant windows facing the east. He recognized several of his new friends playing chess at one of the tables and they acknowledged his passing with friendly nods. One of them, a short, burly Marine Sergeant who had lost his left hand, had become a confidant. His name was Wally Walker and he hailed from Yuma, Arizona.

Brown halted to let several civilians walk past him. A young woman was pushing a double-amputee in a wheelchair, with several little boys following behind them. The wife looked up at Brown and gave him a fragile smile and he nodded. As they went off he turned back to the nearest elevator just as its doors opened.

Then he froze. Emerging from the lift were his parents, Leonard and Lola Brown, and behind them his teenage sister, Audrey.

When his folks saw him, they stopped as if someone had pulled them back. This was the first time they had seen their son since he'd returned to the states. Travel from New Mexico wasn't cheap and though they would have come sooner, Brown's own doctors had advised them to wait until he was both physically and emotionally ready. They had complied, though he knew that directive had not set well with his mother.

Now they were just standing there looking at him and the moment he'd dreaded was unfolding. He saw how faces registered the sight of him and his missing limb. It was as if despite knowing he'd lost the leg, the Browns' acceptance of the reality was just now becoming a cruel and harsh truth. He could see the pain in their eyes and it hurt him deeply.

Tears gushed out of Mrs. Brown's eyes and she closed the gap between them in a single heartbeat, wrapping her arms around her son and crying.

"Oh my baby, my poor baby boy."

Twenty minutes later Brown and his family were seated at a round table in the hospital's large, open cafeteria where the food was excellent. Lucas was doing his best to eat a plate of fried chicken and mashed potatoes, while answering his parent's barrage of questions while their own meals were obviously getting cold.

Audrey, God bless her, was enjoying her bowl of gooey mac-and-cheese too much to utter a word. Instead she'd only nod, take a sip of her soda and then go back to eating.

Brown loved all three of them dearly and did his best to placate their concerns.

"Are you sure they are treating you properly," his mother asked for the tenth time since they'd ridden down the elevator. She was a tall, lithe woman with black hair she kept at shoulder length. He could see tiny traces of gray strands starting to reveal themselves. Like Lucas, her skin was a light cocoa hue whereas his father, Leonard Brown, had inherited dark coloring that testified to his Jamaican roots.

"Yes, Ma, they are treating me well." He managed to swallow a piece of chicken, and wiped his greasy fingers with a napkin. "They treat everyone here fine. Really. They have some of the best doctors and nurses in the whole country working here."

"That's good to know," Leo Brown nodded. "That Doctor Altman who's been calling us on the phone sure sounds like a nice fellow. We're anxious to meet up with him."

"He should be making his afternoon rounds in about another hour," Brown glanced at his wristwatch. "And you're right, Pa. He's an okay hombre. I'm sure you and Ma will both like him."

He picked up another piece of the crispy chicken and had it almost to his mouth when his father said what he'd been afraid to hear.

"Well, I guess this pretty much puts an end to your football career."

"Leo!" Mrs. Brown turned to her husband angrily. "Not now!"

"Its okay, Ma," Brown came to his father's defense. "Pa's only stating the truth. I've had lots of time to think these past few weeks and mostly just about that. Not gonna be any athletic scholarship in my future. I've resigned myself to that fact. I'll just have to change my plans is all."

"Well, you still got the G.I. Bill," Audrey joined in at last, wiping her full lips from spots of cheese sauce. She was a beautiful girl with a small round nose and piercing brown eyes. Her soft curly hair wrapped around her face like an animated bonnet.

"That I do," Brown smiled at his baby sister. At sixteen, she was becoming a very smart young woman. He could imagine his father's determination in keeping the boys at Cumberland High in Santa Fe at a safe distance. Leo Brown didn't keep his bird hunting shotgun by the front porch door just for the sake of convenience.

"The question is, what am I going to use it for? At this point, I really don't know exactly what I want to do next. Sure college is okay, but unless I've got a real goal, I'd just be wasting my time. And the government's money."

"Seems to me you always liked English," Lola Brown recalled. "You always got high marks in all your English classes and Mrs. Cody said your essays showed genuine writing talent."

"You think I should be a writer?" Brown grinned. That was a surprise.

"Well, why not? Your letters home were always easy to read, Lucas."

"She's right," his father nodded. "You got a way with words, boy. Reading them letters made me feel like I was right there with you."

"Well, I'm flattered you'd say that, but honestly, I don't think I could ever do that for a living. I mean, writing you about Nam and what I was doing was personal and real. I don't know if I could just make something up like them big time writers do."

"Maybe you could write poems or essays like Langston Hughes," Audrey added as she licked her spook clean. Her bowl now empty.

Lucas Brown held a hand up. "Okay, can we just talk about this later? My chicken's getting cold and I know yours must be too. After we eat, we'll go back up to the ward and I'll introduce you all to some of the guys.

"How's that sound?"

His mother smiled radiantly and reached out to touch his hand. "It sounds wonderful, Lucas. And you're right. Let's eat."

She turned around to look at Audrey who merely shrugged. "I'm all done. Can I go see what they got for dessert?"

Father Mike Moore came out of the elevator and walked out into the hospital's main lobby. Even though it was almost midnight, there were still a few people working behind the main desk and he spotted two of the janitorial staff moving down the hall in the opposite direction. The hospital had so many staff offices besides the patient facilities; it took a huge maintenance crew to keep everything working smoothly.

A Catholic priest for twelve years, Father Moore visited Walter Reed at least four times a week either to say Mass in the hospital's chapel or to meet with the patients in need of counseling and spiritual support. He'd been assigned this duty five years earlier and he found it personally rewarding as he never failed to marvel at the strength and fortitude of the young men and women he administered to.

Though tired after a long day, Fr. Moore never left the hospital without looking at the first floor chapel. When he arrived there, he glanced past the half-open door and saw was a young black man seated in the front pew with his head bowed. The non-denominational room was beautifully decorated to either side by paintings depicting spectacular landscapes from around the globe, while to the front, a small stone altar was set and behind it three tall stained-glass panels. The light from above was diffused to allow for a gentle, quiet atmosphere.

The room served both the patients and often times their relatives. It was a haven where a few moments of peace might be found amidst much pain and suffering.

Father Moore had always been impressed with just how effective the little room could be for troubled souls.

And now, apparently, here was another. He entered the room and walked up the carpeted aisle. "Hello," he said softly not wanting to startle the man.

Lucas Brown raised his head and looked at the priest. "Oh, hello. Ah.. am I okay to be here?"

"But of course you are," Fr. Moore assured him. "It's not my intention to interrupt your private time, young man."

"Oh, it's okay, padre. I'm not much for praying anyway. I was just trying to see if the Big Guy would have some answers for me."

"The Big Guy?"

Brown pointed to the ceiling. "You know, Him."

"Ah, yes," Fr. Moore smiled then pointed to the pew. "Would you mind if I joined you?"

"Sure, I'd like the company."

The priest sat and extended his hand. "I'm Father Moore, one of the chaplains here."

Brown took the offered hand and shook it. "Corporal Lucas Brown, padre. I've seen you around. I'm a Baptist myself."

They were both silent for a few minutes. Fr. Moore couldn't help notice

Brown's missing limb and the set of crutches set against the bench to Brown's left side.

"Are you all right, Lucas? If you don't mind my asking?"

"Naw. Guess it's part of your job, ain't it?"

"Exactly. Catholic or Baptist, we men of the cloth all work for G...ah, the Big Guy."

Brown gave Moore a weak smile. "I guess you do."

"I sense something is troubling you, Lucas. Would you like to talk about it? Please, I'm not trying to force anything here. If you want to be alone, I'll just go."

"It's okay. Really. I guess I'm just not as tough as I thought I was."

"Tough, how?"

"Well, you know, losing my leg back in Nam. When I got here, I had all kinds of feelings."

"I'm sure you did. You suffered a traumatic injury. That's only natural, my boy."

"Right. It's just that I worked it all out in my head, you see. I knew there was nothing I could do that would change anything. I'm a cripple now and will be from now on. Still, I didn't let it beat me."

Moore looked into Brown's clear brown eyes. This was an exceptionally brave soul.

"That's most admirable of you, Lucas. But the fact that you are here, alone, at this hour... Has something happened to make you question your resolve?"

"Yeah, I guess you could say that. You see, my folks showed up this afternoon. They flew in from Santa Fe. That's where I'm from."

Fr. Moore nodded. "I'm told it's a lovely city."

"It really is, padre."

"So this was the first time you saw them since you returned to the states?"

"Yes. I thought I could handle it okay and for the most part I did. But after they left tonight, I could see the pain in my Dad's eyes."

"I'm so sorry, Lucas. I'm sure it must be difficult for them as well."

"Yeah. See, that's what I hadn't given much thought to until they were here. It was as if I'd let them down."

"Lucas, that's not true. It's not your fault you were wounded. I'm sure they understand and love you despite the injury."

"I know that, padre. It's just that me and Dad always talked about me going to college and playing football."

"Ah...and now that's no longer possible."

"Padre, why did God do this to me. To us? I just don't understand it, no matter how I try."

"Lucas, I wish I had an answer for why bad things happen to good people like you. It is one of the great mysteries we men of faith wrestle with every day."

Fr. Moore sighed and reached out and grabbed Lucas' right shoulder. "Lucas, God didn't do this to you. The war, a cruel and senseless fact of our existence, is responsible in the end. It's we who create the evils in this world, not Him. God created you because He loves you, Lucas Brown, and as long as you live on this earth, He always will. You can take my word on that."

Brown's eyes suddenly began to fill with tears and then he was crying uncontrollably.

Father Mike Moore moved closer and wrapped his arms around the young man and hugged him. Brown buried his face in the priest's chest.

"I know...padre..." he said between sobs. "I know...it just hurts so much."

Fr. Moore wouldn't let him go until all his tears were shed.

In the following days, Lucas Brown felt as if a heavy weight had been lifted off his shoulders. It was obvious it was because of his meeting with the priest. Fr. Moore's words of comfort and encouragement had supported his own faith taught to him by his parents as a child. With those beliefs strengthened, he'd fully enjoyed the remainder of his family's visit over the next few days. When they finally had to go back to Sante Fe, their parting had been both sad and hopeful.

"Whatever you decide to do, Lucas, you know me and your Ma will support it one hundred percent," Leo Brown told his son at the same time shaking his hand man to man.

"Thanks Pa, that means a lot to me."

His mother and sister had followed with hugs and kisses on the cheek and then they were off heading for the airport and the flight home. Brown felt a tinge of loneliness after they had left but soon he was back in the exercise room and once again working the routine Paul Rainer had created for him.

The tall, muscular trainer was already there when Brown arrived and was happy to see him.

"Yo, Lucas. Ready time to do a little stretching and lifting?" Rainer wore sneakers, black sweat pants and an Army green tee-shirt. He'd been a Ranger before returning to civilian life and his new occupation. From the first meeting, Brown had recognized the freckled faced Rainer as a kindred spirit.

Never one to shirk physical training, Brown actually liked putting his body through its paces from push-ups to sit-ups; it felt good building up an honest sweat. Sure he couldn't run anymore but that didn't mean he couldn't be strong and that's where the weight training came in.

After fifty push-ups, a task that had once been easy but now a challenge due to his missing limb, Rainer had Brown take a five minute breather before tackling the barbells set against the wall. After a drink of water, Brown took a seat on a long wooden bench and Rainer handed one of the five pound weights.

"Okay, kid, start with some arm curls. Then if you're up to it, we'll move on to the big stuff."

Brown took the small barbell in his right fist and then began lowering and raising it in an easy, relaxed motion while counting off. After he'd done twenty, he switched the weight to his left hand.

He was almost done when Rainer tapped him on the shoulder and pointed to the main door. "Looks like you got company, kid." Brown saw his doctor, John Altman and another fellow entering. They spotted Brown and Rainer and started across the room towards them.

"Hi, Doc." Brown set the black painted hand weight down on the floor. He grabbed the white towel draped around his neck to wipe the sweat from his face. Then he pushed himself up on his one leg careful to keep his balance. *Yeah,* he thought, *I'm learning all kinds of new tricks.*

"Lucas, Paul," Altman greeted smiling at the pair. "Glad to see you here."

Altman was an affable man in his early fifties, with graying hair and round cheeks custom made for his ever present smile. Dressed in his usual white jacket and holding his clipboard in his free hand, he always exuded a professional care and sympathy Brown had taken to immediately upon their first meeting. Doc Altman had served as an Army Medic in Korea and upon his discharge from the service, gone right into medical school.

He didn't waste anytime introducing the man beside him. "I'd like you both to meet Dan Wilcox. He's a medical engineer."

Wilcox was short with a pudgy middle. He wore loafers, gray slacks and short sleeve white shirt with a pen holder in his breast pocket. His corn yellow hair was long and he had granny glasses barely dangling at the tip of his small round nose. The word nerd came to Brown's mind immediately.

"Hello," Wilcox grinned foolishly extending his hand. "Nice to meet you, sir."

Brown could sense his awkwardness and tried to put him at ease as they shook hands. "Sir won't be necessary, Mr.Wilcox, I'm just a plain old infantry grunt. And call me Lucas. Okay?"

"Ah, sure, Lucas. Thanks."

There was a gap of silence, then Dr. Altman continued. "Lucas, Dan is here to talk to you about fitting you for a prosthetic."

"A what?"

"A prosthetic. It's an artificial leg…"

"I know what a prosthetic is, Doc," Brown held up a hand. "I just never gave it any thought is all."

"Well, you should as you're a viable candidate for one," Altman explained. "A prosthetic would help you regain your mobility and you wouldn't need those crutches any longer."

The silence returned as Lucas Brown looked from the doctor to the small, grinning fellow.

"So, I guess that's what 'medical engineer' refers to?" he nodded at Wilcox. "It's what you do."

"Exactly, sir...ah...Lucas. The science of artificial limbs is expanding all the time and great progress has been made in recent years to make our new prosthetics both strong and lightweight."

The guy sounded like he was a car salesman. Brown looked at him intently doing his best to keep his own reluctance at bay.

"Can they help me run again, Mr.Wilcox? Can an artificial leg do that?"

The nerd never blinked once but his smile evaporated into a look that matched Browns. "Actually, yes, they can."

Over the next two weeks, Brown and Dan Wilcox saw a lot of each other. Bit by bit Brown came to appreciate the small man's unabashed enthusiasm for his work in fitting amputees with prosthetics whether arms or legs. Every time Wilcox started in on the wonderful progress made by modern manufacturers and the amazing alloys used in building these devices, his face would light up like a child lost in a toy store.

Which, when he reflected upon it, Brown saw Wilcox's passion was just that; only for more adult and serious toys. On their first meeting, he'd spent an hour telling Brown about the use of carbon-fiber-reinforced-polymer and how each prosthetic was individually molded to the wearer. The fiber in the limb had the capabilities to store kinetic energy built up from each step taken and then, like a spring, allow the wearer to run or jump...almost exactly like a real leg.

At times, it all seemed too good to be true and Brown could only nod his head as Wilcox rambled on. Eventually the young engineer arrived one day with a camera and measuring tape and began cataloging data examining and then measuring Brown's stump.

"This is where it starts," he said as he carefully measured the length of Brown's right leg from kneecap to the sole. Then he wrapped the tape around the left stump and jotted down its thickness. "We want the attaching socket to match perfectly. Later this afternoon we'll make a plaster cast of your stump rising to mid-thigh. From that will mold the plastic leg socket so that when you put it on for the first time, it'll fit perfectly. We want it to feel like it's a true extension of your body."

Brown just looked at him and shook his head. "No offense, Dan, but I'll believe it when I see it."

"Oh, ye of little faith," Wilcox chuckled. "What do your folks think about you getting a new leg? Or have you even told them yet?"

"Oh, I told them. Mama was a bit surprised but seemed to accept the idea."

"And your Dad?"

"Ah, well, that's pretty much old school, if you get my meaning."

Wilcox finished writing numbers in his small black notebook then slipped it into his back pocket. "What? He thinks we're going to give you some kind of wooden pirate peg leg?" He rolled up the measuring tape and that went in right pants pocket.

"Uh, huh. He didn't so say in those words, but that's what it sounded like."

Wilcox picked up his expensive camera off of Brown's bed and aiming down at the left leg, began to adjust the lens focus. "Well, he's going to be in for one hell of surprise when he sees it."

"Yeah, well so will I," Brown said leaning back against the stacked

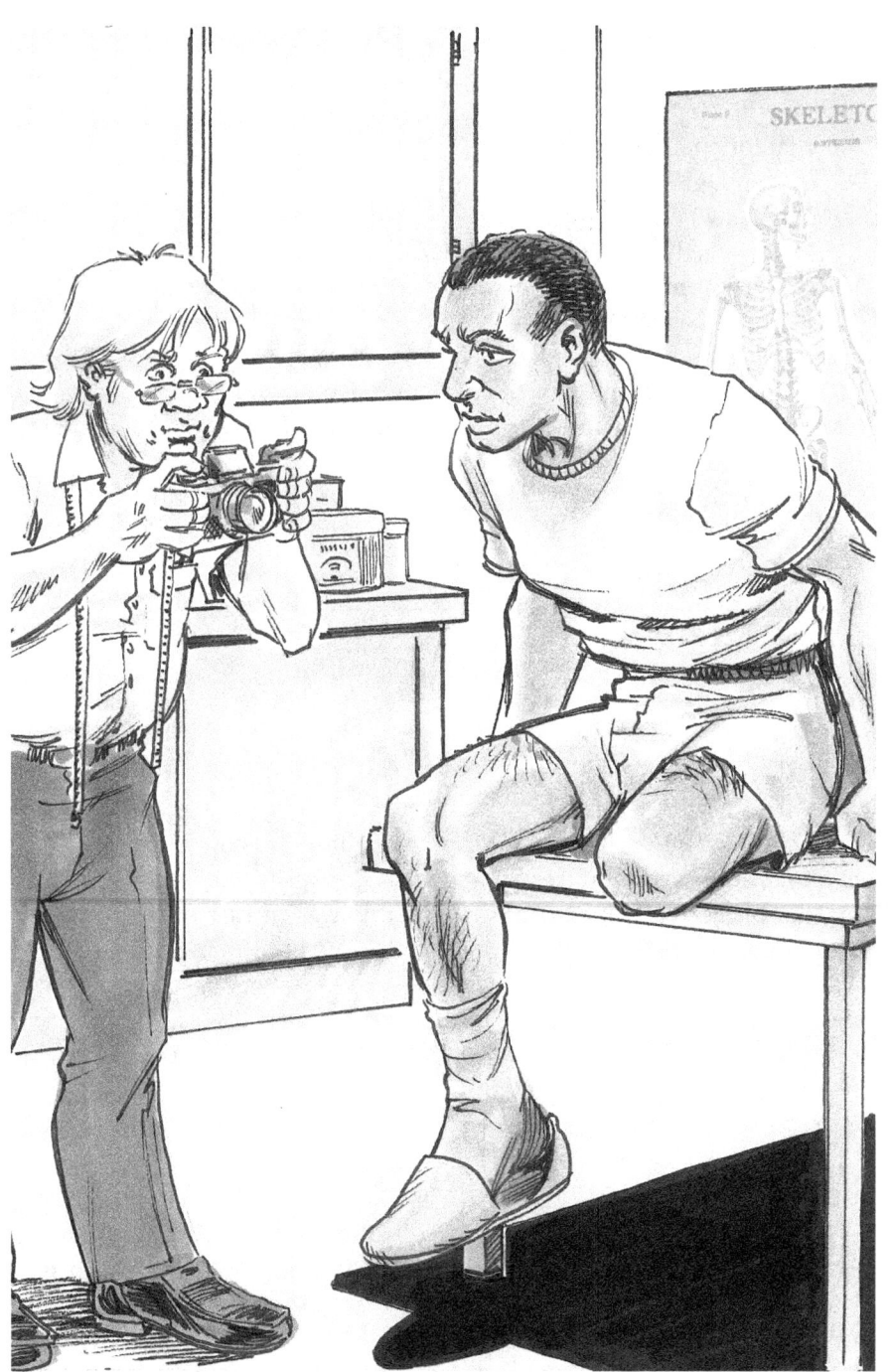

"...when you put it on for the first time, it'll fit perfectly."

pillows while watching Wilcox snap his pictures. "You almost done?"

"I am," the engineer capped his lens and smiled. "Want to take a hike down to the cafeteria for a coffee. The nurses won't be here with the casting material for another two hours."

"You buying?"

"Don't I always?"

"Well, you're the rich engineer wizard."

"Ha, very funny. Let's get you out of the ward for a little while."

"All right….as long as we can talk about something else other than robotic legs."

Wilcox started laughing while Brown rolled down his pajama leg and closed it with a safety pin. Then he twisted around and dropped his right leg to the floor and grabbed his crutches.

"No promises," Wilcox warned as they started down the corridor. "I'm a man who loves his work."

"Yeah, well you keep doing that and I'm gonna whack you across that big old brain of yours with one of these crutches. Don't think I won't."

"Okay, okay. I've been warned."

The following weeks flew by for patient Lucas Brown. As Dan Wilcox had told him, several nurses and physical therapists worked together to make a plaster cast of Brown's stump. This was in turn used to shape the durable socket joint that would attach to it. As soon as that socket was completed, a pretty young nurse named Wendy Songer, taught him the proper way to clean it daily and for the very first time gave him gray colored stump socks. These also had to be washed daily. The plastic socket reminded Brown of a giant egg with the top cut off. Around this half was affixed a small leather belt that he would use to wrap around his upper thigh after he'd slipped his stump into the socket.

Naturally all this practice only made him more anxious to finally see the entire prosthetic. During one session with Nurse Songer, Wilcox had appeared with a little booklet with color photos of the various artificial legs Brown could choose from. Half were shaped to appear like a real limb while the others looked like tall erector sets with all the segments exposed. It began from the socket to a hip joint, then a pylon and rotator just above the knee joint down to the final polymer pylon that rested firmly in the molded foot.

"You're kidding, right?" He asked his new friend. "People actually go with this naked scarecrow leg?"

"Honestly, Lucas, it's a whole lot more practical and durable. The imitation leg is twice as cumbersome and fragile. Whereas the primary model is strong and reliable. Even if you…"

Wilcox stopped in midsentence and dropped his eyes.

"What? You were going to say if I fall."

"Yes." Wilcox met Brown's gaze. "Look, the normal time for most amputees to adjust to a prosthetic limb is between two and six months. And there's a learning curve. You'll have to learn a whole new sense of balance."

"I get that."

"Do you?" Wilcox pressed on. "Lucas, when you step on a rock with your leg, nerve endings feel that. They immediately send a signal to your brain and your body instantly adjust its balance so you don't slip or fall. That's not going to happen now. Although strong and dependable, your prosthetic won't be sending you any messages at all."

"So how the hell am I suppose to walk on it. Let alone run?" Brown was getting riled and Nurse Songer was clearly uncomfortable. Wilcox motioned her to leave and she did so hastily.

Realizing what he'd done, Brown apologized. "I'm sorry, Dan."

"No need, really. I've been doing this for a few years now and though I can't possibly comprehend what you and other amputees feel, I can share with you my experiences in the hopes they will help you to use the prosthetic properly and effectively."

For a second neither said a word. Finally Brown cocked his head. "Okay, so tell me. If I can't feel the damn thing, how do I compensate?"

"With your other senses and your entire body." Wilcox moved away from the bed and pointed to the floor. "You are going to learn to walk not just with your legs, but with your eyes, Lucas. To take in the ground before you and when you put down your new leg, be aware of it carrying your weight and how you'll need to shift your hips and establish a solid rhythm." Then Wilcox stepped forward with his left leg firmly. "It's all about a straight, confident posture and trust in that the leg we're making for you will do its job.

"If you can do that, then pretty soon you'll be out of here and back to your own life. Maybe not exactly like you left it, but pretty damn close."

The conviction in Wilcox's voice was legitimate and Brown smiled.

"Well, all right then. What are you doing wasting time around here? Go make me my new leg?"

Wilcox pointed to the catalog. Brown picked it up off his bed and handed it to him.

"Okay, you convinced me. Give me the scarecrow stick. If it don't work, I can always use it to kick your ass."

It was a warm August day three months later when United Flight 2280 touched down in Sante Fe shortly after two in the afternoon. The temperature was kissing 90 degrees as Cpl. Lucas Brown, dressed in his class A dress uniform stepped out of the passage tunnel and into the small air-conditioned terminal gate area. Walking stiffly, he moved along with the other passengers who had been on the flight from Baltimore. With each passing day, he was adjusting to the feel, or lack of such, with his new metal left leg.

"Lucas! Over here!" It was Audrey, waving at the end of the plastic seats to get his attention. Her smile was as big as the moon. She had on frayed denim shorts, a dark blue cotton short-sleeve shirt and white sneakers with ankle high socks.

He moved towards her only to realize she was rushing at him full tilt, arms wide open. Brown braced himself and caught her in his arms barely able to keep his balance and not fall over.

"Whoa there, little sister!" he laughed. "Hey, have you gotten taller since the last time I saw you?"

She looked up him and smiled. "Shut up and hug me."

He was happy to comply. She buried her head against his chest and for a second he was worried she might start crying.

"I've missed you so much, big brother."

"And I you, little sister. You don't know how good it feels to be back home." Saying the words, he realized it was almost three years since he'd left New Mexico, never mind his hometown of Cumberland.

She broke their embrace still excited. "You ain't home yet. Come on, I've got the car parked in the nearest lot."

"So how come it's you picking me up, anyways? I was expecting Ma and Pa."

"Er...I can't tell you that. It's a surprise."

"What? Hey, don't tell me they've got some kind of shindig going on?"

"Lucas, please, just don't ask. Okay? They really wanted it to be a nice surprise for you."

"Okay," he gave in. "Now where's baggage claim? I've got to get my duffel bag."

"This way. It's on the first floor."

They stepped behind others waiting at the top of the escalator and Audrey paused to look down at his lower half. With his green pants, she could barely see his foot in the black oxford shoe. He caught her looking and beat her to the punch.

"It works just fine, kid."

"Really. You can't even tell. I mean, you walk like...ah..."

"Like I always did."

"Right. Was it hard getting used to it?"

It was their turn and she stepped down first. He followed her carefully, stepping off on his right foot. A new habit he could never forget.

"It was awkward those first few months," he confessed. "But the folks at the hospital wouldn't quit on me. Every day New Peg and I got use to each other more and more."

"New Peg?" She looked back up at him as the escalator lowered them. "You named your artificial leg New Peg?"

"Well I wasn't going to call him Old Peg, was I?" He did his best to keep a straight demeanor, but in the end burst out laughing.

"Aw, you big lug. You ain't changed a bit."

"Well, thank you. I'll take that as a compliment."

Brother and sister quickly discovered that baggage carousel number three was the one about to unload the cargo from his flight. Brown positioned himself between other former passengers as the giant wheel came to life and began to spit out various colored luggage. Within minutes he spotted his khaki green duffel bag with his last name stenciled across it. As it rolled past, he grabbed it with his right hand and hoisted it up over his shoulder. Then, carefully watching his step, he moved around and rejoined Audrey.

"All right, all set. Let's go."

"This way." She pointed to the glass doors and they were off. As they came out onto the sidewalk, he could see the airport was as hectic as ever with private cars, taxis and buses all vying for a spot along the curb. The heat was brutal and the sun blinding. He'd have to pick up some decent sunglasses once he was settled in back home.

Audrey turned to the right and he followed her lead. As they came to a cross-walk that led to a giant parking structure, he heard people yelling. Across the street, moving back and forth in some pre-arranged pattern, twenty or so young people with long hair and leather vests marched carrying homemade signs. One girl, with long yellow hair and goofy cartoon glasses held a bullhorn and was screaming into it.

"HELL NO, WE WON'T GO!" she wailed at the people coming and going out of the main entrance. "VIETNAM IS THE RICH MAN'S WAR!"

"What the hell is this?" Brown nodded to the group of hippies.

"It's a protest against the war," Audrey told him. "They're happening all over the country."

Cpl. Lucas Brown, now a civilian, shook his head.

"Come on, Lucas, the car's in here."

He started to walk again only to have an acne faced young man holding a placard call out to him. "Hey, G.I. Joe, how many Vietnamese babies did you kill over there?"

The girl with the bullhorn saw him and joined her companion. "HELL YES, ANOTHER BABY KILLER…WITH BLOOD ON HIS HANDS."

Brown couldn't believe what he was hearing. He dropped his duffel bag to the cement and balled his hands into fist.

Seeing this, Audrey grabbed his right arm. "No, Lucas! Please, let it go! They're not worth it."

"I ain't no baby killer. They got no right to call me that!"

"I know. But they're too stupid to know any better. Please, for me, Lucas. Let's just go."

The protester kept jeering him, but Audrey's words were the only ones that mattered. If he did anything, he'd only embarrass himself and his family.

"You're right," he sighed, picking up his duffel bag again. "They ain't worth it. C'mon, let's get out of here."

They reached the automatic doors and were soon in the cool darkness of the parking garage, the chanting dwindled the further they moved away from it. Still, as he followed his sister, Lucas Brown couldn't help but think, *What the hell is wrong with those people?*

By the time Audrey Brown drove their father's 65 silver Toyota Roadrunner into the driveway at the end of the White Birch Street cul-de-sac, the ex-soldier had calmed down. It was an hour long drive to the midsize town of Cumberland, New Mexico. Even though it was late afternoon and twilight was still a ways off, he couldn't help but react to the dozen or so cars parked on the street framing their house. Some of them he recognized as belonging to family while others he'd never seen before.

"What the hell?" he mouthed as his sister stopped the car and shut off the engine. The twin garage doors were open and he could see his mother's Suburu sedan in the left bay while the one to the right was empty.

"I told you they wanted to surprise you. They're all out in the backyard. Dad fired up the grill and Mom made the decorations."

"Decorations?"

Audrey climbed out of the car, tossing the keys in the air. "You didn't think she was going to let you off that easy did you?"

Brown retrieved his duffel bag from the back seat and asked the loaded question. "Just how many people are back there?"

"Oh, about fifty or sixty. Granny Brown is there, along with most of our relatives and half the neighborhood."

"Shit." He looked at his smirking sister. "What's so funny?"

"You. You survive a year in a jungle war and are afraid to confront a bunch of people who's only crime is that they all love you and are happy you are home."

Brown wanted to argue, but he couldn't. She was right and even though it was not the quiet homecoming he'd wanted, there was no way he could disappoint his parents. "All right, let's get it over with."

Audrey ran over, took his left arm in hand and together they marched around the side of the garage to the waiting gathering.

The first thing Brown saw when they turned the corner was the giant banner stretched up over two poles behind the picnic table that read WELCOME HOME LUCAS. And then somebody shouted, "Look, they're here." And just like that, he was swept up in a sea of happy faces, all of them familiar from his mother to his best high school pal, Steve Kantor. Arms hugged him, hands slapped his back and matronly lips touched his cheeks.

The soldier had come home.

After managing to shake hands and say hello to most of the assembled folks, Brown excused himself saying he needed to get out of his jacket and tie and put his sack away. His parents agreed and let him slip into the backdoor to the kitchen. From there he went through the main hall and up the stairs to his room on the left side of the second floor. Carefully climbing each step, he immediately thought of Nurse Songer cautioning him to take things slow. He smiled at the memory. Next to his room was Audrey's with a full bath in between. The right side of the floor was occupied by his parent's master bedroom and bathroom.

The door to his room was open and his mother had left the two corner windows open as well to let in fresh air. Walking in, his writing desk was against the left wall under the big poster of his hero, Jim Brown, in action on the football field. Dead center of the polished wood top was his Remington electric typewriter, and behind that several paperback reference titles ala a dictionary and thesaurus plus a thick world atlas. How many school assignments had he banged away on that machine? Too many to count. To the right of the desk was a bureau on which was his old portable radio.

To his immediate right was a small closet and directly opposite the desk and chair was his bed. The window between the bed and bureau looked out onto the street outside, while the window over the bed gave him a view of the backyard and the woods beyond it.

The room was exactly as he had left it three and a half years earlier. Brown sat on the bed, and took off his cap. He took a breath and then said a prayer of thanks to the Almighty. He held his tears in check.

Fifteen minutes later, his jacket and black tie removed and hanging in his closet, Lucas Brown rejoined the party rolling up his sleeves as he walked out the back door.

"Here, you look like you could use one of these," Steve Kantor handed him a cold can of beer. Brown could see his father's big cooler by the picnic table filled with ice and drinks. He popped the lid and took a long swallow.

"Man, it's so good to see you again," Kantor declared. Like Brown, he was a tall, rugged fellow with pale skin and long yellow hair testifying to his Germanic roots. He and Brown had both been on their high school football team together. After school, Kantor had been drafted by the University of Alabama and thus given a college deferment from the draft.

"How's school going?" he asked politely. "You made the first squad yet?"

"I'm working on it, brother. I'm still only a sophomore. They got me on the back-up bench but I'm not planning on staying there forever."

"I hear yah."

"Hey, speaking of football, your Dad told me earlier that Coach Halwell is going to stop by later." Halwell had been their coach at Cumberland High. "He heard you were coming home said he wanted to see you."

"That'd be great." Brown slapped Kantor on the arm. "But right now I could eat a horse. And I see Dad's got some hot dogs and burgers ready go. C'mon, let's grab some grub."

The picnic table was covered with bowls and plates overflowing with various homemade dishes. He recognized his grandmother's signature potato salad next to the bowl of sugar glazed carrots. Much of it had already been devoured by others and he wasted no time grabbing a paper plate and filling it up. Atop everything he'd spooned up, his father set a big, fat juicy hamburger smothered in melted cheese on a sesame seed bun.

"Bet they never fed you like that in the army," Leo Brown laughed, while waving his stainless steel spatula over the grill flames. He was wearing his favorite bib apron with a cartoon of the fairy tale three little pigs dancing on the front.

"No, Pa, I can't say they ever did. Thanks."

Thus the first day of his homecoming went smoothly, and Lucas Brown truly enjoyed the company that had made it a point to welcome him properly. After the incident at the airport, it was nice to know some people hadn't forgotten their patriotism. Once everyone had eaten, a few of his cousins suggested playing some horseshoes. There was a track his father had set at the back end of the yard and as soon as someone had retrieved the U shaped irons from the garage, the first game was under way. He and Kantor teamed up to take on all challengers.

When it came time for Brown to throw, he lined up his throw carefully eyeing the iron spike in the distance and then swung his horseshoe back to throw. He stepped off on his left leg and for a split second his body tensed. Then his arms completed the toss and the horseshoe flew swiftly towards its target. It smacked into the post and dropped away from it by six inches.

Kantor and the others cheered, while he took a long deep breath, grateful no one had seen his momentary wobble. He remembered Dan Wilcox's early advice back at Walter Reed about taking things slow and careful like. It was vital he remember the things he'd learned in his therapy. His artificial leg would serve him well only if he remained constantly aware of its actual limitation.

"Good shot, Brown," a familiar voice said from behind him.

He turned to see Charles "Chuck" Halwell approaching him, a warm, knowing smile on his black face. Halwell was of average height, with sharp facial features, that included a thick nose, square jaw and two gray eyes that could cut into a person like twin laser beams. His bald head wore his battered and beloved New York Mets baseball cap, an ever-present anchor to his having been born and raised in the Bronx.

"Coach," Brown took his mentor's hand and shook it firmly. "It's great to see you, sir."

"Cut the sir, crap, kid. You'll make me feel older than I really am."

"Yes, sir...ah, Coach. Whatever you say."

"That's better. So, how you enjoying civilian life?"

"Aside from six months in Walter Reed, I can't rightly say just yet, Coach. I'm still feeling like a fish out of water."

"Understood, military life will do that to you."

Brown recalled Halwell's stories of his days in the Marines. He'd heard enough of them when Coach was running them through their drills on the football field. He was a tough taskmaster who expected nothing less than one hundred percent from his players. It was a philosophy the Marines had taught him and he never failed to apply it to his coach methods.

"Look, you boys go on and finish your game here," he said looking at the others with Brown. "I'll go grab a brew." Then back to his former star running back. "Soon as you're done. Come find me. I'd like to talk to you one on one. If you're willing?"

"Sure, Coach. Whatever you say. Shouldn't take me 'n Steve more than a few minutes to whip these suckers." His cousins heard the jibe and starting hurling back their own insults.

Halwell chuckled and nodded. "Good, don't be too long. I gotta get home before my wife wonders where I've run off to this time." And with that he walked off in search of a beer and some friends to chat with.

Lucas Brown loved that man.

It was another thirty minutes before Brown could get away from his pals and go looking for the Coach. He found Halwell and his father, seated at the furthest end of the yard in folding lawn chairs under the shade of several Alligator Junipers. At first he wondered why they'd sequestered themselves until he saw the big fat Panatelas they were smoking. His mother abhorred smoking and would only allow his father to do so outdoors. She especially hated the heavy rich odor of his cigars.

Brown grabbed a chair and carried it over to join them.

"Want a smoke?" Leo Brown asked as his son dropped down on the red canvas lawn chair. He tapped his shirt pocket where the top lid of the cardboard package was visible.

"Ah, no thanks, Pa. Bad enough you'll be catching hell from Ma as is. I ain't about to have her come after me too."

Coach Halwell blew out a puff of thick white smoke and chuckled. "Some things women just don't understand. Ain't that right, Leo?"

"Agreed," the elder Brown replied. "Gotta have a few vices or life can get boring on yah."

"Well, it's been thrilling enough for me already," the young veteran declared. "I'm ready for some quiet in my life."

The Coach pointed his cigar at him. "Which brings up a good question. What are your plans for the future, Lucas? And do you even have any?"

"I don't rightly know," Brown answered honestly. "I mean getting used to not having to take orders and such is going to be strange for a while." He looked down and slapped his left knee. "Especially with this new piece of fancy leg of mine. I ain't got a clue what comes next."

"Well, have you given any thought to going to college?" Halwell knew it might be a touchy subject, but his concern for the young man was overriding being awkward. "I mean, for real, boy. To get an education and make something of yourself."

"Damn it, Coach. I just don't know. You know how bad I wanted to play college ball. With what happened and all, it would seem kind of weird now. Hell, I don't even know what I'd be good at."

For a second neither Halwell nor his father said a word. Brown hoped that was the end of the matter. He wasn't that lucky when he saw his mentor's eyes bore into him.

"Look, Lucas, would you be willing to take a ride with me to UNM next Friday?"

"You mean in Albuquerque?"

"Yes. The Dean of Admission there is an old friend of mine and I'd like

"Would you be willing to take a ride with me to UNM next Friday?"

for you to talk with her. If you're willing?"

Brown wanted to say no. He saw the expression on his father's face. Neither of these men would relent and he realized his best course of action was simply to acquiesce. After all, he wasn't committing to anything. Just a friendly drive with the Coach.

"Okay," he told them. "I'll go. But just so you both know, I'm not promising anything. Understood?"

"Understood," his father chuckled. "Now why don't you be a good and dutiful son and go get me and Chuck here another Bud."

Before going to bed that night, Lucas Brown went into the bathroom to fill a pan with warm water. While doing so, he noticed the new steel hand rail screwed up against the shower wall. Audrey told him his father had put it there the day after they had come home from their visit to see him at Walter Reed. It was similar to the railings used in that hospital to assist leg amputees when taking a shower. Leave it to his Pa to know that.

He was quiet going back to his room as his parents and Audrey were already asleep. It was close to 1 A.M. Over his shoulder was draped a terry cloth towel and face cloth.

He set the pan down next to his bed and then went and shut the door and flicked off the overhead light. Now the room was lit solely by the gooseneck lamp between his typewriter and radio. He had his radio on at its lowest setting as to not bother Audrey. At the moment Dionne Warwick was asking musically *Do you know the way to San Jose?* He stripped to his shorts, draping his clothes over the back of his chair. As he sat down on his bed, he thought about the music he'd listened to while in Nam. When he'd enlisted, the Beatles and the Supremes were the hottest groups in the country. Since his time at Walter Reed he'd become familiar with Marvin Gaye, Simon & Garfunkel and something called the Credence Clearwater Revival.

Brown unstrapped the socket from around his upper leg. His prosthetic was made up of four parts; the foot, the pylon, the all important rotator and then the socket. Balancing it on his left knee, he reached down and soaked the wash cloth. He squeezed out the excess water and then carefully washed out the interior of the socket in which his stump had rested all day exactly as he'd been taught. Keeping it clean would be a crucial part of his hygiene from now on.

That done, he set his leg up against his bureau and then gently shoved the pan up to his desk. He peeled off the gray colored socket sock and tossed it to the floor. Walter Reed had sent him home with a half-dozen of these. They had to be kept clean. For the next few years of his life, his stump had to be fully protected from all infections.

Balancing himself on his right leg, he stood, reached over and shut off the radio and the lamp. Then he took a hop backwards, dropped down to his bed in the gray gloom and pulled the covers over himself, while adjusting his position. He'd left the windows open and as he rested his head back on his pillow moonlight filtered into his room.

For a few minutes, the reality of where he was seemed hard to grasp even with all that had transpired. But then he realized something was missing from his life. Something he'd grown accustomed to while in that far off tropical land. The noises of war. The constant shelling barrages out on the perimeters of the camp, the never ending cacophony of bullfrogs and other night critters.

And there was no whirring sound of choppers overhead. Everything was silent.

Blessed, beautiful silence.

"So, I've looked over your high school transcripts, Lucas and your grades seem skewed towards the social rather than hard sciences," Mrs. Sierra Montez noted, looking down at the open folder on her desk. All the while she balanced a Winston filter cigarette between her lips and the fingers of her right hand.

"I was never good with math and science," Brown admitted, fidgeting slightly in his chair in front of her desk. Coach Chuck Halwell was seated on his left looking on.

"You seemed to have had a flair for history and English," Mrs. Montez noted looking up at him while pushing her large glasses back up her straight nose. She was an attractive woman in her late thirties with Hispanic features such as her dark complexion and jet black hair. Not one for frivolities, she dressed conservatively in a light green blouse and brown skirt with the only touch of make-up being pink colored lipstick which left a noticeable ring around the butt she was smoking. No earrings or other jewelry except for a silver wedding ring.

From where he was sitting, Lucas Brown guessed that the three framed photographs to the right, center and left of her neatly organized desk were of her family.

She was also the Dean of Admission for the University of New Mexico. The three of them were seated in her office in Hodgin Hall, the oldest building on the UNM Albuquerque campus.

"History has always fascinated me, Ma'am. And I love reading, so learning about all those different authors was fun for me."

"Good for you," she smiled taking one last drag. She blew out a puff of smoke and then mashed the remains of her cigarette into the glass ashtray beside her telephone. "Tell me Lucas, while in high school, did you give any thought to college at all? I mean before you were drafted."

Before answering, Brown glanced over at Halwell. "Well, I'm sure you've already noticed that I lettered in sports all four years."

"I did. Coach Halwell told me how good you were at football."

"Yes, Ma'am. It was my hope to maybe play college ball some day. Like my grades, I'd guess you can say I was an average player and so was never offered a scholarship anywhere."

He paused and lowered his head for a second. This was the part he would have to get used to; the fact that he was now disabled. "What with my condition now, that's not ever going to happen, I suppose."

"No, most likely not." Sierra Montez always prided herself on her talent to empathize with others. It sprang from her genuine concern and she found herself liking the young man seated before her a great deal. "Tell me, Lucas. Were you awarded anything else besides a Purple Heart for your service?"

"Excuse me, Ma'am?"

"Well, Chuck here told me something about your actions that led to your losing your leg. My father was in the Air Force for twenty-years, retired a Colonel. I'm no stranger to that world."

"They gave me a Silver Star, Ma'am. Though I really didn't do anything any other of my buddies wouldn't have done."

"I see. Lucas, I think you're an exceptional young man and I'd very much like you to consider being a student here."

"Ah, I don't know, Mrs. Montez. I mean, I do want to go to college and all, but I'm not even sure what it is I want to do with my life yet. How would I know what classes to take?"

"There's no need for you to rush into anything, Lucas," she explained. "Why don't you enroll for the coming semester and I'll assign you a course counselor. He or she will help you choose whatever prerequisite courses you need to take."

"Pre...what?"

"Those are just the general courses," Halwell clarified. "The stuff all the students have to take. You get those out of the way first and then later on, you can decide what it is you'd like to major in."

Brown folded his hands together over his lap and looked from Halwell to Mrs. Montez for a few seconds. This was nothing he had planned for himself while recovering at Walter Reed. Still, the Coach was going out of his way to help him and he knew it was an opportunity that might not come again.

"All right. I guess I'm in."

"Excellent," beamed Mrs. Montez. She reached into a desk drawer and removed several documents which she then passed over to Brown. "These are general admission forms. Simply fill them out and mail them back to me as soon as possible. You might also want to make copies if you are planning on taking advantage of the G.I. Bill to help pay for your tuition. They do require such and if you've any questions about that, feel free to contact me."

"Thank you," Brown rose out of the chair holding the papers. "For everything."

Mrs. Montez stood and came around the desk and offered her hand. "No, Lucas, thank you...and welcome to the Lobos."

As the walked out of Hodgin Hall and started for the parking lot where Coach Halwell had parked his Toyota pick-up truck, Lucas Brown couldn't help but admire the campus and its beautiful adobe inspired architecture. All done in muted sand colors, the buildings looked as if they had sprung up intact right out of the rough, hot earth. Looking across the street, he could see desert hills on the horizon under clear, brilliant blue skies. It was a spectacular August day.

"You did super in there," Halwell said slapping Brown on the arm.

"Thanks, Coach. I mean, for all of this. Don't know if I'd ever gotten around to doing anything like this on my own."

"S'all right, Lucas. All of us need a little nudge every once in a while. Say, it's after one and my stomach's growling. You in a hurry to get back home?"

"No, sir."

"Well what do you say we have some lunch? There's a restaurant just around the corner from here that serves the best damn chili I ever ate. What do you say? It's on me."

"Sounds great, Coach. Thanks."

They skirted the open parking lot and turned down the sidewalk with Halwell happily leading the way.

"Yeow!!! That's hot!" Lucas Brown's eyes had doubled in size as the first mouthful of chili hit his mouth. He waved a hand over his face and then grabbed the big glass of ice cold Coke in front of him. He swallowed half of it in one gulp. When he put it down, there were tears in his eyes.

"I warned you," Coach Halwell chuckled, seated across the small table from him in the Firehouse Kitchen. The eatery had once been an actual firehouse at the turn of the century. When the new owners realized the value of its downtown location, they were quick to purchase it and convert the abandoned building into a two-story restaurant. The bottom portion was half tables and chairs; the other half being the kitchen located in the closed-off back room. On hot summer days, both garage bay doors were left open allowing patrons to get some fresh air while enjoying their meals. Stairs to the right side of the front entrance led to the second floor also filled with more tables and chairs. A small bar was built along the back wall to serve drinks, both alcoholic and non with a dumbwaiter having been cut into the floor in which meals rose up from the kitchen and dirty dishes went down.

What had caught Brown's attention upon their entering and being seated on the first floor was the original steel fire pole still standing in the middle of the spacious area. A glance upward proved it was still firmly attached to the top ceiling and Coach Halwell told him management did allow students to drop down for the fee of one dollar, which was then donated to the Albuquerque Fire Department.

"Damn," Brown gasped trying to catch his breath. "What do they make that stuff with, gunpowder? It about burned my tongue off."

"Bet your stomach feels warm too," Halwell was amused. He pointed to the basket of cornbread on the table between them. "Liquids won't put out that fire. You need to take a bite of the cornbread. It will absorb the spices. And take smaller bites."

Brown picked up a piece of the fresh yellow bread and took a bite. He nodded and set it down on his napkin. "Gotcha." He took up his spoon again and this time scooped up a smaller portion of the Mexican meat and beans dish. He carefully chewed it and as soon as the heat began to radiate, he quickly took another bite of cornbread.

Seeing his young friend would survive the meal, Chuck Halwell returned his attention to his own bowl of the fiery entrée. Unlike Brown, Halwell had a glass of cold milk next to his dish along with a cornbread square.

As they ate, Halwell, between bites, explained his familiarity with Mrs. Montez and the campus. "I was the Assistant Football Coach here after graduating from the University of San Diego. The Head Coach back then was Ryder Johnson, one of the best coaches in the game and I learned a whole lot from him.

"When the coaching position opened up at Cumberland High, it was Johnson who urged me to apply for it. Told me I was good enough to run my own program and with his encouragement, I took the job."

"How long were you here?" Brown asked after another sip of Coke.

"Almost six years." Halwell's eyes took on a far-off gaze and Brown imagined his old coach was mentally reliving some pleasant memories. "It was hard to leave, Lucas. I'd made so many friends here, and Maggie wasn't all that keen on it either. We had Mary by then and she was five months pregnant at the time with Chuck Junior. But in the end it proved the right thing to do. We also made sure to keep in touch with all our friends here.

"I guess the lesson here is never be afraid of change. Getting too comfortable sometimes can stop a person from growing, both in body and in spirit."

Brown nodded in agreement. During his four years at Cumberland High School he'd heard lots of Halwell's mini-sermons. It was one of the reasons he'd come to appreciate and love the man; he never stopped wanting what was best for his students both on and off the field.

Both of them were nearly finished eating when a patron coming down the stairs spotted Coach Halwell and called out. "Well, as I live and breathe, if it isn't Chuck Halwell!"

The man who had called out was middle-aged, short and stout, with graying hair and a thick mustache of the same color. He had on black slacks and a UNM sweatshirt over his white shirt and tie.

Coach Halwell stood a stuck out his hand. "Harry Irwin," he greeted as the two men shook hands. "They still haven't kicked you out yet?" At that both men laughed loudly.

"They can't replace me, Chuck. You know that. Who else would put up with Monaghan's bullshit?"

After another good laugh, Halwell pointed to Brown who by now had risen from his chair. "Harry, this is one of my former students and players, Lucas Brown. Lucas, meet Harry Irwin, he's the dude they replaced me with when I left."

"Nice to meet you, kid," Irwin said taking Brown's hand in a firm grip. "So what position did you play?"

"Running back," Brown supplied.

"You a student here?"

"Looks like I will be. Thanks to Coach Halwell."

Irwin took this in and then raised an eyebrow at his old friend. "He's a bit old to be a freshmen, Chuck. What's the story?"

"Why don't you sit down and join us. Lucas and were just about to have some desert and I'll tell why we're here. If you've got the time?"

Irwin looked at his wristwatch. "You got thirty minutes. And desert is on me. Fair enough?"

"Fair enough," Halwell smiled and he and Brown sat. Irwin took the empty chair while waving at the passing waitress. He ordered three pieces of strawberry cheesecake and coffee for all of them.

"Okay, Chuck, I'm all ears."

By the time the three men had finished their delicious cheesecake deserts, Halwell had told Assistant Coach Irwin of Lucas Brown's history; both as his star running back and then his recently being discharged from honorable service to his country. The tale ended with Brown's current status as a new incoming college freshmen.

Irwin had remained genuinely attentive during the story; every now and then glancing over at the stoic Brown. It was clear the lad was uncomfortable with his former coach's praises. After Halwell finished, Irwin looked at Brown with new respect.

"That's quite some story, Mr. Brown," he began. "I'm wondering, have you given any thought to our sports program here at UNM?"

It was the last question Lucas Brown was expecting and it surprised him. Coach Halwell was also taken aback.

"Harry, didn't you hear what…"

"About his losing his leg," Irwin put a hand up to stop his old friend. "I'm not deaf Chuck. I'm not asking him to play. That wasn't my question."

"Then I'm afraid, I don't understand what your question is?" Brown declared confused.

Irwin leaned forward over the table. "If what Chuck just told me is true, then I'm going to assume you know a whole lot about the sport of football. Correct?"

"Well, yeah, I guess I do."

"Excellent. Then you also know there is a whole lot more that goes into putting a team on the field, than just the players themselves. You got the coaches, the support staff, cheerleaders…"

"Whoa, you asking me to be a cheerleader?"

"No, I'm asking if you'd like to help us as an equipment manager."

"You mean keep track of stuff, keep it squared away and ready when the players need it?"

"Exactly." Irwin looked to Halwell and then back at Brown. "The job is currently being done by Dave Sansone, he's very good at it. But he's a senior this year and I'm thinking he could use a hand, what with everything else he has going on to graduate next Spring.

"And if you were interested, it would give you an entire season to learn from him as well as get to know the team personally. What do you say?"

Brown sat back in his chair weighing the man's offer. Finally he asked one last question. "Why me? I mean, I'm not looking for pity, sir. It's the last thing I want. I can take care of myself."

"Of that I've no doubt, Lucas. But here's the thing. All college teams, even ours, are made up of kids. Most of them still wet behind the ears with little or no real life experiences. But no one can say that about you. And I'm thinking, Coach Monaghan sure would appreciate having someone with your maturity on his staff. Someone maybe our kids might look up to and respect. Someone they might even learn from…and I'm not just talking about football.

"Brown, I don't want just another kid; I want a man on board. What do you say?"

Brown looked at Halwell who shook his head. "Don't look at me, Lucas. This is your call."

Lucas Brown scratched his chin and then grinned. "I take it this means I can get into all the games for free?"

The next two weeks were a whirlwind for the ex-G.I. His father and sister had helped him pack the family car and driven him to UNM only a few days after his initial visit. But not before Lola Brown handed him a large paper bag filled with sandwiches and baked goods she'd made the night before.

"Ma, they have cafeterias at the school. I'm not gonna starve."

"You just be sure you get your three squares a day, young man. And stay away from them potato chips and all that soda. They'll rot your teeth, never mind give you a belly like your Uncle Luis."

"Yes Ma'am." Lucas Brown wrapped her up in his arms and gave her a kiss on the cheek.

Upon arrival at the main campus, they received directions from passing students to the dorm where he would be staying. Per their request, they were happy to see his room was on the first floor and it was a single. The Resident Assistant was a post-grad student named Arch Williams, an overweight, friendly fellow with freckles over his chubby-cheeks. He went out of his way to help the Browns carry in some of the things they had brought to include Lucas' typewriter and extra clothes.

After his dad and Audrey had left, Williams took the time to introduce him to his neighbors on the first floor. Later that afternoon, he lead a group of them on a walking tour through the campus itself so as to acquaint the freshmen, including Brown, with locations of the various halls where they would find their assigned classes. It was a cool, sunny autumn day and everyone was enjoying being outdoors.

Although he did walk with a noticeable stiff-legged gait, Lucas Brown didn't shy away from letting others know of his prosthetic left leg. For the most part, his fellow students accepted his disability with a nonchalant attitude. He hadn't tried jogging with it yet, but hoped to do so once he

was familiar with the various areas which would be the most suitable for
him; preferable flatland with as few dips and rises as possible.

He had signed up for three courses; Psychology 101, English Lit and
World History. The first two were on Mondays and Wednesdays, with the
history class on Tuesday and Thursday afternoons leaving his Friday free.
Having been out of the entire school process for four years, his advisor,
one Henry Jenkins, had suggested starting with a small work load and
he'd readily agreed.

What had made Brown anxious was his first meeting with Assistant
Coach Irwin at the Dreamstyle Stadium where the first official intra-
squad football scrimmages were being held. He had been told to be there
for three on Friday afternoon and purposely arrived an hour early to get a
better look at the place before everyone else showed up.

There were several maintenance people working in the stadium when
he arrived and one of them pointed to the main tunnel that led to the
green playing field. The stadium was impressive as he walked over to the
nearest goalpost. He could hear the riding lawn mower before he saw it
as it came up the sidelines. The driver was an older man wearing a UNM
baseball cap and poplin jacket with earphones over his ears to protect him
from the engine's loud roar. Seeing Brown, he gave him a wave before
zooming back down the other side of the field leaving behind the sweet
smell of cut grass.

"Lucas," a voice called out from behind him. "You're a bit early."

Harry Irwin, wearing his familiar crimson and silver sweater, the
Lobos colors, marched up to him carrying a clipboard while around his
neck dangled a blue plastic whistle. Wrap around sunglasses covered his
eyes.

"I just wanted to take a look around before everyone else showed up,"
Brown said as they shook hands.

"Gotten all squared away with your classes, dorm and that stuff?"

"Yes, sir. It's still kind of strange and all."

"How so?"

"Seven months ago I was in the jungles dodging VC bullets and mortar
fire. Now I'm a rookie freshman trying to figure out what the hell I'm
doing here."

Irwin chuckled. "Don't worry, Lucas. I'm sure you'll adjust soon
enough. And you can quit the Sir stuff, okay. Coach will do just fine here."

"Gotcha."

The lawn mower came charging in their direction and Irwin pointed to the wooden benches along the sideline yard in front of the stadium bleachers. "Come on, let's get out of this guy's way before he runs us down with that thing."

As they approached the benches, a group of young men appeared coming out of the tunnel; most of them carrying burlap bags of equipment.

"And here come the guys," Coach Irwin said with pride. "Great. Now I can introduce you to Dave Sansone, the senior Equipment Manager I told you about. He's the tall, skinny guy with the wild black hair sticking out everywhere and chin beard."

Looking at Sansone, Brown was reminded of the character Shaggy from the Scooby Doo cartoons.

In the next few minutes Brown shook hands with ten players who were part of the first team; all of them either juniors or seniors. As he was chatting with several of them, other players arrived and eventually the Head Coach himself, Carol "Buster" Monaghan accompanied by his Defensive Coach Wally Peterson and Offensive Coach, Chris Donaldson. All of them were big men but it was Monaghan who stood out being well over six feet tall with a body-builder's physique, close-cropped iron-gray hair and a face that looked as if it had been carved out of granite.

With his presence all talk ended abruptly and all eyes turned to the man. It was a sign of respect Brown admired. Much like that given a superior officer in the army.

"All right, gather round," the Head Coach commanded. "In a few minutes, Coach Peterson and Coach Donaldson will be dividing you up into squads and start putting you through your paces. As most of you know, tomorrow will be our first full team practice along with try-outs for new players.

"We lost some good men and it will be up to you to take their places. Some of you may even earn the attention of a few NFL scouts. Of that I've no doubt. But as always it is going to take nothing but hard work and dedication. I expect nothing less from any of you."

Monaghan paused for a moment then looked over to Coach Irwin. "Coach Irwin, I believe we've a new member on the support team. Would you like to introduce him to us?"

Irwin smiled and pointing to Brown, indicated he should come with him. Together they went over to stand alongside Monaghan.

"Guys, some of you have already met Lucas Brown here. He's going to be helping Dave as Assistant Equipment Manager this year. Lucas just finished four years in the Army and earlier this year finished a tour of duty in Vietnam."

Brown was embarrassed not knowing if he should say anything or not. Then Coach Monaghan walked over and slapped him on the arm.

"Welcome to the Lobos, Brown. We're proud to have you with us."

Several of the players yelled out welcoming cheers and Brown felt truly welcomed for the first time since leaving the army.

"All right," Monaghan was all business again. "What are you ladies waiting for? Get on that field and show me what you got!"

UNM was a member of the NCAA Division One Mountain West Conference and the initial few games of the new seasons were played away. The first was with the Air Force Academy in Colorado which they won and the second in Wyoming and there they lost by a single point. Coach Monoghan was a rigid taskmaster and Lucas Brown soon learned he pushed his men hard, regardless of the previous week's results.

Practices were held three times a week, usually in the late afternoon and went until dark when the stadium lights had to be turned on. Still, Brown's love of the sport colored those long hours added to his own class work. He'd never shied away from a challenge and his college life was no different.

He had eventually found a nice, flat course through the campus and jogged three miles every morning before going off to breakfast. He loved being outdoors just as the sun was rising, its majestic appearance always lifted his spirits as he moved along between the various halls and parking lots. Although it was early, he wasn't the only brave soul running along the empty streets. Dozens of other students came and went along their own paths. He imagined many were field and track athletes.

One bright and clear Wednesday morning he was nearing the end of his run when a voice called out behind him. "Geez, old man, is that how fast you can move?" He barely had time to turn to his left as a freckled face young woman with dark brown hair tied in a ponytail came past him. She was huffing and moving fast. Something that was impossible for him. Over the weeks, he'd learned to jog along at a turtle like pace, forced to compensate for his artificial limb. He didn't like it, but had resigned himself to accepting a slow jog was better than no jog at all.

Now this pretty girl was jeering at him. For a second Lucas Brown took his eyes off the ground to look at her. She had on green sweatpants and a matching jacket with white sneakers and was rapidly moving away. Which was how he failed to see the small pothole in the road and as his left shoe dropped into it, he lost his balance. He fell hard, his hands out to brace himself, a loud cry escaping his lips.

"Oh, God!"

Brown looked up to see the girl rushing back to him, genuine concern on her face. He sat up and looked at the tiny piece of dirt stuck to his palms. He wiped them against his pants as he looked down at his left shoe.

"Are you all right…" She saw the metal of his prosthetic now exposed rising up out of his sneaker. "Oh…I'm so sorry."

"For what?" He smiled extending his hand. "I could use a hand up."

"Oh, right." She grabbed his hand and he used her pull to get back on his feet. "What I said before, about you being an old man and…"

"Hey, it's all right. Really. I guess I do move kind of slow these days." He realized she was still holding on to his right hand. "Ah..my name's Lucas and you can let go now."

"Right." She laughed nervously. "Sorry."

"You really should stop saying that. I'm fine, really. Not the first time I've gone down and most likely not the last."

For a second neither said anything. Her eyes were a lively green and he liked how they looked at him directly without any guile at all.

"Aren't you in Prof. Anderson's World History class with me?"

"Yeah, I am. Oh, my name's Lucy. Lucy Jennet. I'm a freshmen."

"Me too, though an old one for sure."

He saw the puzzle in her eyes. "Look, I was just about done with my run. Can I buy you a cup of coffee at the diner on Silver Street? It's only a block away."

She bit her lower lip as she mulled over his offer. "I guess so. Sure. I don't have a class until ten this morning."

"Good. And my full name is Lucas Brown for the record."

"Nice to meet you, Lucas Brown. And as for the coffee, it's on me. I won't take no for an answer."

"Lucy, I never argue with a lady."

"Oh, God!"

"So when you going to ask her out?" Dave Sansone asked Lucas Brown as he packed footballs and measuring tape into a maroon-colored duffel bags. He and Brown stood by the home side benches next to a two-seat motorized cart. They stored the collected gear in the back of the mini vehicle. The afternoon's practice session had ended only a few minutes earlier and most of the team was now in the showers.

"Hey, I only met her this morning," Brown replied picking up a few white towels off the ground. Players used them to wipe sweat off their faces after several hours of grueling exercises.

"But you are going to, right?" Sansone was a good-natured clown, as Brown had come to learn working with him. The young man loved nothing better than ribbing his friends to get a laugh out of them.

"I don't know, Dave. I mean, maybe. She was nice and…"

Suddenly a voice yelled out. "HEADS UP!"

Brown turned to see a spinning football rocketing down toward's his friends head. Without thinking, he dropped the towels, took two quick steps and reached out his hands to intercept the pigskin missile.

"Yeow!" Sansone gasped, as he stumbled back a step. Brown, holding onto the football, looked across the field at the team's quarterback, Dan Conklin and team kicker Russ Andrews.

"Nice catch," Conklin called out. "Toss it back, will yah."

After the regular practice session had ended, Conklin had suggested to Andrews that they stick around. Andrews had missed a field goal kick in their last game, Monaghan wasn't very happy about that effort. As Conklin was the guy who held the ball for Andrews' kicks, he was okay with putting in extra time.

Lucas Brown twirled the football in his hands for a second. Every time he held one, it brought back memories of his days playing the game he loved.

"Oh, what the hell," he said as he turned around and took two quick steps. Right, left and then keeping his balance, let go of the football at waist height and kicked it with his right leg. Soon as his shoe made contact, he centered his balance, afraid he'd topple over as he'd done that morning. But this time he was strong and all that happened was the football flew through the air all the way to the other side of the field where Conklin and Andrews were standing by the goal posts. Both were stunned and Conklins raced backward several yards to catch it.

Dave Sansone gasped. "HOLY SHIT!"

"What?"

"I didn't know you could kick like that?"

Before Brown could say anything, Conklin and Andrews came running over. Conklin was of average height with a slim body that made him wiry when slipping away from oncoming rushers during a game. He was also in the ROTC program and would be going into the Army after graduating the following Spring. He and Brown had hit if off immediately, with Conklin always ready to buy him a beer. Most of the time just to hear Brown talk about his experiences as a grunt.

"Damn it, Lucas," he blurted out still holding the football. "Can you do that again?"

"Yeah," Russ Andrews echoed. "That's one of the longest kicks I've ever seen." Andrews was short and stocky. He was a junior and this was his first year as the team's number one kicker. He was good, but still unsure of himself.

Conklin tossed Brown the football. "Go on, do it again."

Brown looked at the trio, all of them anxious for him to repeat what they had just witnessed.

"All right," he acquiesced. "But I'm most likely going to fall on my ass this time."

He gripped the pigskin tight in his hands and moved away from the others by a few yards. Then he squared his shoulders and took a deep breath. Again he stepped off on his right leg fast, brought the artificial leg up and down, and dropped the football just as he swung his right leg up hard.

Contact. The football shot into the air.

Brown felt his balance wobble, tried to steady himself but couldn't adjust in time and fell on his butt.

None of the other three laughed. They were too busy watching the football soar high and far beyond the goal posts into the stands.

"I told you," Brown chuckled as he started to pick himself off the ground.

Dan Conklin rushed over and helped him up. Then he brushed the grass off Brown's arms, grinning. "Lucas, my man, we have got to tell the coach about this."

The following day, as Brown and Sansone were getting things squared away in the locker room before the players arrived, Harry Irwin walked in and greeted them.

"I hear you did some kicking last evening, out there on the field," he told Brown. "Is that true?"

"You should have seen him, Coach," Sansone cut in excitedly using his hands to demonstrate how the egg-shaped ball had soared through the air. "Lucas kicked half way across the field way up into the seats."

"Is that true, Lucas?"

"Well, yes. But it was nothing, Coach. Just a lucky kick is all."

"Hmm, well Conklin already told Coach Monaghan and he'd like to see you do it again before practice today."

"Oh. Okay, I guess."

"Good, then I'll let you guys get back to it."

As Irwin exited, Dave Sansone slapped Brown on the arm. "OOWEE… what do yah think of that, my man?"

Brown scratched the back of his head. "Hell, I don't know. Most likely nothing but a big waste of everybody's time. That's what I think."

By the time practice was under way two hours later, Irwin found Brown and escorted him to the center of the field. Coach Monaghan was there along with the Offensive Coach, Wally Peterson. Peterson was a rugged ex-NFL pro with beefy arms and salt and pepper hair who was always chewing gum to dampen his excess energy. Now he was tossing a football around in his hands and grinning.

"Here he is," Irwin said as he and Brown approached them.

"All right," Monaghan nodded. "Brown, Dan Conklin tells me you're a good kicker. Is that so?"

"I guess. I used to fool around kicking back in high school. It was just something to fool around with."

"Then try fooling around now," Monaghan said and Coach Peterson flipped the ball into Brown's hands.

"From right here?" Brown looked around. Various squads were doing drills everywhere on the field.

"Yes," Monaghan replied. "Just kick it towards the poles. Either side of the field. Your choice."

"Yes, sir."

Lucas Brown opted to kick towards the eastern end of the field. That way he wouldn't have the descending sun in his eyes. He took a few steps away from the others to get his balance ready, then a long deep breath.

What the hell, he thought, *here goes nothing.*

Then, as he had done before he moved off on his right leg, followed through with the left and then kicked the pigskin with all his might. It flew off the toe of his shoe in a curving arc all the way across the field and hit the crossbeam of the goal posts.

Brown turned around, his heart beating wildly in his chest. The three coaches were all looking at him as if he'd just performed a magic trick they couldn't solve.

Monaghan looked to Irwin. "Get him signed up and ready. Also make sure there aren't any NCAS rules against a player with prosthetic leg."

"You got it, Coach. I'll get right on it."

Monaghan tapped the clipboard in his hands. "Brown, starting next week, you'll be working under Coach Peterson here. That is if you want to play?"

"Play, Coach? I don't understand."

"Then let me spell out it. Russ Andrews is a decent kicker, but he can't do what you just did in a million years. So if you want to be our second kicker, the position is yours. But I need an answer now.

"Yes or no?"

Lucas Brown smiled. "Yes, sir! Damn straight, yes, sir!"

The following week the Lobos flew to San Diego where they lost by a touchdown. After having worked with Coach Peterson that previous week, Lucas Brown went along with the team, but didn't suit up.

"Be patient," Peterson offered while chewing away on a stick of Juicy Fruit gum. "You're coming along fine, but I can see some hesitancy when you step off. Just watch Andrews for the next couple of weeks, then you'll get your shot."

Brown had no reason to question Peterson's decision. He liked the big former New England Patriot tackle and it was easy to see the man knew his football. Like Monaghan, he was a no-nonsense leader on the field and the players respected him for that. They were becoming better players because of him.

On week two they were in Idaho taking on Boise State and came away with a two point victory. The flight home was a celebratory one. They were only a half hour from Albuquerque when Dave Sansone, seated next to Brown, leaned over and said, "Coach Irwin told me next Saturday is it, amigo."

"Is what? The game with Utah."

"No, goofball. You're going to suit up. No more just watching from the sidelines."

"Pretty much what Peterson told me back in San Diego."

"Yeah, well you might want to give your folks a call and let them know."

"Right. Please, don't let me forget. My Pa would kill me if he missed it."

At that point the pilot announced they were preparing for their final descent and went through the regular routine of asking all passengers to make sure they were buckled up and seats were in their upright positions.

As Brown rested his head back against the seat, he recalled the phone call he'd made to his family after Monaghan had officially made him a part of the team. Apparently their inquiries with the NCAA had returned with all thumbs up. There were no regulations against a player with a prosthetic leg. Although still cautious, Monaghan had spoken with the school legal department and they recommended Brown sign an extra insurance waiver releasing the school of any liability should he injure himself severely while playing. Brown considered that only fair as the school was under no obligation to let him play.

Of course the reactions back home had been mixed. Though his father and Audrey had been thrilled by the news, Lola Brown not so much. She thought it was foolish and dangerous but in the end, he convinced her he would only be on the field to kick. Coach Monaghan had made it very clear that if he even attempted to run and tackle anyone, he'd be off the team in a heartbeat.

As the wheels of the Southwest 707 touched down and bounced on the tarmac, Brown knew the week ahead would be intense. Was he ready for it? And more importantly would he be ready the following Saturday? Somehow he had a hunch the week ahead was going to be the fastest week in his entire life.

He wasn't wrong.

Thirty-eight thousand Lobos fans rose to their feet and cheered as their beloved Lobos came onto the field. All were fit, eager young men anxious to get their game under way against the Utah Utes. The last man to come out of the tunnel was Lucas Brown, dressed in the Crimson and Silver uniform of the UNM Lobos with one slight alteration; the left pants leg had been cut away earlier in the week during practice. He'd found that his artificial, metallic limb was hampered by the tightly stretched pants material. In the end, after conferring with the coaches, it was decided to simply remove that piece of cloth.

Naturally his appearance didn't go unnoticed as those nearest to the tunnel mouth had a very good view of this most unique member of the team.

But Brown was oblivious to any stares directed his way. When thirty-eight thousand fans cheered, the noise was wonderfully deafening. As the Lobos made their way to their sideline benches, Brown kept staring up into the bleachers. He knew his parents were up there somewhere, along with Coach Halwell and a certain freckled-faced young woman with whom he'd had coffee that very morning.

Before they had parted ways outside the cafeteria, Lucy Jennet had risen to her toes and planted a kiss on Brown catching him completely off guard. Then she was gone, calling out, "Good luck, Lucas!! Kick a field goal for me."

As he removed his helmet, the memory of her lips on his was still fresh. Dave Sansone was standing off to the side, near the mini-cart and motioned him over.

"You ready, big guy?" Sansone had been on the field hours before the front gate had opened to the public. He had containers of water, Gatorade and lots of towels ready along with bandages and ice packs in case they were needed. Now he was leaning back against the cart, arms folded over his chest, wearing his Lobos sweatshirt.

"As ready as I'm ever going to be," Brown replied. He backed-up to the small cart and dropped onto the seat. "Damn, it Dave. I'm nervous as hell."

"That's only natural, amigo."

"Yeah, but what if I mess up."

Sansone's eyes widened and his mouth fell open. "What!! The great Lucas Brown mess up! Oh dear God, I think the entire world will collapse for sure. This could be the end."

Try as he might, Brown couldn't help but laugh. Sansone was always able to loosen him up and he'd done it again. With his exaggerated miming, he'd simply reminded the player of what he knew; in the end, one leg or two, he was still only human.

The Utes won the coin toss and elected to receive. Russ Andrews kicked off and they returned the ball to their twenty-five-yard line. The game was on.

As Brown watched, he recalled Monaghan's advance scouting report. Both teams had equal win-loss records and were fairly matched. Whereas Utah's quarterback was a returning player and noticeably more aggressive than Conklin, who was still developing his throwing arm. By the end of the first half the score was 7 to 7.

At the start of the second half, the Lobos scored a touched down but Andrews missed the extra point kick. So, going into the third quarter it was 13 to 7. As expected, the contest was hard fought, with both defensive squads digging in and stopping their opponents from scoring. The fans on both sides loved it.

Minutes after the fourth quarter began, the Utes' quarterback threw a long bomb of a pass that was caught by his speedy receiver; touchdown. Score 13 to 13. Then they were able to score an end-run conversion. So, two points separate the gridiron battlers.

Score 15 to 13. The Lobos trailed by two points.

The Lobos came back more determined than ever and Dan Conklin led the Lobos to within thirty yards of the Utes' end zone when the drive stalled out. Andrews came out and missed the field goal. He came off the field dejected as the Utes started their next drive.

Time clicked away and the Lobos defense did its job magnificently. The Utes kicked the ball away and the Lobos once again fought their way up the field only to have Conklin miss his target and have his pass intercepted. Fortunately, the Utes runner only gained a few yards. Dejected, the offensive squad left the field and once again it was up to Coach Donaldson's squad to hold the line.

And they did. The Lobos dug deep and only gave up ten yards before forcing the Utes to give up the ball.

As Dan Conklin and his pals positioned themselves on their own twenty-yard line, all of them knew the game clock was now also their foe. They had all of six minutes to cross eighty yards. For the next few plays, Conklin kept the Lobos to short end runs, avoiding going up the middle. His running backs were doing their job and after two successful first downs, one of them fumbled the ball. There was an instant pig-pyle and Lobos fans held their breath. When the referees pulled all the players off, it was to the relief of the fans that Lobos Chuck Williams had been the first to reclaim the football.

Regrouping, with third down and twenty-yards, Conklin threw a short pass but his receiver was brought down five yards short. They were now at the forty-yard line and it was fourth down.

Monaghan called time out. Then he turned to Coach Irwin. "Get Brown."

Seeing Irwin signal him, Lucas Brown grabbed his helmet out of the mini-cart and hurried over. Sansone had said something but he hadn't heard what it was. He knew his time had come and it was as if everything else in the world was now shut down.

"This is it," Harry Irwin said pointing to the field, where the team was awaiting him. One of the receivers had come off the fields and they passed each other. Brown finished strapping his helmet on.

Dan Conklin was standing seven yards behind his center. He looked at Brown and yelled, "Show 'em what you got, Lucas!"

Brown took his place four paces behind the quarterback and then gave Conklin a thumbs-up. He took in a long breath, looking past their own line at the Utes in their red and white uniforms. Way behind them, across the field was the goal post.

Conklin was screaming out numbers. Brown's eyes were on his hands. Then the football was snapped and Conklin pulled it out of the air, turned the stitches forward while Lucas Brown propelled himself forward. Conklin set one end of the ball down, Brown's right leg touched the ground, then his left went out, landed and he twisted his entire body bringing the right up in a fast graceful kick.

He never felt the kick. He only heard the thump sound and then the football was tumbling through the air and high over the empty half of the playing field.

Lucas Brown watched it go and he thought of trainer Paul Ranier, Doctor John Altman, Nurse Songer, Engineer Dan Wilcox and Father Mike Moore. All of them responsible for his being there as that brown missile continued on its way.

The time clock whistle blew.

The football cleared the uprights.

Thirty-eight thousand people screamed.

And Lucas Brown thought, *We did it!*

THE END

I CAME HOME

I joined the Army in 1965 for a three years enlistment well aware the Vietnam conflict was in full swing. I qualified for clerical training and did two months of rough winter basic at Ft. Dix in New Jersey. I remained there for two additional months to become a Personnel Specialist. Upon my graduation from clerk school, I was assigned to a training battalion at Ft. Ord, California. You could say my first two years were pretty cushy, what with being a small town New Hampshire boy, California was an eye-opener. These were days of the supposed sexual revolution, flower-power and war protesters. The times, as Bob Dylan sang, were a-changing.

Then, early in the summer of 1967 I was ordered to Vietnam where I would serve my final year of enlistment. I was, as Stephen Crane wrote, off to see the elephant. I was in-country from that summer to the following year and in late June of 1968 came home and returned to civilian life. While I was in Vietnam, I wrote a weekly column for our hometown paper, the *Somersworth Free Press*. Perhaps the most significant piece was the one actually printed two weeks after I was back in the states. It was the story of my visiting the U.S. Army morgue where the bodies of young American soldiers were embalmed before shipping their remains back to their families.

I won't bore you with numbers. A large part of my generation died in that little Asian country. Many came home wounded, both physically and mentally. I was one of the lucky ones. This story is the only story I've ever done related to that time in my life and is dedicated to all those young men who never came back. I think about them all the time.

RON FORTIER – Comics and pulps writer/editor is best known for his work on the Green Hornet comic series and *Terminator – Burning Earth* with Alex Ross. He won the Pulp Factory Award for Best Pulp Short Story of 2011 for "Vengeance Is Mine," which appeared in Moonstone's The Avenger – Justice Inc. and in 2012 for "The Ghoul," from the anthology Monster Aces. He is the Managing Editor of Airship 27 Productions, a leading New Pulp Fiction publisher and writes the continuing adventures of both his own character, Brother Bones – the Undead Avenger and the classic pulp hero, Captain Hazzard – Champion of Justice.

In 2017, he was awarded the first, Pulp Grand Master by the Pulp Factory.

Fortier also writes the highly popular Pulp Fiction Reviews blog.

You can find him at (www.Airship27.com)

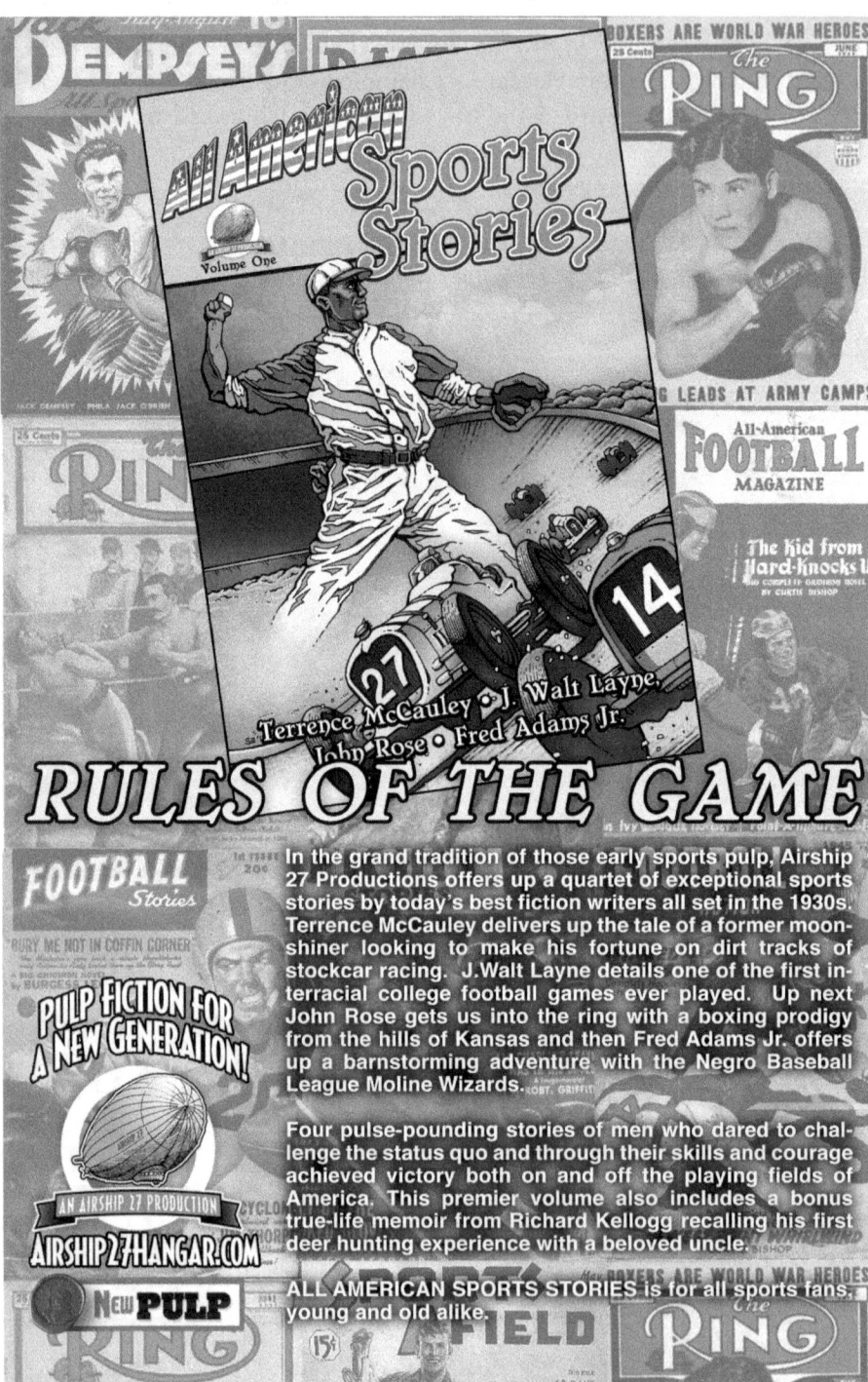

RULES OF THE GAME

In the grand tradition of those early sports pulp, Airship 27 Productions offers up a quartet of exceptional sports stories by today's best fiction writers all set in the 1930s. Terrence McCauley delivers up the tale of a former moonshiner looking to make his fortune on dirt tracks of stockcar racing. J.Walt Layne details one of the first interracial college football games ever played. Up next John Rose gets us into the ring with a boxing prodigy from the hills of Kansas and then Fred Adams Jr. offers up a barnstorming adventure with the Negro Baseball League Moline Wizards.

Four pulse-pounding stories of men who dared to challenge the status quo and through their skills and courage achieved victory both on and off the playing fields of America. This premier volume also includes a bonus true-life memoir from Richard Kellogg recalling his first deer hunting experience with a beloved uncle.

ALL AMERICAN SPORTS STORIES is for all sports fans, young and old alike.

PULP FICTION FOR A NEW GENERATION!

AN AIRSHIP 27 PRODUCTION

AIRSHIP27HANGAR.COM

NEW PULP